SPECIAL MESS~~AGE~~

THE ULVERSCR~~OFT FOUNDATION~~
(registered UK cha~~rity~~
was established in 1972 to provide funds for
research, diagnosis and treatment of eye diseases.
Examples of major projects funded by
the Ulverscroft Foundation are:-

- The Children's Eye Unit at Moorfields Eye
  Hospital, London
- The Ulverscroft Children's Eye Unit at Great
  Ormond Street Hospital for Sick Children
- Funding research into eye diseases and
  treatment at the Department of Ophthalmology,
  University of Leicester
- The Ulverscroft Vision Research Group,
  Institute of Child Health
- Twin operating theatres at t~~he~~ Western
  Ophthalmic Hospital, Lond~~on~~
- The Chair of Oph~~thalmology at the~~ Royal
  Australian College~~ of Ophthalmologists~~

You can help further th~~e work of the~~ Foundation
by making a donatio~~n or leav~~ing a legacy.
Every contribution is gratefully received. If you
would like to help support the Foundation or
require further information, please contact:

THE ULVERSCROFT FOUNDATION
The Green, Bradgate Road, Anstey
Leicester LE7 7FU, England
Tel: (0116) 236 4325

website: www.foundation.ulverscroft.com

Wendy Soliman was brought up on the Isle of Wight in southern England but now divides her time between Andorra and western Florida. She lives with her husband Andre and a rescued dog of indeterminate pedigree named Jake Bentley after the hunky hero in one of her books. When not writing she enjoys reading other people's books, walking miles with her dog whilst plotting her next scene, dining out and generally making the most out of life.

AT THE DUKE'S DISCRETION

When Cristobel Brooke's father, jeweller to the rich and famous, is brutally murdered, Crista flees to her uncle's small village close to Winchester. But the criminals pursue her, forcing her to fall in with their plans. Lord Amos Sheridan, brother to the Duke of Winchester, is intrigued by Crista. Astounded when she becomes implicated in treasonous acts, Amos is determined to vindicate her. With the duke's backing, Amos and Crista launch a daring scheme to expose the villains. Meanwhile, Crista finds herself falling slowly in love with Amos. But he is a duke's heir, and she a nobody with a criminal past . . .

Books by Wendy Soliman
Published by Ulverscroft:

LADY HARTLEY'S INHERITANCE
DUTY'S DESTINY
THE SOCIAL OUTCAST
THE CARSTAIRS CONSPIRACY
A BITTERSWEET PROPOSAL
TO DEFY A DUKE

MRS DARCY ENTERTAINS:
MISS BINGLEY'S REVENGE
COLONEL FITZWILLIAM'S DILEMMA
MISS DARCY'S PASSION

WENDY SOLIMAN

AT THE DUKE'S DISCRETION

Complete and Unabridged

ULVERSCROFT
Leicester

First published in Great Britain in 2014

First Large Print Edition
published 2015

A catalogue record for this book is available
from the British Library.

ISBN 978–1–4448–2655–5

Published by
F. A. Thorpe (Publishing)
Anstey, Leicestershire

Set by Words & Graphics Ltd.
Anstey, Leicestershire
Printed and bound in Great Britain by
T. J. International Ltd., Padstow, Cornwall

This book is printed on acid-free paper

1

Winchester, England 1818

Amos Sheridan's efforts to distract Nate's attention away from Martha's ample bosom proved woefully ineffective. With an impatient roll of his eyes, he slammed his empty tankard down and dealt his brother a sharp nudge in the ribs.

'Ouch!' Finally, Nate turned towards Amos, albeit with a scowl. 'What was that for?'

'Time to go, little brother.'

'Damnation, just when things were getting interesting.'

Amos suppressed a smile. Nate's fascination with Martha, the comely barmaid at the Crown and Anchor tavern in Shawford village, was as predictable as it was diverting. Martha's eyes had lit up an hour previously when Nate and Amos walked into the taproom. True to form, she had flirted outrageously with Nate ever since, frequently leaning her elbows on the bar and pushing her breasts together to better display her décolletage.

Nate had not long returned to Winchester since finishing his tenure at Oxford, and was thirsty for the pleasures of life. Martha would not disappoint.

'Drink up, Nate,' Amos urged.

'We will not be missed.' Nate waved a negligent hand, his attention firmly focused on Martha's bosom again. 'There's time for another tankard of this excellent ale.'

'Mother has guests, and since she has gone to considerable trouble to arrange this dinner to welcome you home, it would be the height of bad manners to keep her waiting.'

'Perdition, so it would be.' Nate removed his elbows from the bar and blew Martha an exaggerated kiss. 'Until later, Martha my love.'

'Good evening, your lordships.'

'And good evening to you, Jeggins,' Amos replied to the landlord, picking up his hat and ushering his reluctant brother towards the door.

Jeggins inclined his head in the direction of his departing customers. That was about as deferential as it got in this establishment, which was one of the reasons why the Sheridan males frequented it. The residents of Shawford and Compton had come to an unwritten agreement to let them be themselves, and didn't badger the life out of them for favours or with obsequious behaviour when they showed themselves in the villages.

There had been a duke at Winchester Park since Norman times, and that title was currently held by Amos's older brother, Zachary. One of the few characteristics the feuding residents of the two villages shared was a fierce pride in their duke. They claimed the Sheridans as their own and were aggressively protective of the family's privacy, as well as their right to behave as well or as badly as anyone else.

All four of the boys had done their level best not to disappoint on the bad behaviour front.

'Don't worry,' Amos said, slapping Nate's shoulder as they took their horses from the ostler in the inn's mews and mounted up. 'Martha will still be there tomorrow.'

'Not sure I can wait that long,' Nate replied morosely. 'She's whet my appetite.'

'It's what she does,' Amos said, pushing his new stallion into a canter as they cleared the village streets and headed across three miles of common land to reach Winchester Park.

'I wouldn't know.'

Amos's laugh echoed above the whisper of the soft breeze as he continued to give his lively mount its head. 'Don't tell me you didn't find distractions in Oxford. If you spent all your time studying, the family name will be sullied beyond redemption.'

'Never fear, I lived down to the standard you three set for me.' Nate drew level with Amos and grinned. 'Oxford seems a devilish long time ago already.'

Their horses had decided to race one another. Fiercely competitive, neither brother saw reason to stop them and leaned forward instead, laughing as they urged them on. Conversation between them was temporarily suspended while they gave their full attention to the speeding animals. They were still neck and neck when they were forced to slow in order not to excite the young horses grazing in Winchester Park's paddocks.

'An honourable draw,' Nate said, patting his sweating mount's neck.

'Nothing honourable about drawing,' Amos laughed. 'Sheridans play to win. We must arrange a proper race sometime soon, with all four of us taking part. It will be like old times.'

'Best not let Annalise hear about it,' Nate said, referring to the older of their two sisters, 'or she will insist upon being a part of it.'

'And most likely beat the lot of us.'

Amos failed to suppress a prideful grin. Annalise, when still very young, had badgered him to allow her to ride astride. Amos had seen little harm in her doing so while on the privacy of the estate. It had not occurred to him that at nineteen, having taken the *ton* by storm during her first season, she would not have put aside her tomboy pursuits in favour of more feminine occupations. With the benefit of hindsight, he ought not to be surprised. Annalise had inherited the same hellfire tendencies as her brothers, but had learned to disguise them a little better.

The brothers surrendered their mounts to the grooms who ran out to take them, and entered the imposing house by a side door. Faraday, the family's faithful butler, materialised to take their outer garments.

'We're fearful late, Faraday,' Amos said. 'Unavoidably detained.'

If Faraday could smell the reason for their delay on their breath, he did not give the slightest indication. 'Her Grace is not yet down, my lord. I believe you have just enough time.'

'Right then, we'd best look to it.'

The brothers took the stairs two at a time and parted on the upper landing. A short time later, Amos, impeccably attired in beautifully tailored evening clothes, descended the stairs at a more moderate rate. He found all three of his brothers already in the drawing room, glasses of whisky in their hands. Zach acknowledged Amos's arrival and poured a drink for him.

'I hear you have been leading our youngest brother astray,' he said.

Amos snorted. 'He hardly needed any leading.'

'I would imagine not,' Vince said. 'Especially if Martha was involved.'

'What do you devils know of the luscious Martha?' Nate demanded in a possessive tone.

The three eldest Sheridans had a good laugh at Nate's expense.

'Martha is a family tradition,' Zach explained, clapping Nate's shoulder. 'Just place yourself in her capable hands, little brother. She will see you right.'

Nate looked affronted. 'I'm hardly a greenhorn, I'll have you know. I don't need tutoring.'

This statement provided the brothers with another cause for amusement. 'Trust us,' Vince said. 'Until you have sampled Martha's delights, you know next to nothing.'

'It's all part of the dispute between the villages,' Amos explained.

'Martha is?' Nate's eyebrows disappeared beneath his thick thatch of hair. 'I don't see how.'

'Shawford and Compton both claim credit for having us, the Sheridans, living in their environs,' Zach explained, even though Nate knew it perfectly well.

'And as Winchester Hall is equal distance between the two,' Amos added, 'the dispute will never be resolved through fair means.'

'Ah, now I understand.' A slow smile of comprehension graced Nate's disgustingly even features. 'Martha is Shawford's secret weapon.'

'You see,' Vince said, grinning, 'that expensive education wasn't completely wasted.'

'Perhaps not,' Zach replied. 'But it won't be complete until Martha has got her claws into our baby brother here.'

'She looks upon it as a rite of passage to educate us all,' Amos said, topping up his glass.

'And who are we to stand in the way of good honest competition between the villages?' Vince demanded to know.

'What competition?'

Annalise walked into the room in a rustle of pale yellow silk, curls dancing around her lovely face, her eyes alight with interest. Portia, at sixteen the baby of the family, was at her side, her much plainer face alive with excitement because she was to dine with the family when guests were present. Not due to be presented until the coming season, society was still new and interesting to Portia. Amos idly wondered if he had ever exhibited such enthusiasm himself and when he had become so jaded, so bored with the entire social rigmarole.

He watched his siblings contemplatively, wondering about the unfairness of life. Being born into wealth and privilege ensured they would enjoy the very best of the amusements society had to offer. It ought to have been enough but, to top it all, they had been blessed with good looks, elegance, and engaging charm. All of them except poor Portia, that is. In spite of their mother's lack of stature, all the brothers topped six foot and Annalise, much to her annoyance, was taller than average. Portia on the other hand was short and, as she herself cheerfully put it, the runt of the litter with a face like a wrinkled prune. It wasn't true, of course, especially when she wasn't being compared to her sister. Portia had a lively wit, an enquiring mind and charming personality. Simply put, Amos adored her and felt fiercely protective of her, as did all of the Sheridan brood.

'Nothing that needs to concern you,' Zach replied to Annalise's question.

'Which is precisely the response I would have expected.' Annalise wrinkled her pert little nose in disgust. 'You boys find all sorts of diverse pursuits to discuss, but the moment we get anywhere near you, you change the subject. How are Portia and I supposed to learn anything interesting about life if you insist upon being so secretive?'

'How many offers of marriage was I asked to entertain for your hand during your first season?' Zach asked in a tone of mild amusement.

'Oh, that. Bah.' Annalise flapped a hand. 'I am far too young to think of matrimony.'

'You're nineteen,' Amos reminded her. 'More than old enough.'

'Most young ladies look upon it as a duty to marry in their first season,' Vince pointed out.

'*I* am not most young ladies.'

The brothers shared an exasperated glance. 'That is certainly true,' Nate said, speaking for them all.

'Well, I don't intend ever to marry,' Portia said airily. 'Unlike Annalise, no one would want me for anything other than my fortune.'

'Darling, that simply isn't true,' Annalise protested. 'You are interesting, clever, and amusing, whereas my head is full of air, and I can barely string two intelligible sentences together.'

'Gentlemen don't like women to be clever. It makes them feel inferior. Besides, why should I have a man telling me how to behave when I can stay here and do precisely as I please?'

'Rather like our brothers do.' Annalise sent the brothers in question a teasing smile. 'Well said, Portia. Zach, you have no business berating me for not accepting any of those stuffy proposals, when you are a duke and have a duty to marry and produce an heir. Besides, you are thirty, which is positively ancient. If you leave it very much longer, you will probably lack the stamina to beget said heir.'

All four brothers spluttered on their drinks.

'What must Zach do precisely to beget an heir?' Portia asked with an air of such innocence as to make the brothers dissolve into fits of laughter.

'I am glad to find you all in such good spirits,' the dowager duchess said, walking through the door that Faraday held open for her. 'May I ask what you find so amusing?'

'Our sisters are an endless source of entertainment,' Zach replied. 'When they are not irritating the life out of us, that is.'

The duchess sent her eldest son a look that told him she didn't believe a word of it and seated herself beside the fire, accepting a glass of champagne from Faraday's tray.

'It is very pleasant to have you all together like this. It has been too long.' She raised her glass. 'Welcome home, Nate.'

'Thanks, Mother, it's good to be idle for a

change. All that studying takes it out of a chap.'

'Is that so?' Amos replied, biting back a smile.

'Certainly, although I dare say Zach will find me an occupation soon enough.'

'If he does not then I certainly shall,' their mother replied. 'Your sisters and I need escorting on an excursion to Winchester over the coming week. We must set our minds to Portia's wardrobe for her come-out.'

Nate's horrified expression caused more amusement amongst the brothers, but he was saved from finding a way to excuse himself from the engagement by the arrival of their guests.

As Amos intermingled with their neighbours and friends he thought his mother was right about one thing. A close-knit family, it had been too long since they had all been at home at the same time. He watched his mother, elegant and charming still although she was now well into her fifties, and wondered how she could have produced four such strapping sons when she herself was so diminutive. But what she lacked in statue was more than compensated for by her style and steely determination to maintain the family honour. Anyone who mistook her easygoing manner for weakness was not left in ignorance as to her true character for very long.

Amos had been severely worried about her when their father died three years previously. The two of them had been so much in love, right until the very last. Even a boisterous family of six could not quell the affection between them. Amos and Zach had thought her heart might actually fracture beneath the weight of her grief, and nothing any of them said or did seemed to comfort her. She recovered from her loss in time, but a light in her eyes had been permanently extinguished. She devoted herself to her children, and turned her attention to Zach in particular. Never tiring of introducing him to young ladies whom she considered suitable duchess material, she allowed her annoyance at his tardiness in selecting one to become increasingly apparent.

Unfortunately the brothers had seen for themselves just how harmonious their parents' marriage had been, and that example now worked against the duchess. None of them were in any particular hurry to embrace matrimony as a consequence. For his part, Amos was absolutely determined not to become leg-shackled unless he found a lady who could inspire him to similar devotion. Despite being inundated with potential candidates whenever he showed himself in society, Amos had yet to find a female who moved him to the extent he would sacrifice his freedom for her sake.

Zach, he knew, was similarly minded. Although, as Annalise had so artfully just reminded them all, expectations rested on his shoulders which, sooner or later, he would be obliged to fulfil. Hopefully, he would do so before Portia's prophecy of physical incapability became a reality.

During dinner, the conversation turned to the annual garden party their mother threw to celebrate her birthday. It had become quite a tradition over the years. Both sets of villagers attended and managed to behave with civility towards one another, at least until the ale supplied in strict rotation by the competing inns in the two villages loosened tongues and opinions. Their father had been a firm believer in supporting local businesses. His widow and Zach maintained that tradition, spreading their custom with conscious consideration for the ongoing competition. The duchess sought to fill Portia's wardrobe, and doubtless replenish her own and Annalise's in Winchester rather than London. It was a consideration that was noted and appreciated by local tradesmen.

She would almost certainly look to smaller establishments in Shawford and Compton for additional items. Amos smothered a smile, reminding himself to tell Nate the taproom at the Crown and Anchor made a very convenient place to wait while the ladies selected their purchases — a chore, he had reason to know from painful past experience, that took up a considerable amount of time. Once he was privy to that knowledge, Nate's enthusiasm for escort duties would likely undergo a marked improvement.

'As to the addition to your silverware, Your Grace,' Palmer, the local squire, remarked during dinner. 'Have you thought to look anywhere other than Shawford this year?'

Amos wondered what the devil Palmer was playing at. Their late father had always commissioned a new piece of silver to add to his wife's growing collection to coincide with her birthday celebrations, where it would be set on display for all to admire. That duty now fell to Zach and, like his father before him, he only ever went to Mr. Chesney in Shawford for that purpose. Chesney's work was quite exquisite and even Compton residents reluctantly conceded they had no one skilled enough to compete with him.

'Whatever can you mean, Mr. Palmer?' the duchess asked, looking up from her roasted guinea fowl. 'I would not insult Mr. Chesney by even thinking of going elsewhere.'

14

'No insult was intended by the question, Your Grace. It is just that Chesney's health is no longer robust.'

'He is unwell?' Amos asked. It was the first he had heard of it, and not much local gossip escaped him. He visited the Crown and Anchor's taproom at regular intervals for precisely that reason.

'His eyesight is failing him, my lord, although he is too stubborn to admit it. The delicate filigree work he undertakes can only add additional strain.'

Amos exchanged a loaded glance with Zach. Neither of them particularly liked or trusted Palmer, although if pressed, neither could have said why. He was supposed to be neutral when it came to the competition between the two villages, but Amos suspected that he favoured Compton.

'If his eyesight is failing,' Amos said, fixing Palmer with a steady gaze, 'what possible reason could he have for remaining in business? I cannot persuade myself he is short of blunt and he is definitely approaching retirement age.'

'He takes prodigious pride in his work, Amos,' the dowager said. 'Since he enjoys our patronage, perhaps he is reluctant to let us down.'

'I have business in Shawford tomorrow,

Mother,' Amos replied. 'I shall call upon Chesney and assess the situation for myself.'

'Thank you, Amos,' the dowager replied. 'That would put my mind at rest. I would not wish to offend him, but nor would I wish him to feel under any obligation to this family.'

2

Cristobel Brooke wiped perspiration from her brow with the back of her hand. Her back ached from the amount of time she had spent crouched over her workbench. She was desperate to move her cramped muscles, but couldn't afford that luxury until she had completed her task. She leaned further forward, peered through the magnifying glass attached to the leather band circling her forehead and bit her lip as she carefully applied the soldering iron to the delicate filigree necklace she had almost completed. This was the difficult part. Too much solder and the silver would run, causing ugly blobs. Too little and the gemstones would fall out.

'There, that should do it,' she said aloud, feeling a great sense of satisfaction.

She put her solder iron aside and picked up tweezers. She used them to carefully remove excess chips of solder before applying flux solution to the wire arches with a brush and placing the necklace aside to cool. The sapphires, embedded between tiny seed pearls, made an unusual and highly attractive arrangement that would, hopefully, be remarked upon, leading to further commissions for her uncle's establishment. Crista thought of Lady Middleton, about whose rather fat neck her masterpiece was destined to reside, and sighed. Hardly the best showcase for her talents.

'Beggars cannot be choosers,' she muttered, placing both hands on the small of her back and finally indulging in a luxurious backwards stretch. She sighed with pleasure when her muscles unknotted themselves.

'Talking to yourself again, Miss Brooke.'

Crista abruptly sat upright, heart pounding but the rest of her freezing at the sound of the indolent voice she had grown to despise. She was perfectly sure speaking to herself was a far better alternative than conversing with the owner of that voice but saw little profit in antagonising the man by saying as much.

'I did not hear you come in,' she replied, without looking round.

'I have been watching you for some time and enjoying the view.'

She felt his gaze rove insolently over her body. Clad in the tight-fitting breeches and the man's shirt she wore when working, Crista felt disadvantaged. Her face heated with anger, as it always did when she was in the man's presence. She clenched her fists and closed her eyes, fighting the urge to give him the set-down he so richly deserved.

Instead she ignored him and, still with her back to him, reached for a velvet display case in which to place her now cooled creation.

'You were engrossed in what you were doing.' His boots rang out on the stone floor as he moved closer and peered over her shoulder at the completed necklace. Crista felt his coat brush against her back and his breath, hot and heavy, peppering her face.

'Magnificent,' he said softly. 'You have excelled yourself.'

'I have done my job.'

'Such a shame no credit will find its way to your door.'

She removed the leather band from her forehead, where it was starting to chafe, and tossed it aside. 'I do not do this for personal acclaim, Mr. Reece, as you well know.'

He was still too close for comfort, and so Crista stood up and packed away her equipment.

'I fail to understand why we cannot be friends.' He watched her intently as she moved around the workroom, his penetrating stare causing her to shiver. It felt as though he could see right through her. She found it as unnerving as his ridiculous suggestion that they be friends. Odious man! Friends did not coerce one another into acting against their consciences. 'I could do a very great deal to enhance your reputation, if only you would be nice to me.'

'Release my uncle and me from our obligation, and I am sure we can enjoy a very congenial friendship,' she replied, crossing her fingers behind her back. She would see herself in the workhouse before she *ever* befriended this callous popinjay. Besides, she knew very well what he really required from her, and it had little to do with friendship.

'Alas, my hands are tied.' He sounded convincingly regretful. 'Were it up to me then . . . '

Voices coming from the shop caught the attention of them both. Crista's uncle was speaking with a customer in very deferential terms.

'Hello, what do we have here?' Reece moved towards the door and placed an ear against it. He listened for a moment, and then scowled. 'One of the Sheridan clan, unless I mistake the matter. What the devil does he want?'

'The duke's family always calls upon my uncle for their jewellery requirements.'

'We thought to have put a stop to that.' Reece eyed Crista with suspicion. 'I do not trust your uncle any more than I trust you. I had best go out there and keep a watchful eye on him.'

'Do you think you should?' she asked capriciously. 'Whatever would your masters say?'

He grasped her arm so tightly it brought tears to her eyes. 'Just so we're clear, I am in charge here, and I make my own decisions.'

'Whatever you say.'

Crista was tempted to point out that Reece's presence, so out of place in her uncle's shop, would raise speculation. She refrained, thinking perhaps that would not be such a bad thing, although she could not have said why. At least it would rid her of Reece's loathsome company, and give her an opportunity to eavesdrop. Her uncle was sometimes secretive about their commissions for fear of placing too much burden upon Crista. Poor Uncle Charles. She felt for him excessively. He possessed the fierce Chesney pride that made it a torment to admit to being anything other than completely self-sufficient. Crista ought to know because she inherited the same trait. She had yet to decide if it was a blessing or a curse.

Reece had the temerity to place his grubby hands on her waist to move her aside. She had an aversion to being touched generally, even by people whom she admired. Reece most certainly did not rank amongst that select group. Startled by his action, her instinct was to grab her still cooling soldering iron and brand him with it. He chuckled, as though reading her mind, and swaggered into the shop before she could act upon that increasingly compelling impulse. She expelled a frustrated breath, promising herself that when the time was right she would have her revenge upon Reece and the people he worked for. Crista's patience — not one of her strong points — was fast reaching its limit.

Fortuitously, Reece left the door between the workroom and shop slightly ajar, affording Crista a glimpse of her uncle's aristocratic visitor. My goodness, what a fine sight to behold, she thought, suppressing a gasp of admiration. The tiredness left her limbs as she observed him. Even Reece prowling around the shop like a strutting peacock failed to annoy her, as it usually would have. Instead, her eyes were all for his lordship. Which one was he, she wondered, moistening lips that suddenly seemed inexplicably dry.

She had seen each of the four brothers in the village at different times but couldn't tell them apart. All of them were tall, broad-shouldered, dark-haired, and dark-eyed. The duke stood a few inches taller than his brothers, as though being first born had afforded him that right. She hadn't spoken to any of them. Indeed, she had no wish to draw attention to herself, and every reason to fade into the background. Even so, the sight of those brothers, the sound of their educated voices, spontaneous laughter and the charm and elegance evidenced in their mannerisms, had left a mark on her. She came away from those sightings understanding what had not previously been obvious to her. The Sheridan family did not follow the example set by aristocrats who put themselves above their company, expecting all and sundry to behave with deference. Quite the opposite, in fact. The Sheridans appeared to be as comfortable with farmers and fishermen as they probably were with their equals. Crista now understood why the villagers took such vicarious pride in them.

'Certainly we can do something special for Her Grace this year, Lord Amos,' her uncle said.

Ah, so he was Amos Sheridan, the second son. Crista had heard he was the sibling responsible for the horse stud at Winchester Park. It was a great success. Well, of course it was! Everything that family touched turned to the equivalent of the precious metal Crista spent her days working with. When she had time to herself, she often walked on the common land between the village and Winchester Park and observed one or more of their lordships charging across it on horseback. Lord Amos was the most familiar sight, but she had never seen him at such close quarters before. His large frame filled her uncle's establishment with an inundation of masculine power and smooth formidability that made Crista feel inexplicably warm.

Something stirred deep inside her — some dormant feeling that curled through her body and settled pleasurably in her abdomen — as she continued to observe him. She was angered by a reaction over which she had no control. Through no fault of her own, enough of the control she had once exerted over her own activities had already been wrested away from her. She did not require handsome gentlemen with charming smiles, sophistication, and poise stalking her thoughts. Even so, there was something about Lord Amos that defied her best endeavours to remain immune. Ye gods, she must be more tired than she realised since such whimsical fancies did not usually have any place in Crista's world.

'That is remarkably good of you, Chesney,' Lord Amos replied amiably. 'But, excuse me, I heard tell your eyesight is not what it once was. Are you perfectly sure the strain

24

wouldn't be too much for you?'

How extraordinary, Crista thought, that he should know of her uncle's malady and seem genuinely concerned about it.

'Your lordship is remarkably well informed.'

Lord Amos shrugged those impossibly broad shoulders. 'It's a small village.'

'Pray do not to listen to rumours put about by establishments in Compton, for I am persuaded that is where this whimsy must have originated.' Lord Amos raised a brow, but said nothing. 'I am perfectly able to be of service to your lordship. I can no longer do the close, intricate work, it is true, but I have a very able assistant who more than adequately serves me in that respect.'

'An assistant?' Reece blurted out, his face like thunder.

'You?' Lord Amos turned towards Reece and raised both brows this time, as though he couldn't quite believe such a dandy would be prepared to get his hands dirty. Clearly there was more to his lordship than a handsome face and easy manners.

'I have that honour.' Reece recovered quickly and executed an elegant bow.

'Hmm, I see.'

When it became apparent Lord Amos did not care too much for what he saw, Crista warmed to him a little more.

'I am sure we can meet your request for something out of the ordinary to mark the occasion.'

'Stop fishing for compliments, Chesney. All of your work is out of the ordinary, and well you know it.'

Uncle Charles inclined his head. 'Your lordship does me great honour.'

'I speak as I find. However, as I was saying, Her Grace turns sixty this year. The duke's commission for an additional piece of silver will not change, but I am charged by the duke to seek your advice on something more personal. A gift from her children to mark the occasion.'

'Perhaps a special suite of jewellery? A necklace, earrings and bracelet in gold or platinum, with ruby and diamond settings.'

'I'm listening.'

So was Crista. As her creative mind whirled with possibilities, her excitement grew.

'Would you like me to draw up some suggestions for your consideration?'

'Hmm, the duke will need to be involved in the decision.' Lord Amos rubbed his chin. 'How quickly can you have something to show us? We do not have the luxury of time on our side, for which I must take the blame. I ought to have spoken to you about this matter long before now.'

'A week should suffice, my lord.'

'A week? But that will only leave you with another week to make the pieces, once we agree upon them.'

'The planning often takes longer than the execution. Besides, for you, my lord, anything is possible.'

But only if we forget all our other commissions, Crista thought. Obviously, they would do so, but still, if anything went wrong with the pieces for the duchess there would be no time to correct the mistakes.

'Very well then, a week it is. I believe Her Grace intends to visit Winchester on Tuesday of next week, which will keep her occupied for the entire day. Would it be convenient for you and your assistant to call at the Park during the morning?'

Crista clapped a hand over her mouth to prevent a nervous laugh from escaping. Reece, Uncle Charles's supposed assistant, didn't have the first idea about jewellery design and construction. Intimidation and thuggery was more his forte.

'We would be honoured, my lord.'

'Very well then, Chesney,' Lord Amos replied with great good nature. 'We shall look forward to seeing you then. Reece,' he added with far less warmth, nodding abruptly to that individual as he headed for the door.

'Good day to you, my lord,' Uncle Charles replied, opening the door for him and standing back to allow his visitor to don his hat and leave the establishment.

When Lord Amos was safely out of the way, Crista pushed through the door from the workroom.

'A suite of jewellery, Uncle,' she said mildly.

'What the devil do you think you're playing at, Chesney?' Reece asked at the same time. 'You said nothing to me about a special commission.'

'I did not know his lordship would make the request,' Uncle Charles replied, turning sideways to wink at Crista. 'Remaining in favour with the duke is vital to the success of my business.'

'You do not have time for special commissions,' Reece said, scowling. 'The work you undertake for my masters must take priority.'

'Not at the expense of my relationship with Winchester Park,' Uncle Charles replied with determination. 'If I lose that connection I will go out of business, and since I refuse to become part of your infamous deception by accepting payment for what you force us to do, I must earn a living somehow.'

'You already enjoy the duke's patronage.'

28

'At the duke's discretion. It could be withdrawn at any time.'

And would be, Crista thought, if any of the Sheridan family even suspected what she and her uncle had been compelled by Reece and his masters to do for them. She shuddered. Not only would the Chesney name be thoroughly disgraced, but Compton village would ensure that everyone who was anyone heard all the particulars of their spectacular fall from grace.

That simply could not be permitted to happen.

'Don't think to play me for a fool,' Reece said, grabbing her uncle's lapels and pulling him hard against his own body. Uncle Charles, who did not enjoy the best of health, gasped for breath. Crista was infuriated.

'Let him be, you despicable brute!' she cried, looking around frantically for a weapon.

Reece emitted a rough snarl and pushed Uncle Charles forcibly away from him again. He stumbled, his glasses slipped down his nose, and only Crista's quick thinking in grasping his flailing arm prevented her uncle from falling to the floor. Crista helped him to a chair and fetched him a glass of water.

'I know you are accustomed to getting your way through brute force,' Crista said to

Reece, sending him a damning glance. 'But that will not serve on this occasion. If my uncle suffers from your rough handling then he will be unable to work, which means I will not be able to work either.'

'I can always think of ways to keep you gainfully employed, m'dear.' He leered at her, his gaze insolently resting on her thighs, visible in her tight-fitting breeches.

'You are certainly welcome to try,' Crista replied, crouching beside her uncle to satisfy herself he was recovering. 'Can I fetch you anything else for your comfort, Uncle Charles?'

'Bless you, child,' he replied, wheezing. 'I shall be quite myself again in a moment or two. I am not quite in my dotage, yet.'

'Then you will be able to tell me what you plan to do about this visit to Winchester Park,' Reece said, impatiently tapping his fingers against a glazed display cabinet. 'It won't take the duke five minutes to realise I know nothing about jewellery.'

'Then you should have remained in the back room during his lordship's visit.'

'I did not trust you to deal with the man alone.'

'What could I have said or done to concern you?'

Reece curled his upper lip. 'Just remember

who you're dealing with.'

As if we could forget, Crista thought malevolently.

'I shall take Crista with me to the Park,' Uncle Charles said decisively.

'You can't — ' Reece replied.

'How can you?' Crista asked at the same time.

'I shall tell their lordships the truth.' He carelessly lifted his shoulders. 'Unlike you, Reece, I have not forgotten how to be honest. I shall explain that you are my niece, Crista dear, and do all the design drawings for me nowadays.'

Crista narrowed her eyes at her beloved uncle, pleased to see a little colour returning to his face. She wondered what mischief he was planning in exposing her to the Sheridans. They had been so careful to keep her involvement in his business a secret, but she refrained from asking in Reece's company. Reece stepped forward, leaned over Uncle Charles's chair and pressed his face close.

'Make sure you don't try anything underhanded, or it will be the worse for you. The day has yet to dawn when an old man and a slip of a girl get the better of Edward Reece.' He picked up his hat and pushed it onto his head. 'You know what's at stake if you step out of line.' He opened the door to the street, paused when he was halfway through it, and turned back to look at them both. 'I shall be watching you both very carefully. Very carefully indeed.' Once again his gaze lingered on Crista. 'Especially you.'

3

'You think there is some truth in what Palmer told us about Chesney?' Zach asked, arranging himself in an elegant sprawl behind his imposing desk in the library at Winchester Park.

'Palmer always flaps like a headless chicken,' Amos replied from his chair on the other side of the desk that had been their father's and his father's before him. 'But there is something in what he had to say on this occasion, much as it pains me to admit it.'

'In what respect?'

Amos took a moment to gather his thoughts. He liked Chesney and appreciated his extraordinary skill. He had often thought he was wasted in such a small community. Had he set up shop in London, he would have been assured both a rich clientele and the reputation he deserved. Even so, facts had to be faced. The man was no longer in the first flush of youth.

'Chesney was a little too defensive when I asked him about his eyesight.'

'No one likes to acknowledge they're

getting old. Take it from one who knows.'

'Quite right, old man.' Amos sent his brother a roguish smile. 'But there was more to it than the toll of advancing years, although I can't put my finger on precisely what.'

'Perhaps you are seeing shadows where none exist.'

'Perhaps, but there's no mistaking the fact I took a dislike to his assistant. The man was dressed in the fashion of a gentleman, which he most decidedly was not, and he had soft hands.'

'You held his hand?' Zach asked with a wicked grin.

'Don't be such an ass.' Amos grinned as well. 'I happened to notice his hands. I was immediately suspicious of him because looked out of place in that shop, and Chesney seemed uncomfortable in his presence. That would not be the case if they worked together and Reece enjoyed Chesney's confidence.'

'Hmm, even so. I wouldn't imagine making jewellery is hard on the hands.'

'Oh, all right then, his hands were too clean, and the knave was too smooth by half.'

'You don't like the man, I understand that much,' Zach replied, idly fiddling with a silver paperknife, 'but if Chesney is happy with his work, who are we to interfere?'

Amos stood up and paced about the room.

'I wish I knew why I felt so uneasy about the entire incident.' He ran a finger along the spines of a shelf of books. 'There was something else odd about the business. I left the shop, then remembered I hadn't asked about the necklace Mother ordered for Portia's come-out. As I turned back I glanced in the window and saw a lad come out of the workroom at the back of the shop.'

'What of it?' Zach frowned. 'Have you fallen from the irascible stallion of yours and taken a knock to the head? You are making no sense.'

'It was almost as though the lad had been listening to our conversation.'

Zach shrugged. 'I dare say Chesney has an apprentice. What's so odd about that?'

'Nothing, but there was something very odd indeed about the actual apprentice. Prettiest lad I've seen in many a long year — '

Zach waggled his brows. 'Don't tell me your tastes have changed.'

Amos fixed His Grace the Duke of Winchester with a withering glare that made its recipient roar with laughter.

'The lad in question seemed to have a great deal to say for himself in front of his employer.'

'But what did he have to say when you went back into the shop? No doubt the sight of Lord Amos Sheridan in all his splendour gave him pause.'

'I didn't go back in.' Amos shook his head. 'Damned if I know why, but something stopped me. It felt like I would have been intruding.'

'It sounds to me as though you don't have enough to do with yourself, if you're still fretting about an incident that happened a week ago.'

'On the contrary, the stud is keeping me fully occupied. The services of our stallions are increasingly in demand.'

Faraday entered the room. 'Mr. Chesney is here for his appointment, Your Grace.'

'Very good, Faraday. Show him into the drawing room.' Zach stood up. 'Well, little brother, I shall take a look at this assistant who so bothers you and see if I share your concerns.'

Amos and Zach strolled the length of the vestibule and entered the drawing room. Amos drew in a sharp breath when he was met by Chesney and not Reece but a young lady in a pale green muslin gown and with a straw bonnet perched on top of an array of chestnut curls. He and Zach exchanged a glance. Zach moved forward to greet Chesney but Amos remained rooted to the spot, his gaze locked upon the young woman as

36

understanding came crashing in on him. He knew now why the interlude in Chesney's shop had bothered him so much.

This young woman with the most arresting silver-blue eyes was the *lad* he had seen through the shop window.

'Chesney.'

Crista watched the duke stride across the room, hand outstretched. His uncle shook it and offered the duke a deferential bow.

'Your Grace. May I present my niece, Miss Cristobel Brooke.'

'Miss Brooke.'

Crista curtsied to the duke. He took her hand and raised her from that curtsey, smiling so infectiously that Crista couldn't help smiling also.

'It is both a surprise and a pleasure to make your acquaintance, Miss Brooke,' he said. 'I was unaware Chesney had a niece. Where have you been hiding her, Chesney?'

'Crista came to live with me a short time ago, Your Grace.'

Lord Amos stepped forward, shook her uncle's hand and turned to her. Once again she curtsied, but this time she also blushed. Lord Amos's gaze was so intense, so penetrating, it was as though he could see inside her head and read her thoughts. When he took her hand a deeply disturbing jolt rocked her body and turbulent heat fogged her brain. She sought for her dignity and self-control, which had chosen a most inconvenient time to desert her, and found herself wallowing in a tangle of chaotic emotions. She fought her deepening blush when, with a knowing smile that implied he was accustomed to making females' senses reel, Lord Amos released her hand.

'A pleasure, Miss Brooke,' he said. 'What happened to your assistant, Chesney?'

'He is indisposed, my lord.'

Crista was sure Lord Amos muttered something along the lines of his hoping it was nothing trivial, causing her mind to warm to him in harmony with her already overheated body.

'I took the liberty of bringing Crista with me today because she has a knack for design,' Chesney said. 'She has drawn up a few proposals for your perusal.'

'Pray, take a seat, Miss Brooke, and I will ring for refreshment,' Lord Amos said.

Crista had been warned to expect great civility from the duke and his brothers, but their willingness to entertain them to tea took her by surprise. She seated herself on what had to be a Chippendale sofa. She recognised the striking characteristics peculiar to that great craftsman — the gracefully shaped

38

back, uninterrupted seat cushion covered in deep cream fabric, and traditionally beaded legs. Crista, who appreciated beauty and skilled workmanship, had never imagined she would ever sit upon such a fine piece of furniture and was terrified she might slop her tea over the priceless fabric.

She glanced around the magnificent, tastefully appointed room, taking in some new aspect to delight her each time she turned her head. A select few very tasteful, and doubtless rare and expensive ornaments rested on the superb black marble mantelpiece. An ornate chandelier, probably of bronze and gold and elaborately ornamented, made her yearn to examine the workmanship more closely. The walls were dominated by four large pictures, probably painted by a famous artist whose work she appreciated but did not recognise. The decoration leaned heavily towards a Moorish influence, as evidenced by the ceiling, which caught her attention and elicited a gasp of delight.

'I see you are admiring our ceiling, Miss Brooke,' Lord Amos said.

'Yes, indeed. I have never seen anything to compare to it.'

'I believe the inspiration came from Turkish palaces.'

'Ah yes, that would account for the canopy

of trellis work.' Her gaze fell upon the border displaying flowers, peacock's feathers, and ornamentation of a rich hue and delicate texture. 'Just imagine the work that went into producing such an ambitious ceiling,' she said in a tone of reverent awe. 'It is remarkable.'

Lord Amos's attention was claimed by something the duke said to him and Crista allowed her mind to wander. As the gentlemen chatted briefly amongst themselves, Crista took the opportunity to examine the brothers. The duke was very handsome, with easy manners and considerable charm. She'd heard rumours of countless women living in expectation of receiving his address, only to be disappointed. Crista could appreciate why ladies of quality threw their respective caps at him. Even if he had not been such a fine specimen of male beauty, his rank and wealth was such that any misfortunes of nature could be easily overlooked.

Appealing though the duke was, it was Lord Amos who held her interest. The connection she had felt to him when she saw him in the shop intensified the moment he walked into this room. She had looked up at him, caught his gaze, and felt as though the air had been sucked from the room. It was most peculiar. Crista had had her share of admirers over the years, but she had never felt the need to lose her head over any of them. Now she had met a gentlemen who excited her interest, but he was so far above her he might as well have been Chinese. She could not decide what made her even think about him in such terms. Hopefully it was nothing more than a momentary lapse brought on by her strained circumstances.

Lean-limbed and broad-shouldered, Lord Amos wore skin-tight bias-cut breeches in a light shade that showcased well-turned legs. She was absolutely sure his superbly cut green coat, resting so well upon his shoulders, did so without the need for padding. His silk waistcoat was patterned in muted shades of green and cream, and his neckcloth, elegantly tied in an intricate and fashionable manner, was secured with a superb emerald pin. A gold fob chain spanned his waist, disappearing into his waistcoat pocket, whence presumably sat his watch. The chain appeared to be a belcher link, she noticed absently, wondering who had made it for him, and if she could have done a better job of it.

'Ah, here is tea,' Lord Amos said when the butler entered the room, preceding a footman bearing a loaded tray. 'Can we persuade you to pour for us, Miss Brooke?'

Crista felt a moment's anxiety at the prospect of being the centre of attention. Her fear of spilling the tea, or worse, dropping the exquisite bone china cups, intensified. Reminding herself of the painstakingly intricate work she carried out on a daily basis without mishap helped to sooth her skittish nerves and she rose to the challenge with a serene smile.

'With the greatest of pleasure.' She lifted the heavy silver pot and filled the first cup. 'Milk and sugar, Your Grace?'

'Lemon, if you please.'

Naturally, sliced lemon had been provided in accordance with the duke's tastes, and Crista added a slice to his saucer before handing him his cup. She was pleased her hand barely trembled, and the cup did not give her away by rattling in its saucer. I shall remember this moment, Crista thought as the duke politely thanked her, and tell Amelia's children about the time I poured tea for a duke and a lord.

'And for you, Lord Amos?'

'Just milk, I thank you.'

'How do you find life in Shawford, Miss Brooke?' Lord Amos asked when they all had their tea and sat drinking it. 'It seems extraordinary you have lived here for a few months, and yet I have not had the pleasure of seeing you in the village.'

She arched a brow. 'How can you possibly know that, my lord? The village is always busy. I should be surprised if you would notice me amongst the throng.'

He fixed her with an intense look, his eyes radiating elusive warmth. 'Believe me, I would not have forgotten.'

'Oh.' *Lord in heaven, what does he mean by that remark?*

'You have designs for us to see, Chesney,' the duke said, casting what appeared to be a warning glance in Lord Amos's direction. Warning about what, Crista wondered.

'Indeed, Your Grace.' He picked up the rolled parchments he had brought into the room with him. 'Perhaps if we could put these on the table, you will get a better idea of what Crista has in mind for Her Grace.'

'Good idea.'

The duke rang the bell. It was answered almost at once by a footman who cleared away the tray, freeing up the table for their use without the need to vacate their chairs. Crista felt inexplicably nervous as her uncle unfurled her sketches. It was one thing knowing that she, a mere woman, had come up with the designs, but entirely another for these gentleman to accept them. They appeared enlightened, not unduly concerned about a woman being the designer. But still, when it came right down to it, they were probably like most of their sex and would

43

deem her suggestions unworthy for no other reason than that she was their architect.

'This first suggestion calls for rubies and diamonds and is, if you will be guided by me, gentlemen, by far the most suitable.'

Two dark heads pored over Crista's sketches. Before they could ask any questions, the door opened and another gentlemen joined them. He looked so much like the others that he had to be another brother.

'Ah, Vince, there you are,' the duke said.

'Sorry, I was riding the eastern perimeter with Philson, and time got away from me. We need to start work on that dry stone wall before winter, Zach. How do you do, Chesney.'

Uncle Charles stood up and bowed. 'Lord Vincent.'

The newcomer's glance landed on Crista, and a slow smile illuminated his handsome features. 'I say, will someone introduce me?'

'This is Miss Brooke, Vince,' Lord Amos said. 'She is Chesney's niece and responsible for these rather excellent designs. Miss Brooke, this is my brother, Lord Vincent Sheridan.'

Crista stood and curtsied. Lord Vincent bowed over her hand. 'Your servant, ma'am.'

'Do sit down, Vince, and stop crowding Miss Brooke,' Lord Amos said. 'You must excuse us, Miss Brooke, but we have often been told that as a pack we are a little overwhelming.'

'Just be thankful our brother Nathanial is escorting our mother and sisters to Winchester today,' the duke said, smiling. 'Which means you are spared all four of us at once.'

'I am not so feeble I cannot withstand your company, gentlemen.'

Crista was horrified by her spontaneous reaction. She could see she had surprised the gentlemen and shocked her uncle.

'I am very pleased to hear it,' Lord Amos replied with an enigmatic smile. 'Look at this, Vince. What do you think?'

'Very ambitious, but different enough to stand out,' Lord Vincent replied after taking several minutes to carefully study Crista's design, stretching her nerves to breaking point.

'What is all this delicate work around the settings, Miss Brooke?' the duke asked.

'Filigree, Your Grace, constructed by cutting gold solder into fine chips.'

'I see.'

The gentlemen looked briefly at Crista's other designs but came back to the rubies and diamonds almost immediately.

'I have some very fine Burmese rubies in stock, Your Grace, if this design suits. In ancient times, the ruby was said to signify power and vitality,' Crista told them. 'It has been called the king of gemstones. Warriors embedded rubies in their skin to give them courage and protection before going into battle. They were considered a talisman to ward off danger, evil, and bad dreams.'

'How very interesting,' the duke said, fixing her with a speculative expression. 'Can I ask why you have not recommended diamonds?'

'I feel persuaded Her Grace must already have an abundant supply,' Crista replied.

'Quite so. My father gifted many to her.'

'What else can you tell us about rubies?' Lord Vincent asked.

'In days gone by, they were symbols of power.' Crista leaned forward, warming to her theme. 'It is also said they have healing powers which assist blood circulation.' At a warning glance from her uncle Crista abruptly fell silent. 'My apologies, gentlemen, I sometimes get carried away with my enthusiasm.'

'Not in the least.' Lord Amos sent her a smouldering smile. 'Do tell us more.'

'Well, rubies are supposed to ease transition by providing clarity, my lord. And the diamonds surrounding them represent pure and unbreakable love.'

The brothers shared a prolonged glance. Crista laced her fingers together in her lap, aware she had overstepped the mark. She ought to have remained silent and allowed her uncle to sell her suggestions to the duke. One of Crista's many failings was permitting her enthusiasm for and knowledge of jewellery to overcome social mores. On this occasion she had probably cost her uncle a valuable and prestigious commission. She really was a sorry excuse for a niece. Her uncle had taken her in when she was badly in need of his protection and all she had done to show her gratitude was to visit her troubles upon him. She had never liked herself less.

'Excellent,' said the duke. 'Then rubies it must be.'

'Really?' Crista's head shot up, surprise and delight causing her to spontaneously blurt out, 'Oh, how wonderful!'

'After such an impassioned plea, Miss Brooke, we would not have it any other way. How quickly can the pieces be ready?'

4

'What did you make of that?' Vince asked when their visitors had departed. 'Those jewellery designs were exceptional, and done by a chit of a girl, too. She cannot be above two and twenty.'

'It explains your interest in Chesney's apprentice,' Zach said, grinning at Amos.

'She is deuced attractive and intelligent,' Vince agreed.

'Miss Brooke's presence raises more questions than it answers,' Amos replied thoughtfully. 'Why does she feel the need to dress in male clothing? Why does she undertake Chesney's design work? If his eyesight is still good enough to make intricate jewellery then he ought to be able to sketch.'

'His assistant does the close work, remember,' Zach pointed out.

'Supposedly.' Amos still had his doubts about that. 'Chesney has always taken great pride in the uniqueness of his designs and guards that aspect of his work jealously. It makes no sense for him to cede that part of his business to a young girl.'

'He doesn't look as strong as he once did,' Vince remarked.

'Which would explain his need for an assistant,' Zach pointed out.

'An assistant who didn't see fit to keep an appointment with a duke.' Amos scowled. 'Does that not strike you as odd, Zach? You are by far and away *the* most important person around these parts, and your patronage can make or break an establishment. Can you think of another single occasion when a craftsman ignored a summons of yours?'

'I don't suppose the man can help being indisposed,' Zach replied mildly.

Amos shook his head. 'It's damned odd, that's all I know.'

'The points your Miss Brooke made about rubies and diamonds were inspired,' Zach said. 'It was as though she understood Mother's sorrow at our father's passing.'

'Healing powers, ease of transition, and diamonds representing pure and unbreakable love.' Amos nodded. 'The same thought occurred to me.'

'Miss Brooke must be a romantic at heart,' Zach said.

'Why have we not seen or heard anything of her before now?' Amos asked. 'Unless we are losing our touch, one of us would have noticed her.'

'She certainly seems to have caught your attention now,' Zach replied, sharing an amused glance with Vince. 'All that chestnut hair, those most unusual eyes, her lively spirit, and intelligence make for a compelling combination. But have a care. She is respectable and not of Martha's ilk. You can look, you can admire, but that's as far as it goes.'

'Thank you for your advice, Your Grace,' Amos replied drolly.

'My pleasure.' Zach grinned at both brothers and led the way towards the dining parlour. 'Come along, it's time for luncheon.'

Amos brooded through the meal, his head full of the mysterious Cristobel Brooke, prepared to wager all was not as it appeared to be with that young lady. Why else would she choose to hide herself away in her uncle's workshop when she ought to be enjoying the pleasures of village society? The thought of any of the young traders in either village sniffing around her petticoats filled him with protective instincts that were as strong as they were inexplicable. Miss Brooke was not his responsibility.

And yet, he had never felt such a fierce attraction towards any female. Even before formally meeting Miss Brooke today, catching a glimpse of her in her breeches and still thinking her to be a lad had been a defining moment, like turning a corner in his mind.

He jerked upright when a possibility occurred to him. When riding home in the early evenings across the common land between the village and Winchester Park, on several occasions he had seen a mysterious woman walking there. Most villagers chose to walk by the canal, waving to the regular passage of loaded barges moving to and from the wharf near Shawford Mill. For that reason, a lone woman on the common was unusual enough to stick in his mind, especially when that woman possessed a profusion of distinctive chestnut hair. He had raised a hand in greeting once or twice, but the woman disappeared into the tree line, as though she did not wish her solitary ramble to be interrupted.

Amos was convinced now the woman had been Miss Brooke. He was equally convinced she had secrets, was in some sort of trouble, and mistrusted any well-intentioned offers of help. His instincts told him he had hit upon the reason for her reclusiveness. Amos was determined to find out why and resolve her difficulties for her.

Beyond that point, he was unwilling to speculate.

An early opportunity to put his plan into action occurred the following evening. Nate had badgered Amos into a visit to the Crown and Anchor. Leaving Nate to flirt with Martha, Amos took a stroll down the main street. The businesses were closed for the evening, and there was no sign of life in the vicinity of Chesney's shop. Amos glanced up at the two stories above, where lights showed in several windows. Chesney had done well over the years and could probably afford to live elsewhere but chose to remain living over his business. Amos supposed Miss Brooke must now reside there with him.

He slipped down the alleyway to one side of the premises, which led him to the workshop at the rear. Light spilled from the window, presumably because Chesney or his damned assistant were hard at work on the commission for Amos's mother. Not wishing to be caught in the embarrassing position of snooping, Amos flattened himself against the wall and cautiously chanced a glance through the window.

'What the devil?'

Amos blinked, thinking his eyes must be playing tricks on him. He took a second, longer look but nothing had changed. Miss Brooke, clad in her masculine attire, was bent over a workbench, not sketching but soldering jewellery in what appeared to be a professional and competent manner. He leaned back against the wall, cogitating. If she was now undertaking all the jewellery making, it would explain the male attire. Skirts and petticoats would hamper her movements. He could also understand why she was reluctant to take credit for her art. Most men were insufficiently enlightened to accept a woman could be capable of holding down a traditionally male occupation, and would resent her talent if they knew about it. The question was, why did she need to do the work instead of her uncle? Where had she learned her trade, and what part did Reece play in the deception? The name Brooke, in connection with jewellery, rang a vague bell, but he couldn't think where he had heard it before. He would ask his mother. If anyone knew, it would be her.

Amos stole another glance at Miss Brooke's figure, still bent close to her work. She straightened up as he watched, appeared to sigh and massaged the small of her back with both hands. Her face looked drawn and tired. She wore a magnifying glass attached to some sort of strap that circled her forehead. She removed it, tidied her equipment and extinguished the lights. So she ought. It was gone nine in the evening and she must be exhausted. What was her uncle thinking of, keeping her working so late into the night?

He headed back towards the Crown and

Anchor deep in thought. The more he learned about the enigmatic Miss Brooke, the more curious about her circumstances he became.

★ ★ ★

Crista had the strangest feeling she was being watched. She glanced through the window, but there was no one there. She had been working since seven that morning, with hardly a break and was weary to the bone, almost too tired to stand. Was it any wonder she was imaging things? She critically examined the emerald-studded bangle she had just completed. It was far too ostentatious for her taste, but exquisitely made, if she did say so herself. She wished she could take more pleasure from the result, but that was impossible. What she was doing was against the law, and against every principle she possessed. She was not a criminal by nature and felt nothing but contempt for the things she had been forced to do.

She heard the door open behind her and when her skin crawled she knew, without turning around, it was Reece come to check on her progress.

'Is it completed?' he asked.

She kept her back to him. 'I told you it would be.'

'You had better not have skimped just because you have designed jewellery for a duchess.'

Crista was tempted to throw the bangle at his face. She resisted only because it might be damaged if it fell to the floor, which would mean more work for her putting it right.

'See for yourself.'

Reece picked up the bangle and examined the workmanship minutely. She continued to tidy away her equipment, not caring about his opinion. He gave it anyway.

'Superb,' he said.

Crista said nothing.

'I need a necklace to match.'

'That was not part of the agreement.'

'Nevertheless, you will do it.'

Crista stood up, placed her fisted hands on her hips and glowered at him. 'I cannot, not now. I must finish the commission for the duchess. After that, we shall see.'

He took a menacing step towards her. To her considerable annoyance she instinctively backed away, giving the impression she feared him. She did, since he was a bully with an unpredictable temper and took especial pleasure in intimidating helpless women. But that didn't mean she should show her fear.

'Do I need to remind you what is at stake if you fail to do as you're told?'

He stood so close his rancid breath, smelling of whisky and rich food, peppered her face. When he reached out, as if to touch her, Crista's temper erupted. She felt behind her for a weapon, something to make this contest of wills more even. Her hand closed around the wooden handle of her soldering iron, still warm from recent use. She whisked it towards his face, close enough to singe his whiskers. He jumped back, murder in his eyes.

'What the devil — '

'You are not the only person capable of intimidation. Never, ever try to touch me again.'

He sneered at her. 'You will do as you are told.'

'I will do as I see fit. I shall finish the commission for the duchess, and then we shall see about your wretched business.'

'You have no choice.' Reece back away from her, and Crista returned the soldering iron to her bench. 'You are too good at what you do for us to let you go. We have a plethora of customers eager to benefit from your expertise.'

She tossed her head. 'That must make you very proud.'

'No, m'dear, it makes me very rich, which is all that concerns me.'

'I do not have the slightest difficulty believing you. Even so, I will not make anything else for you until I have seen to the duchess's requirements, and there is an end to the matter.'

Reece appeared to realise she was in earnest, and she had the satisfaction of watching him snarl his agreement. She knew her victory would be fleeting and he would find a way to make her pay for it.

She saw Reece out, locked the door firmly behind him, and trudged up the stairs, almost too tired to lift her feet. She hated the person she had been forced by circumstances to become. Enough was enough! She wanted to be able to walk down the street with her head held high and her conscience clear. She paused on the top step and nodded decisively. Regardless of the risk to others, it was time for her and her uncle to stand up to Reece.

★ ★ ★

Reece strode away in a disgruntled frame of mind. Cristobel Brooke had chosen an unfortunate time to develop a rebellious streak. It would have to be curtailed before she did something to overset their very profitable scheme. He fingered the bangle she had just finished making, now safely wrapped

57

in a velvet cloth and secured in his pocket. She really did have the most exceptional talent. It was a disappointment that she was unprepared to be more reasonable. She worked for them under duress, refusing all payment for her services. If she was more realistic about her circumstances, she could soon become a wealthy woman of independent means. Well, that was females for you. Not an ounce of sense between the whole damned lot of them. Was it any wonder that men ran the world?

Why her refusal to accept payment should bother Reece so much was a puzzle. If Miss Brooke declined her share, it meant more for the rest of them. She remained detached from their nefarious activities, never showing any curiosity about the pieces she made for them, and her attitude of superior disdain infuriated him. He would break through her reserve if it was the last thing he ever did. Edward Reece was not prepared to be gainsaid, especially by a chit of a girl who had precious little to be superior about.

His mood lifted when Reece reminded himself that no one would ever guess this bangle was the work of a woman rather than that of a skilled tradesman. Well, like it or not, she would be producing a very great deal of the same for Reece over the coming months.

Reece would just have to give her a little reminder of what was at stake if she even thought of refusing.

Miss Brooke had something about her that fascinated Reece, which possibly explained his disappointment at her aloof attitude. Reece enjoyed more than his share of success with the fairer sex, but Miss Brooke seemed oblivious to his charms. Her attitude baffled him. She was not exactly beautiful, nor was she well-born and, since her father's death, she had no means of supporting herself. She couldn't use her skill as a jeweller once her uncle retired, which he would soon be forced to do. No other respectable establishment would employ a woman to do a man's work, no matter how skilled she was.

Perhaps it was her disinterest in him that had made Reece want her the moment he set eyes on her. Unfortunately, Reece was under strict instructions to let her be, at least until she had outlived her usefulness. Only the thought of doing precisely as he pleased with her when their business was complete kept Reece's lust in check, though his imagination still sometimes spiralled out of control. He could, and did, purchase as many women as he felt the need for, but they were willing. There was something about a reluctant one, about the way Miss Cristobel Brooke looked down her pert little nose at him that heated his blood. It didn't help matters that she dressed in men's attire. Attire that graphically displayed every delectable curve on her body.

Reece slowed his pace, hampered by his reaction to such thoughts. He had been within a hair's breadth of pushing her across her workbench and having his way with her in retaliation for her rebelliousness. She had no business talking back to him in such a fashion. Being entertained at Winchester Park had given her ideas above her station, and that attitude could not be permitted to flourish, but he was unsure how far to push her. She was not as biddable as her weak father had been, and threats against her uncle and sister would only get him so far. The wretchedly naive girl had standards. Reece blew air through his lips as he strode on towards his destination, frequently glancing over his shoulder to ensure he was not being followed. He could have told her having standards didn't fill empty bellies and that God helped those that helped themselves, but why bother? Still, she would find out soon enough, if she continued to defy him.

Much as he hated to admit to his inability to control her, Reece knew she was too important not to pass on intelligence of her rebellion, which was why he was making this unscheduled call. He made a habit of always covering his own back, thinking it better to share even the smallest concern with his employer, rather than seem inefficient if matters ran out of control. His loyalty and straightforwardness had seen him rise fast within the ranks of the organisation he worked for, and he had no desire to see that situation come to an end because of a chit of a girl.

He reached the manor house on the edge of the village occupied by a respected resident whose reputation was beyond reproach. Miss Brooke knew nothing of his involvement in this business. Reece lifted the front door knocker. It was answered by a maid who dipped a curtsey and stood back to allow him in. He handed her his hat and gloves.

'Is the master expecting you, sir?'

'Just tell him I'm, here, Mary. There's a good girl.'

'Wait here then.'

Reece patted her rear, causing her to giggle. She was obliging that way, always willing to lift her skirts without a fuss if Reece had an itch that needed scratching. She was grateful for the attention and the monetary reward. He suspected that she provided the same service for her employer.

'He's in the library, sir,' Mary said, returning quickly. 'He said to go through.'

61

Reece tapped on the library door and entered the room. The gentleman seated behind an imposing desk put his quill aside and looked up at Reece.

'I hope there is a good reason for this unexpected visit,' he said in a quiet, yet steely tone.

'I thought it best to come in person to inform you Chesney has taken a commission to design a special suite of jewellery for the duchess's birthday.'

'Damn it, man, why did you permit that to happen?'

'I could hardly stop him.' He shrugged. 'Lord Amos came to the shop and Chesney took me by surprise by suggesting the idea.'

'You think Chesney planned this as a means of disrupting our business?'

'Very likely. He's a wily old fox. But the girl didn't know what he had planned. She seemed as surprised as I was to hear about it. Then both of them had to go up to the big house and show them designs.'

The gentleman scowled. 'The Sheridans have seen the girl?'

'Well, I could hardly go. They would have caught me as a fraud in a heartbeat. She's supposed to have drawn up designs. Well, no *supposed* about it. She did.'

'When did they go to the Park?'

'Yesterday.'

'And I am only just hearing about this?' The gentleman's scowl became lethal.

'You were in London, sir. I came tonight, having heard of your return.'

'Hmm, this is deuced inconvenient. I wish I knew what they made of the girl drawing up the designs. Is there any possibility they might realise who she is?'

'Unfortunately, I have no way of knowing. I doubt she would be foolish enough to drop any hints, given she *is* now involved with us. No one will ever believe she helps us against her will, especially since we can prove her father's involvement.'

'I hoped the rumours circulating about Chesney's eyesight would turn the Sheridans against him. Obviously, that didn't work, and their continued patronage will slow our business down considerably.'

'I realise that, but it will only take a week for the duchess's work to be completed.'

'We have other commissions due before then. We are already running behind.'

Reece extracted the emerald bangle from his pocket and placed it on his employer's desk. He picked it up and examined it closely. 'Superb,' he said with evident satisfaction. 'But what of the necklace we need to go with it?'

'She says she won't make it until she has done the duchess's commission.'

The gentleman thumped his clenched fist on his desk. 'Perdition, since when did a slip of a girl start calling the shots in this organisation?'

'We need her, sir,' Reece said mildly. 'The old man can't work nearly as fast as she does, and she knows it.'

'For the love of God, we didn't have this trouble when her father was alive. Perhaps you should remind her of the consequences if she continues to defy us.'

'She knows well enough, which is the only reason why she helps us. But she is temperamental, and I get the feeling that if we push too hard she will push back.'

'Which will implicate her and her precious family.'

'And put us all in gaol.'

'Hmm, there is that. God preserve me from headstrong women!' The gentleman fell into momentary contemplation. 'I suppose a week's delay can be explained away, but I don't want her to think she has won this particular skirmish or there's no telling what she might try next.' He leaned back in his chair, pausing to think. 'There must be some way to bring her to heel. What does she fear the most, apart from her uncle's health and her sister's reputation, neither of which seem sufficient to make her completely obedient?'

'Well . . . ' A slow smile spread across Reece's face. 'She hates to be touched.'

'I won't have you despoil her. At least not yet. If you strip her of her dignity then she will definitely defy us. Woman are odd that way.'

'It doesn't need to come to that.' *And you don't need to know if things get out of hand.* 'But if I can get to her when she's away from that shop, I can put the fear of God into her.'

Reece's employer rubbed his chin in his cupped hand. 'Do what is necessary to secure her continued obedience.'

'She sometimes walks on the common when she finishes work for the day.'

'Well, that sounds ideal. No one walks there much.' The rigidness left the gentleman's shoulders. 'I will leave the particulars to you to decide, but I don't relish having to tell our London masters we can't control the girl. I placed my faith in you, Reece, because you assured me you could manage matters. Don't make me regret that decision.' He stood up. 'You did right to tell me about this, but don't come back again unless it's absolutely necessary. We cannot be seen together.'

Reece nodded, relieved to have escaped further chastisement. His employer was not a pleasant person to be around when he was displeased. 'You can depend upon me, sir.'

5

Amos had been able to ride almost before he could walk and horses were in his blood. He had never seriously considered doing anything with his life that did not directly involve them. When he finished his tenure at university and was in need of an occupation, he had sold the idea of an innovative new stud to Zach and persuaded him to let him run it. Six years later, it was an established and respected enterprise, having earned a reputation for producing decent Nonius foals, extensively used by cavalry regiments in Europe.

'I am glad you stopped by,' Amos said to Zach as they stood together at the paddock railings, watching the two mares who had arrived the previous week. Zach's two Irish wolfhounds Phineas and Phantom had their noses to the ground, following the trail of rabbits until they became bored and slumped down at Zach's feet. 'I discovered something rather strange last night that I wanted to discuss with you.'

'In the Crown and Anchor?' Zach flexed a brow. 'There are always strange activities in that establishment. One never quite knows what one is likely to see or hear.'

The stud workers gently led the mares inside to prepare them. Both went willingly enough, which was a good sign.

'I left Nate to enjoy Martha and have absolutely no wish to hear about their strange activities.'

Zach laughed. 'Very wise. What did you do while our baby brother was earning his spurs?'

'I took a turn about the village.'

'And your perambulation just happened to take you past a certain jeweller's establishment?'

Amos sent his brother a searching look. 'Am I that transparent?'

'I believe we were all taken with Miss Brooke's passion for her designs, Amos, to say nothing of the lady herself. Her eyes are remarkable, saving her from being plain.' Zach grinned. 'As to her body — '

'Leave her alone. I saw her first.'

'Aha, I though as much.' Zach roared with laughter, startling the horses. 'Sorry, Amos, but I've never seen you like this before. Please tell me you plan to sweep the beguiling Miss Brooke off her dainty feet and stand with her in front of a parson at the earliest opportunity. That way, you and she can beget a dozen children, saving me from the trouble of producing an heir, and also diverting our mother's matrimonial ambitions away from me.'

Amos rolled his eyes. 'Now whose imagination is running away with him? Miss Brooke is charming, but she is not a lady in the true sense of the word.'

'And yet, that is precisely what she appeared to be. She knows how to behave in society.'

'Yes, that thought had occurred to me.' Amos rubbed his jaw. 'I wonder why Chesney has kept her hidden away.'

'Probably trying to keep her safe from people like you.' Zach grinned. 'Anyway, what did you wish to tell me about your nocturnal perambulation?'

'We could not quite understand why Chesney brought Miss Brooke with him rather than his damned assistant, nor why she drew up the designs for that matter.' Amos scratched the back of his neck. 'I felt there was more to it than they let on.'

'Very possibly, but provided they produce the jewellery on time, why should it matter to us?'

'I think Miss Brooke is being exploited in some fashion.'

Amos could see he had surprised his

brother. 'By Chesney? Surely not?'

'No, not by him, but by someone. Anyway, I walked past the shop last night and, of course, it was all closed up. So I slipped around the back and observed Miss Brooke in the workshop.' Amos paused and fixed his brother with a probing look. 'Making the jewellery herself.'

'Good God!'

'My thoughts precisely.'

'Do you imagine Chesney's eyesight really has become so bad that he can't work himself?'

'I'm unsure what to think, but my instincts tell me Miss Brooke is being coerced in some way.'

'Because that's what you want to think. You are attracted to her and want to think well of her. Not that there is any reason why you should not. I hope we are not so unenlightened we would disapprove of a woman taking up such an occupation. Since she is Chesney's niece, it's reasonable to suppose she grew up surrounded by jewellery and learned her skill from the cradle.'

'She doesn't share Chesney's name, so her mother must have been Chesney's sister.'

'If Chesney can no longer do close work, perhaps the girl persuaded him to let her try her hand herself. It would explain why she keeps to herself. If Compton village heard of a woman craftsman, or should I say a woman, plying Chesney's trade because he was incapable, they would take pleasure in shouting it from the rooftops. You know how seriously the two villages take this silly feuding.'

Zach rolled his eyes. 'I am hardly in a position to forget it.'

'Do you imagine her uncle trained her himself?' Amos asked. 'The name Brooke and jewellery are mixed in my mind. I'm sure there is a reason for that.'

'Her uncle, or perhaps there is someone else in her family who encouraged her talent.' Zach slapped Amos's shoulders. 'Anyway, we should respect her secret. I have no objection to a woman making Mother's jewellery. If her work is even half as competent as her passion for it, then our mother will be delighted with her gift.'

'I am glad you feel that way, but something isn't right, and I have a feeling Miss Brooke is urgently in need of our help.'

'Ours, or yours?'

'I have decided to make her my responsibility.'

Zach flashed a raffish grin. 'How very noble of you. But be careful, Amos. Chesney and his niece may not thank us for interfering. They can't very well tell you to go to the devil, as they would if it was anyone else interfered.'

It was time for the mares to be covered. The brothers watched as the stud-hands led them into the covering shed. The stallions were eager to perform their duties, and the matter was soon dealt with. Zach wandered back to the house, his dogs loping along ahead of him, but Amos remained behind, unable to dislodge thoughts of Miss Brooke from his head. Still just in shirtsleeves, he came to a decision. And there was no time like the present to carry it through. He saddled his black stallion himself, mounted up, and left the yard at a canter.

'Come along, Warrior,' he said to the horse. 'Let us see if we can be of service to a lady in distress.'

He turned Warrior in the direction of the common, hoping to see Miss Brooke walking there. Unless she worked late into the evening again, this was the time when he was the most likely to encounter her.

To his intense disappointment, she was nowhere to be seen.

He rode on to Shawford, and walked Warrior down the main road. All of the businesses had closed for the day, with the exception of the Crown and Anchor which, as always, was enjoying a brisk trade. He was about to head on past Chesney's establishment when he saw a familiar figure leave the tavern on foot, heading for the common with a purposeful stride. It was Reece.

On an impulse, he turned Warrior and followed at a safe distance behind, curious to know what he was up to.

★ ★ ★

Crista had worked solidly the entire day on the duke's commission while her uncle concentrated on the silver chalice agreed upon for her collection. Crista would finish the filigree on it just as soon as she could make the time. Thankfully, she had seen nothing of Reece that day. With no interruptions, she had made good progress forming the gold settings for the stones. Next, she must start the delicate filigree that would decorate the pieces.

'My dear, you have been here all day.' Uncle Charles came into the workroom, his brow creased by a frown. 'You will make yourself ill if you continue to work so hard. Allow me to take over for a while. I am not completely past it, you know.'

'I know that, Uncle,' Crista replied, leaning up from her seat to place an affectionate kiss on his wrinkled cheek. 'But I am enjoying doing honest work for a change. I can take pride in it and not feel the need to apologise every five minutes.'

'You have absolutely nothing to feel guilty about.' Uncle Charles scowled, but she knew his displeasure was not directed at her. 'Your father got you into this situation. You and I must now find a way out of it.'

'How extraordinary.' Crista smiled. 'I had reached the same conclusion. The more we do for them, the deeper we become embroiled, and the harder it will be to prove we were coerced.'

'It is time to stand up for ourselves.' Uncle Charles clasped his lapels, his expression grimly determined. 'We need to find out what we are up against so must discover who Reece reports to. He is just the messenger.'

'Yes, we have always known that.' She shuddered when she recalled what had happened to her father. He behaved badly in allowing greed to get the better of him. Even so, he had not deserved the brutal punishment that befell him when his conscience prevented him from continuing with the activities he had been drawn into. 'Do you imagine there is someone in the village?'

'Reece never leaves the district, and receives no visitors to his room at the Crown and Anchor, so we must assume so. After all, he must get his orders from somewhere.'

'How shall we discover who he is in league with, and what help will it be to us if we do?'

'Knowledge is power, my dear. Besides, if we knew more, we could go to the duke. The family is very fair-minded, Crista. I have known them all since they were in short coats.'

'You cannot risk telling them, Uncle.' Crista grasped his hand, filled with alarm that he might do something foolhardy. 'We must resolve this problem alone. Think of Amelia. Besides, even if we could convince the duke we are innocent pawns, we have still broken the law, and such appetising scandal could never remain secret for long. Just think what the residents of Compton would do with it.'

'I know, but I am at the end of my career, and I'll be damned . . . excuse the language, my dear, but I simply will not allow this situation to endure indefinitely. Had they not dragged you into it, it would not have even started, regardless of your father's stupidity.'

'Which is precisely why they involved me. I just wish I knew how they found out about my skills. That question plagues me, keeping me awake at night. So few people knew.' Crista felt tears spring to her eyes. 'Do you have any idea how wretched I feel each time I think of the way you have been used?'

74

'There, there, my dear, don't distress yourself.' Uncle Charles patted her hand. 'Now that we are agreed something must be done, I am sure a means of extricating ourselves will present itself.'

'I would love to see the back of the odious Mr. Reece, but if we do get the better of him, his masters will simply replace him. They will go after Amelia just to remind us what they are capable of and possibly you, too.' She flung her arms around him. 'I couldn't bear it if anything were to happen to either of you. I know Amelia can be selfish and silly, but she is still my sister.'

When she released Uncle Charles, she noticed his eyes were also damp. 'You've spent all your life trying to please others, my dear. I had thought with the demise of your father you would finally have the opportunity to live for yourself and can't tell you how sorry I am at the way things have turned out.'

'Hush, Uncle, it's not your fault.' She offered him a tired smile. 'Together we shall think of a way to get the better of them and expose them for the villains they are. You'll see.'

'That we shall, but in the meantime there is something you could do for me.'

'Anything.'

'Go out and enjoy the evening air for an

hour before Kate has dinner ready for us. You look fearsome pale, and fresh air will revive you. It's a beautiful evening.'

At first Crista shook her head. She had planned to put in at least another hour's work but, now that her uncle had suggested the idea, the call of the outdoors was simply too strong to resist.

'Very well,' she said. 'To please you, Uncle, I shall do just that. Let me tidy up here. Then I had best change into a gown, just in case I encounter anyone and excite their curiosity.'

'Get along with you, child. I shall tidy up for you and I don't expect to see you again until it's time for dinner.'

Crista ran up to her room on the second floor and shed her breeches and shirt. She then uncoiled her hair from the tight bun that had contained it for the entire day, aware from painful experience that if she did not keep it clear of her work, it could easily be ignited. She sighed with pleasure when the pressure on her skull receded, brushed it loose and felt the headache that had been threatening diminish almost immediately. With her hair neatly tied back with a ribbon, she donned an old yellow cotton gown, draped a shawl negligently around her shoulders, and didn't bother with a bonnet. She was unlikely to meet anyone on the common at this hour. Indeed, she had made an art form of avoiding people and their intrusive questions since moving to Shawford.

Feeling giddy with relief at having a moment to herself, she slipped back down the stairs and through the back door. With a light step she headed for the common, determined to make the most of her precious moment of freedom. The air was fresh and warm on her face as she turned it upwards. She breathed deeply of it, happy as long as she didn't think about Reece. She tried, truly tried, to count her blessings instead. She had an uncle whom she loved and respected, a sister on the brink of an advantageous marriage, and she herself was doing what she had always wished to, even if she couldn't take public credit for it.

She followed the familiar track across the common, unsurprised no one else was abroad. She failed to understand why they preferred the canal to this lovely wilderness with its wild flowers, trees in full leaf, and cacophony of sweet bird song, but was glad they did. This small corner of Winchester was hers alone, or so she liked to think, and she was familiar with every corner of it. She felt the knots leaving her muscles as she headed wherever her feet directed her, thinking about her visit to Winchester Park the previous day and the courteous manner in which she had been received. She had poured tea for a duke and two of his brothers.

Only imagine that!

She buried her nose in a bush of wild honeysuckle, breathing in its fragrant aroma, chiding herself when her thoughts returned to Lord Amos. They had done so with disturbing regularity since the previous day. His disarming smile, elegant manners, and animal vitality had had a profound effect upon her. If she shared her worries with him, she felt sure he would find a resolution. She shook her head to dislodge such a whimsical notion. Even if he believed her and took up the cudgels on her behalf, she would have to admit to her culpability, and he would lose any respect he entertained for her. That thought was more painful than the terrifying prospect of challenging Reece alone.

She left the honeysuckle and wandered on. No, confiding in anyone was out of the question, especially Lord Amos. Damnation, was that a horse she could hear approaching? She looked over her shoulder and gasped. She recognised the magnificent stallion being trotted along the path she had just walked. She also recognised the man on its back. It was as though her thoughts of Lord Amos had summoned the man himself. Like her, he was hatless, hair as black as his horse's coat blowing in the wind. He was informally dressed in a white shirt and his habitual tight-fitting breeches, controlling the powerful horse with just one hand, shading his eyes with the other as he glanced around as though looking for someone. Eager not to be caught here alone she picked up her skirts and ran towards the trees. As she breeched their leafy canopy a hand shot out from behind a solid oak and caught her around the waist. She cried out before a second hand was clapped across her mouth, stifling all sound.

'Miss Brooke,' said the voice she recognised, with a sinking heart, as belonging to Reece. 'I have been looking everywhere for you.'

* * *

Where the devil had Reece disappeared to, Amos wondered as he trotted Warrior across the common. He had kept well back for fear of being seen by him, even though it didn't appear to occur to the man he might be followed. He strode along as though late for an appointment and had not once looked back. By the time Amos decided it would be safe to get closer, he had lost the fool. He must have taken the path through the trees, but Amos decided against following his example. There were low branches and rabbit holes everywhere. He would not risk Warrior's welfare for the sake of chasing shadows.

'This is a rum affair, Warrior,' he said, shading his eyes against the lowering sun with one hand as he peered in the direction of the woods that separated the common from Sheridan land, thinking he had seen movement in the treeline. 'What possible business could he have here?'

Unless, of course, he had an assignation with a lady. God forbid he was here to meet with Miss Brooke. The thought was abhorrent and Amos dismissed it at once, satisfied he wouldn't be so attracted to her if she had such poor taste. He shook his head and again focused on the treeline, thinking he saw a flash of yellow. He halted Warrior and looked more closely, but there was nothing there. Then a scream rent the air — a scream that was abruptly cut off. Without hesitation, Amos spurred Warrior into a flat out gallop and headed for the trees.

He discovered Miss Brooke lying on the ground, her forehead grazed and bleeding.

'Lord Amos.' She blinked up at him, her eyes clouded, not with pain but fear. 'What are you doing here?'

6

'You're perfectly safe now.' Amos slid from Warrior's saddle and crouched beside Miss Brooke. 'Your attacker is gone. Are you harmed? Can you stand?'

'I wasn't attacked.' She looked down at her torn and dirtied gown, not at him. 'I caught my foot in a rabbit hole. It was careless of me.'

Amos was disappointed she chose not to be honest with him. A simple fall would not have caused the terror in her eyes. Besides, he had caught a glimpse of the rogue responsible taking off through the trees. The desire to chase him down and thrash the living daylights out of him had been compelling, but he couldn't leave Miss Brooke, possibly injured, without protection. There might be others hiding out in the trees waiting to assault her, also. He had heard nothing about a band of marauders being in the district, but since the end of the war there had been an increasing number of such incidents in rural areas.

Not that he gave the possibility serious consideration. Amos couldn't be sure her attacker had been Reece, but given he had just followed him to an otherwise deserted common, the possibility of anyone else being the perpetrator was remote.

'Here, take my hand and let me help you to your feet.'

She hesitated for a protracted moment before slipping her hand into his, as skittish and unsure of herself as one of his newborn foals. Amos closed his fingers firmly around her palm and pulled her gently to her feet. A part of him wished he could sweep her into his arms and pick her up by less conventional means. The desire to behave recklessly consumed him whenever he was anywhere near Miss Brooke. Stimulated by the touch of her hand, the urge to protect her burned through him like a virulent disease.

'Have you twisted your ankle?'

She cautiously placed her weight on the afflicted limb. 'I don't seem any the worse for wear. Thank you for helping me, Lord Amos, but I need detain you no longer.'

She gasped when she noticed her bodice had been torn and quickly reached for her shawl, tying it across her bosom to preserve her modesty.

'Shall we sit on that log for a moment?'

'I am perfectly all right. There is no need for you to inconvenience yourself.'

Why is she so anxious to be rid of me? 'On the contrary, there is every need.'

He led Warrior with one hand and placed the other on her elbow as he guided her towards the log in question. She took several deep breaths and appeared to recover some composure, yet was still deathly pale. Amos was gripped by the sight of her thick riot of curly hair cascading over her shoulders. If it had been tied back, the ribbon had disappeared during her attack. Thoughts of that attack — of what could have happened to her if he hadn't been there — fuelled his murderous rage and deepened his determination to discover her true reason for being in the district.

Amos had yet to decide if he would tell her that he knew she made most of the jewellery for her uncle but took no credit for it. Amos was willing to wager Reece didn't know one end of a soldering iron from the other. Zach was right to say it was not Amos's concern, but since saving her from being accosted, even the wildest of the horses he bred could not have stopped him from delving more deeply into her business.

'Allow me,' he said, helping her to sit.

Once she was settled, he tied Warrior's reins to stout branch, and the horse idly set about cropping the coarse grass. Amos sat beside Miss Brooke and fixed her with a steady gaze. There was blood on her forehead, but it had stopped flowing and the wound didn't look deep. He extracted a handkerchief from his pocket, moistened the cloth with his tongue, and gently dabbed at the injury. She inhaled sharply but not, Amos suspected, because he had hurt her. Their gazes clashed and a gasp of awareness slipped past her lips. The sound brought Amos to his senses. Damn it, he was here to help her, not confuse the poor chit. He ceded control of the handkerchief to her and she held it firmly against her forehead.

'Thank you.'

'What happened?' he asked for the second time. 'I know you didn't fall.'

She didn't immediately respond. The only sound was the jingling of Warrior's bit as he chomped at the grass, the distant sound of a dog barking, and a melodious chorus of evening bird song. She absently pulled away a piece of the bark from their makeshift seat as the silent awareness of shared sensibility stretched between them.

'Someone did take me by surprise and caused me to fall,' she eventually said, staring off into the distance. 'I did not see who it was.'

Amos was disappointed by her response,

but not surprised. 'I would prefer it, Miss Brooke, if you would either tell me to go to the devil, or be honest with me.'

She gasped and finally gave him her full attention. 'Whatever do you mean?'

'I mean you know who attacked you. It was Reece.'

Her eyes darted wildly in all directions, as though seeking a way to escape from him. She was very afraid of something. Or someone. 'What makes you say that?'

'I saw him walking this way as I left the village. If he cut through the trees, he would have reached your position just before I did.'

'Mr. Reece is not my favourite person — '

'I am very pleased to hear you say so.'

'But he would not attack me.'

Amos screwed up his features. 'There we must disagree.'

'You don't know him so can't possibly judge.'

'I have known men like him. They take what they want.' Amos had difficulty containing his anger, unable to understand why she would protect a man she clearly despised. 'It is fortunate for you I came along when I did,' he said laconically.

'I am very much obliged to you, my lord.'

'I didn't say that in the hope of earning your gratitude, Miss Brooke. Any gentleman would have provided the same service.' He fixed her with an ardent look. 'But if you wish to reward me, I would prefer you to honour me with your confidence.'

Her trilling laughter sounded contrived. 'About what? I don't have any secrets, and even if I did, why would I share them with you? More to the point, why would a gentleman of your stature be interested in my affairs?'

Amos sighed. He had enjoyed sitting on an uncomfortable log at the edge of the common with a young lady who intrigued him. But he was aware that trust needed to be earned, and she was too afraid to place hers in him.

Yet.

What struck him as extraordinary was the manner in which she spoke to him. Her uncle was a skilled and respected craftsman, it was true, but he was not a gentleman. Ergo, she was no lady and ought to be tongue-tied and awkward in the presence of a duke's brother. And yet, she was not — nor had she been when she came to the house. She poured tea for them all as though she was perfectly accustomed to doing so, barely a shake of her hand indicating nerves. Her speaking voice was refined, as were her manners. This infuriatingly secretive young lady was no stranger to good society, and he yearned to know more of her background. But he did not force the issue, instead asking a question of his own.

'Presumably, as your uncle's assistant, Reece lives above the shop?'

'No,' she replied, satisfaction in her tone. 'We do not have to endure his presence there.'

Then why endure it at all? This makes no sense. 'I am glad, at least, for that.'

'Uncle Charles thought it would not be appropriate to have an unmarried man in such a small establishment.'

'I applaud your uncle's morals.'

'Reece resides at the Crown and Anchor.'

Amos's brows shot up. 'Does he indeed? And how does a mere assistant afford that?'

'I believe it's a temporary arrangement, until he can find alternative lodgings.'

Amos was pleased to hear it. A quick word in Jeggins' ear and he would soon know all there was to know about Reece.

A bird shot out of a nearby tree with a loud clatter of wings, startled by something, and startling Warrior in its turn. The stallion jerked its head up, whinnied, and turned on the spot, pawing at the ground. Amos stood up to soothe him. So, too, did Miss Brooke.

'Sit down,' Amos told her firmly. 'You have had a shock and ought not to be on your feet again yet.'

'There's nothing wrong with me.' She walked across to Warrior, and this time her smile appeared more genuine. 'He is magnificent. Did you breed him yourself?'

'Be careful! Warrior doesn't take kindly to strangers.'

She ignored his warning, leaving Amos with no time to pull her clear of Warrior's snapping teeth. Instead he watched, dumbfounded, as his irascible stallion stopped misbehaving the moment Miss Brooke reached out a hand and stroked his sleek neck. He dropped his head into her outstretched hand and even permitted her to place a kiss on his muzzle.

'Remarkable,' he said softly, shaking his head in astonishment. The more he learned about Miss Brooke, the less he understood her.

★ ★ ★

He knew, Crista thought, playing for time as she focused her attention on the stallion, which was no great hardship since she loved horses. He knew it was Reece who had attacked her and now thought ill of her for being untruthful.

She wanted this time alone with her formidable rescuer to last forever. She also wanted him to leave, then she might be able to think straight; an impossible ambition to achieve when he loomed over her, tall, handsome and dangerous, addling her wits and making her forget who she was supposed to be. Why did he not go? It must be obvious she was unharmed. Crista urgently needed to decide what had made Reece deliberately lay in wait for her and try to . . . well, it wouldn't do to consider what he had tried to do. Thanks to Lord Amos's intervention, he had not succeeded. But it was hard to apply her mind to Reece's behaviour with his lordship standing so very close, watching her with unnerving stillness.

'No, I did not breed him.'

His deep, arresting voice intruded upon Crista's introspective thoughts, startling her. He again reached out a hand, and she was most reluctant to place hers in it. The mayhem it caused to her emotions when she touched him was both unsettling and inappropriate. She compromised by walking beside him and obediently resuming her seat on the log, breathless for reasons that had nothing to do with her recent attack. Lord Amos truly was as magnificent as his beautiful horse, a combination of elegance, grace, strength, and coercive charm. Long, thick, flowing black hair framed a face that reflected strength of character, steadfastness, and tough resourcefulness. His broad forehead led to rugged, symmetrical features and a strong, chiselled jaw. His dark blue eyes gleamed with intelligence and, she suspected, missed little. At that moment, they were focused upon her, assessing her in a most disarming manner.

'Warrior was a present from my father, the year before I graduated from university. I broke him myself.' He looked away from her. 'He was the last gift I ever received from him. He died six months after the end of the war.'

'I'm very sorry,' she replied, moved enough by his obvious sadness to daringly touch his arm. 'I lost my own father not so very long ago and so I can understand your pain.'

His fingers briefly touched hers, still resting on his arm. 'And now you are alone in the world.'

'No, I have my uncle, and a sister.' She reluctantly reclaimed her hand.

'A sister.' He appeared surprised. 'Where is she?'

'She lives in London and is to be married soon.'

Crista offered no additional information.

'What of you, Miss Brooke?' he asked. 'I'm sure you have received offers.'

'Me?' The bluntness of his question surprised her. She supposed brothers of dukes could ask lesser mortals intrusive questions whenever the fancy took them. Since he had just rescued her from a difficult situation, she decided not to take offence. 'I am beyond the age of matrimony. Goodness, I am already quite the old maid.'

Lord Amos threw his head back and roared with laughter.

'I am glad you take amusement at my expense,' she said huffily.

'Excuse me, Miss Brooke, I was not laughing at you, but at your perception of an old maid. You cannot be more than one and twenty.'

'I am twenty-two.'

'The perfect age to be married.'

She tossed her head. 'You take a great deal of interest in my affairs, my lord.'

He angled his head and increased the intensity of his piercing gaze. 'That is because you interest me.'

'I cannot think why. Besides, why would I wish to be married and subjected to the tyrannical whims of a man when I am well able to look after myself?'

'Not so very well able,' he replied softly, glancing towards the trees where she had been attacked.

'Oh well, that was unfortunate, but it won't happen again.'

He looked as though he wished to dispute that assertion. 'Do you intend to make a permanent home here in Shawford with your uncle, or shall you undertake your independent life elsewhere?'

'Now you're laughing at me!'

'Not in the least. I find your attitude refreshing, especially since I believe you are sincere in your desire not to marry. That, in my experience, is very unusual.'

'You and your brothers must be hounded by ladies keen to meet with your approval, the duke especially.' She probably sounded as sympathetic as she felt. Even so, she was well aware he had cunningly turned the conversation back to her affairs. He seemed doggedly determined to know all of her business. Unfortunately for him, she had compelling reasons not to be forthright. 'That cannot be easy.'

'We have become adept at avoiding the match-making mamas.'

Crista laughed in spite of herself. 'I am perfectly sure you have.'

They lapsed into momentary silence. Now was the time when he would leave her, Crista thought, since they had run out of things to say to one another.

'The stud at Winchester Park *was* started by me three years ago, at the end of the war,' he said into the silence.

'I beg your pardon?'

'You asked if I bred Warrior. I did not, but my father gave him to me because of all his sons, I was the one who most closely shared his love of horseflesh.' He spread his thighs, rested his elbows on them and dangled his hands into the space between them. 'With the war over, I was in need of an occupation. Our father had recently died, and Zach was the new duke. He needed help, and I persuaded him to let me take over the stud and introduce two Nonius stallions.'

'Nonius?' She looked at him askance. 'They are Hungarian, I think.'

Lord Amos shot her an assessing look. 'You know something of horses, Miss Brooke?'

'I did, at one time.'

'I ought not to be surprised, given the way Warrior responded to you.'

'Why did you choose Nonius stallions?'

He shrugged. 'Someone had to do something to meet the demand for military horses. Depressing numbers of British stock were slaughtered on the battlefields.'

'How awful. Did you serve, Lord Amos?'

'Yes, beside Zach and Vince.'

'Your mother must have been beside herself to have three of her sons in the conflict.'

'She still had Nate. If the worst came to the worst, there was a male Sheridan to keep the family name alive. Papa was still alive at the time and he would have taken a very dim view if we had not all gone.' Amos chuckled. 'As for Nate, he was furious to miss the excitement, but our father insisted he remain in England and finish at Oxford. In the end, the three of us came through with barely a scratch between us.' He shrugged impossibly broad shoulders. 'It hardly seems fair.'

Crista blinked. 'You *wanted* to be injured? Or worse?'

'A good many decent men either didn't come back at all, or were maimed for life.' He shook his head. 'Far too many. We already had more than our share of privileges as a family and then sailed through the conflict without being harmed.'

'You are worried people will think you allowed others to take all the risks?'

Lord Amos seemed surprised by the question. 'What on earth makes you say that?'

'I am sure you have absolutely nothing to feel guilty about, Lord Amos. I suspect you and your brothers were simply better strategists than some of the more reckless officers. I can tell from the way you speak that you cared about the welfare of the men beneath you, as well as your own skin, of course.'

'Yes, I suppose that's true.' Talk of the war had made him seem remote. As though realising it, he turned towards her, smiled, and the grip of winter left his eyes. 'Anyway, that is where I first saw Nonius horses and realised they made equally good equines on the battlefield. They have the right sturdy confirmation, strength, and endurance for it. Zach saw the sense in that argument, and the gamble paid off. We are now well established and in the position of having to turn mares away because our stallions are overworked.'

'They must give you considerable satisfaction.'

Lord Amos stifled a laugh, as though she had said something amusing. 'Nonius horses can be put to a variety of uses that don't involve military manoeuvres. They make decent carriage horses and excel on the hunting field.'

Crista nodded. It was evident from her visit to Winchester Park that the Sheridan family was wealthy beyond imagination and could spend their days in idleness and dissipation if they so desired. She had seen a number of gentlemen in Lord Amos's fortunate position follow that path. But it appeared Lord Amos was blessed with a fierce desire to make himself useful in a venture that satisfied his love of horses and improved his family's finances.

She applauded his sense of responsibility, even though she was not showing much of it herself. Instead of finding excuses to remain here in a ripped gown with a gentleman she barely knew, she ought to insist upon returning to the village before they were seen. She was about to suggest leaving, truly she was, but the words stalled on her lips. She was enjoying herself. When had she last taken pleasure from a mere conversation? Besides, Lord Amos was right about one thing. She *had* had a shock and ought not to walk back quite yet. Dear God, she was pathetic! A kind word and helping hand from a polite gentleman, albeit one with a not altogether civilised aura and quite disturbing charm, and her determination to remain detached evaporated.

'It would be my pleasure to show you the stud when you attend the garden party.'

'Oh, I don't know if I shall be able to — '

'Of course you must come. You designed my mother's gift, and she will want to thank you in person.'

'I had not thought to attend.' She restlessly plucked at the tied ends of her shawl. 'My uncle will need someone to attend to the shop.'

'All business closes for the afternoon in honour of the occasion, and so even if you stayed behind, you would have no customers.' He reached out one hand and lifted her chin with his long, capable fingers. 'I cannot make you out. What are you so afraid of, Miss Brooke?' he asked softly.

'I am not afraid of anything, my lord.' *Except you, when I feel the dark intensity of your gaze boring into me. I cannot think straight for what I see in your eyes.* 'It is just that I don't know many people in Shawford and — '

'Then it's high time you got to know your neighbours. Especially if you intend to remain in the district.' He removed his fingers, and she was unsure if she was more relieved or disappointed at their loss. 'Don't make the mistake of setting yourself apart and giving them the excuse to brand you as aloof. It will cause ill-will.'

'Don't assume you understand my character,' she replied acerbically, regretting the words as soon as they slipped past her lips. Her quick temper would be the death of her yet.

He sighed. 'I can't make any such claim, since you are a lady of mystery.'

She lifted her shoulders. 'I cannot think why you are so interested in my affairs.'

The meltingly gentle smile he sent her lit up his face and sent a spiral of desire lancing through her body. It really wouldn't do to get entangled with a gentleman so far above her in the social structure that he might as well be the king of England. Unless . . . perhaps his intentions were no better than Reece's? He just went about it more intelligently, hoping to seduce her with kindness and consideration rather than brute force.

The thought was unworthy, and Crista swept it aside. She was perfectly sure his intentions were honourable. A part of her was sorry for it. In spite of her desire for independence, Crista maintained a healthy curiosity about the intimacies of the bedchamber. Lord Amos was precisely the right person to satisfy her curiosity in that respect. Not that she would ever make the suggestion. How could she? But the idea had lodged in her brain. It was all his fault, and she was quite out of charity with him as a consequence. He had no business being quite so gloriously tempting, so male, so interested in her, or so . . . well, so everything. Any admiration had always been reserved for her younger, much prettier, far less opinionated sister and interest from such a captivating source confused her.

'You're right, of course.' He looked surprised, presumably because she had taken him to task for his intrusive questions. She suspected few people refused to give him direct answers. 'However, I insist upon your attendance at Mother's party. Who knows, you might even enjoy yourself.'

She tried hard to quell a smile that escaped anyway. 'Since I'm curious to see your stud, and your lovely Nonius stallions, I can't refuse.'

The corners of his lips lifted. 'Then I shall look upon it as a fixed engagement.'

The church clock sounded the hour, causing Crista to jump to her feet, breaking an intimacy that probably only existed in her imagination.

'Goodness, is that the time? My uncle will wonder what has become of me.'

'Permit me to escort you home.'

'There is absolutely no need.'

'I hesitate to disagree with a lady but — '

'But I am no lady.'

'Again, I beg to differ,' he replied softly. 'You are no stranger to good manners and polite society.'

She gasped, blaming herself for getting trapped by her attraction towards him into revealing more of her true character than was wise. 'You quite mistake the matter, my lord.'

His knowing smile told her he was not deceived, but he didn't press the point.

'Come.'

He again claimed her elbow, untied Warrior, and walked beside her back to the village, a respectable amount of daylight separating their bodies. He knew without needing to be told she would wish to enter the premises by the back door and led her straight to it.

'I . . . er — '

'Yes, Miss Brooke?' He lifted one brow in polite enquiry.

'About what you thought you saw on the common.'

He frowned. 'Yes, what about it?'

'I would prefer not to make anything out of it and distress my uncle. He doesn't enjoy the best of health and I don't want him worrying about my safety.'

'Someone needs to worry about it.' Lord Amos's jaw flexed and hardened. 'You may not be so fortunate next time.'

'It won't happen again. Please, Lord Amos, don't make more trouble for me.'

He was quiet for too long but eventually gave her a curt nod. 'Very well, if you're sure.'

'Thank you, I'm perfectly sure.'

'Then I shall keep your secret, but don't expect me to allow Reece to escape punishment.'

'No!' She cried out louder than she had intended. 'No,' she repeated more softly, placing a hand on his arm. 'Please, don't interfere. You have no idea what harm it would do.'

'Shawford and Compton might set themselves against one another, but there is no serious crime in the district, and women are free to move about without fear of attack. If that situation has changed, then the duke will not stand for it.' He fixed her with a firm look. 'And no more will I.'

'But you don't understand. The situation with Reece is personal, a misunderstanding, nothing more. No other females are in danger from him.'

'You ask me to keep your confidence but don't trust me with the truth.' He glanced at her grazed forehead, expelled a deep breath, and reached out to gently touch the curve of her face. 'You are an enigma, Cristobel Brooke, but you are right about one thing. It's not my place to interfere and so I shall let it be.' He paused, before adding softly, 'For now.'

Her spontaneous smile probably reflected her relief. 'Thank you . . . for everything.'

'Here,' he said as she turned to walk through the back gate.

'What is it?'

'I believe this is yours.' He removed her ribbon from his pocket. 'I picked it up from where you fell to the ground.'

'Oh.'

She took the ribbon from him, lifted a hand in farewell, and let herself in. She sensed him standing there beside his horse, watching her, but didn't trust herself to look back, even when she discovered she still had Lord Amos's fine lawn handkerchief clutched in her hand.

7

Reece stumbled through the trees, blinded by a combination of anger and fear. Of all the damnable luck! So few people frequented the common at that time of day. Why had Sheridan come along at that precise moment? More to the point, had he recognised Reece? Curses upon the whole Sheridan clan! Reece didn't seem able to turn around without stumbling over one or another of the blighters.

He stopped his headlong flight away from Amos Sheridan, pausing to straighten his clothing and regain his breath and composure. If he *had* been recognised, if the girl talked, then all hell would break loose. Sheridan would not let matters rest there, and Reece would have risked their entire operation. Ye gods, he knew what the punishment for disloyalty would be. He had been given permission to chastise Cristobel Brooke, as she deserved, but had also been warned to be discreet. Being caught in the act by one of the Sheridans hardly met that criterion, and his masters were unlikely to be lenient if word reached their ears.

Reece leaned against a tree and allowed common sense to gradually overcome his anxiety. She would not mention the incident to her uncle, he decided when he could think rationally again. In spite of the spirited defiance that so attracted him to her, deep down she was afraid of him. With her own eyes, she had seen the fate that had befallen her father. She also knew he could destroy her precious sister and her uncle, her entire family, if she continued with her rebellious ways.

Feeling reassured, he crouched down and peered through the trees, wondering where she was. He didn't think he had hurt her, but he hadn't heard Sheridan ride off or seen any sign of Crista making her way back to the village.

'Perdition!'

Reece thumped his clenched fist against his thigh, scarcely able to believe his eyes. Amos Sheridan, the Duke of Winchester's named heir, was sitting on a fallen tree trunk fussing over a mere shop girl, holding his hand-kerchief to a graze on her forehead. It wasn't difficult to imagine what he expected from her in return.

Reece ground his jaw, infuriated by her double standards. He had tried to be kind to Crista, explaining why it was vital for her to take her father's place in the organisation he served, receiving nothing but haughty disdain by way of return. He had salved his wounded pride by reminding himself she was well brought up, innocent and respectable.

Now he knew differently. An aristocrat had shown her kindness, and she was all but lifting her skirts for him in broad daylight.

It was insupportable!

Reece stood up so abruptly he disturbed a bird nesting in the tree above his head. It flew off with a loud squawk, startling Sheridan's stallion. The horse tried to rear up, attracting the attention of its master and Crista, both of whom got up to calm the beast. Reece couldn't risk remaining where he was in case Sheridan investigated the cause of the disturbance. He slunk off into the trees, tearing his best coat as he forced his way through them, and stumbled onto the track that led back to the village.

He pushed his way into the taproom at the Crown and Anchor and ordered a much-needed tankard of ale from Martha. The sight of the buxom beauty partially quelled his anger, and he sent her a flirtatious smile. She served him and turned to her next customer without appearing to notice. It was strange, but all his efforts to impress the girl had failed. Reece might not be rich or titled, but he was blessed with reasonably good looks and cut a fine figure, though he did say so himself. His attempts to attract members of the opposite sex did not usually end in failure, but first Miss Brooke and now a barmaid found him easy to resist.

Reece supped his ale, brooding upon the events of the day. It had all started to go wrong when Chesney blithely offered to make jewellery for the duchess and then intimated Reece was his assistant. Up until then, he had been able to stay at the Crown and move about without attracting particular interest. He had put it about he was employed by a merchant looking for new markets. That was not uncommon and had satisfied the curiosity of those who troubled to ask. He had originally been sent here to force Miss Brooke to return to London. But when her uncle threatened to close his long-standing business and go with her, she had flatly refused. Reece's masters were so pleased with Miss Brooke's work, they decided to continue running their operation from this most unlikely little village. Reece was obliged to stay and keep control of her.

Now the Sheridans knew he was *supposed* to be Chesney's assistant. If they also discovered he was lodged at the inn, they would wonder why and how he could afford it. He would have to take a great deal more care about his movements now and perhaps make a few enquiries about marketing his imaginary merchandise. One or another of the Sheridans always seemed to be in the Crown, mixing with the locals as though they actually had something in common with them. Damn it, Reece liked the inn and was very comfortable there. Now he would have to find somewhere else to stay.

Or perhaps not. Reece managed a brief smile as an idea occurred to him. If Sheridan put about the story of Reece being Chesney's assistant, Reece could claim Chesney was embarrassed about needing his help. He worried what mischief the residents of Compton would make if they knew about his frailty, and made Reece promise not to admit his true purpose for being in the district, thus accounting for his being accommodated at the inn.

Another thought occurred to him as he drained his tankard and banged it on the bar, impatient for a refill. Chesney was not quite the doddering old fool Reece had supposed. He had deliberately agreed to make the duchess's jewellery to discompose Reece in some way and had succeeded better than he could know since Reece no longer felt in control of the situation in Chesney's shop. He

107

had not told his master as much, but the fact of the matter was, Chesney and his luscious little niece were getting ideas above their station. Rebellious ideas. Could that be why Crista was being so charming to Lord Amos, hoping to enlist his support? Reece's blood ran cold at the thought. He had already decided she would not tell her uncle about the incident on the common. Telling Lord Amos would create a damned sight more trouble.

Reece downed his second tankard of ale quickly and stomped up the stairs to his chamber. He needed solitude in which to think matters through, decide how to keep the old man and the girl quiet, and failing that, how best to cover his own back.

★   ★   ★

Stopping to aid Miss Brooke had made Amos late for dinner. He cantered back to the estate and changed quickly into evening clothes.

'Maynard,' he said to his valet. 'I have a job for you.'

'I already have a job,' Maynard, not one to stand on ceremony, replied indolently.

'This one will take you to the Crown and Anchor.'

'Oh well, that's different.' He brushed the

shoulders of the coat he had just helped Amos into. 'What do you need me to do then?'

Amos spent the next five minutes explaining. Maynard smirked when Amos ran out of words.

'Pretty is she, this Miss Brooke?'

'Don't be impertinent.'

Amos's words wouldn't make a blind bit of difference to his valet's attitude, and he was grateful for it. All of the Sheridan males selected their valets precisely *because* they didn't tend towards the obsequious. They were fiercely protective of their masters, Amos had reason to know, especially in the servants' hall if someone should speak out of turn. They were also loyal to a fault, and in private they tended not only to speak their minds, but also to give sound advice.

'Right ho, you'll do,' Maynard said, opening the door for Amos. 'If you don't need me any more tonight, I'll cut along to the Crown and see what I can find out.'

'Good man.'

It was just the family at dinner, for which Amos was grateful. His mother and sisters were in high spirits, discussing the shopping expeditions they had undertaken during the past few days.

'Nate was a far more willing escort than

any of the rest of you have ever been,' Annalise said cheerfully. 'He was quite obliging and didn't mind how long we kept him waiting as we dithered over our purchases.'

'I can't imagine why,' Zach replied, sending Nate an ironic glance.

'Glad to be of service,' Nate said, looking smugly pleased with himself.

'I dare say Martha used the exact same words,' Vince said in an aside to Amos, making him choke on his wine.

'The rivalry between the villages is getting worse,' Portia remarked. 'Miss Higgins in the haberdasher's in Compton told us that on no account should we purchase Flemish lace from Mrs. Woodley in Shawford.'

'Did she give a reason?' Vince asked.

'Oh yes.' Portia's round face was invaded by a huge smile. 'She pretended to be shocked, and professed to hate being the purveyor of gossip, but had it on the best authority that the lace in question had been smuggled into the country without the duty being paid.'

'How shocking,' Zach said, looking as amused as Amos felt by the endless bickering between the two communities.

'Shame on you, Zach,' Portia said, her grin belying her outrage. 'You are the duke. It is your duty to . . . well, to make sure duty is paid on commodities in the shops hereabouts.'

'Good heavens.' Zach elevated both brows. 'How the devil am I supposed to do that?'

'We received similar warnings about Miss Higgins when purchasing shawls from Mrs. Woodley,' their mother said, amusement lighting her eyes. 'Not about lace, but some other trifling matter.'

'Buttons,' Annalise supplied. 'There is some question, apparently, regarding the quality of Miss Higgins's stock. It was too amusing.'

'It saddens me that the blame for the feud lies with this family,' the duchess said. 'Both villages seek to enhance their standing by exclusive association with us. Your father maintained it was our duty to bestow our custom equally between them, which the girls and I continue to do.'

'Your sons are also slaves to duty,' Nate assured her. 'We regularly visit the Crown, and the Ploughman in Compton, of course.'

The duchess looked upon her youngest son with suspicion. 'Hmm,' she said.

Zach flashed a wry smile. 'Your dedication to duty is an example to us all, little brother.'

'I do my humble best.'

'Are all the arrangements in place for the garden party, Mama?' Portia asked.

'The servants have everything under control. All that remains for us to do is ensure all our neighbours of consequence receive formal invitations.'

'Heaven forbid that we should forget anyone,' Zach said, rolling his eyes.

'Precisely,' their mother replied equitably.

'Whose turn is it to supply the ale?' Nate asked.

'The Crown's,' Zach told him.

'Oh good!'

Nate's three brothers were obliged to smother knowing smiles. Nate and Martha let loose on the estate during the riotous annual garden party could only end one way. They ought to know since it had ended similarly for the three of them.

'Lady St. John today accepted.'

Their mother looked directly at Zach as she spoke. Her eldest son merely lifted his shoulders which, Amos knew, was all the reaction he would allow himself. The lady in question was new to the district, her past even more clouded in mystery than Miss Brooke's. She and Zach enjoyed lively exchanges whenever they met, exciting their mother's ambitions to see Zach married. The fact that Lady St. John was a widow did not seem to deter the duchess, perhaps because she was the first lady Zach had shown even the remotest abiding interest in, much as he tried to deny it.

'Well,' the duchess said, putting aside her

napkin and standing. 'I have things to do, and I am sure you girls have as well. Let's leave your brothers to their port.'

The gentlemen stood, but the port was circulating before Faraday closed the door behind the females.

'Come on, Amos,' Zach said. 'You've barely said two words all evening. What's wrong?'

Amos told them what he had seen on the common, and about Miss Brooke's unwillingness to tell him the truth.

'I wish I had been here to meet your Miss Brooke,' Nate complained.

'I dare say you were usefully employed elsewhere,' Vince replied.

'Yes, well, there were other compensations.' Nate grinned good-naturedly. 'Did you know what Martha can do with her — '

'We know,' his brothers assured him in unison.

'Are you convinced it was Reece who attacked her?' Zach asked, pushing his chair away from the table and resting one foot on his opposite thigh. 'Antipathy might be clouding your judgement.'

'I am absolutely sure. I followed him there myself. If it wasn't him, he would have been close by when she was attacked and would have gone to her aid.'

'I see your point.' Zach fell into momentary

contemplation. 'I advised against interference in her affairs, but this puts a different light on matters. If she's so scared of the rogue she can't bring herself to tell you why, then there must be something odd going on.'

'Does she really make the jewellery instead of Chesney?' Vince asked.

'Oh yes, I saw her with my own eyes.'

'If that got out, then there really would be all out war between the two villages. Just see how much fuss they make over a little contraband lace and questionable buttons,' Nate said.

'What do you plan to do about the situation?' Zach asked.

'I've sent Maynard down to the Crown to ask about Reece. I need to know how long he's been here and what he does with himself all day. I'm fairly sure he doesn't make jewellery.'

'No, he makes eyes at Martha,' Nate said, scowling. 'I've seen him in the taproom, the impudent upstart.'

'You've practically been living in the place yourself this past week,' Vince replied. 'So you should know.'

'I have lost time to make up for,' Nate said, aggrieved. 'I have needs that must be met.'

All his brothers laughed.

'Martha will wear you out if you aren't

careful,' Amos said, topping up his glass and passing the decanter to Nate.

Nate grinned. 'I live in hope.'

'If you need to have Reece followed, let me know,' Zach said.

'Thank you. It might well come to that.'

'Did you learn anything more about the mysterious Miss Brooke?' Vince asked.

'Frustratingly little, other than that her father recently died, and she has a sister living in London who is about to be married.'

'What did the father do to make a living?' Nate asked.

'She didn't say, and I thought it better not to ask.'

'It's refreshing to meet a female who doesn't wish to talk one's ear off about herself and her family,' Vince remarked as he topped up his own glass and sent the decanter on to Nate.

'Shall I meet Miss Brooke at the garden party?' Nate asked.

'She hadn't planned to attend but I managed to persuade her.'

Vince shared an amused glance with Zach. 'His powers of persuasion being legendary.'

'I have my moments.' Amos stretched his arms above his head and yawned. 'It will be interesting to see if Reece attends. If he is what he says he is, then he has every reason to want to be here, but I'll wager ten guineas we don't see him.'

'You won't get any takers around this table,' Zach said, pushing his chair back and standing up.

The rest of them stood also and went their different ways. In Nate's case, that would almost certainly be to the Crown. Amos suppressed a grin, wondering why he had bothered to send Maynard when Nate could have served him just as well, except Maynard was more likely to keep his mind on the business in hand.

★ ★ ★

Crista managed to slip up the stairs without encountering her uncle. She gasped when she looked in the glass and saw her dishevelled hair, her forehead caked in dried blood, her eyes sparkling unnaturally bright. She looked wild, but actually felt alive, truly alive and desirable, all because she had spent ten minutes in conversation with an elegant gentleman who wanted nothing from her. That, in Crista's recent experience, was highly unusual.

Except, of course, Lord Amos *did* want something from her. He had decided to take an interest in her affairs, and the desire to confide in him, to relieve herself of the

116

burden that weighed heavier by the day, had been difficult to resist.

But she couldn't do it.

The only way to ensure she didn't give way to temptation was to keep out of his way. The garden party in five days' time would be too crowded for him to single her out. She didn't take seriously his offer to show her his stud and didn't trust herself to be alone with him, not just because he was so curious about her circumstances. She was ashamed of her acute awareness of him, of the fierce longing that had gripped her when he sat beside her with the purest of intentions. The intelligence and elusive warmth in his eyes as he settled his gaze upon her had the most disconcerting effect. She, who had seen quite enough of the destructive power of one-sided love, ought to know better than to fall for his lethal charm.

Crista washed away the blood on her brow, changed her gown and brushed her hair over her injury so the graze wouldn't show. Pushing all thoughts of Lord Amos aside, she then made her way downstairs.

'Ah, there you are, my dear.' Her uncle looked up from his chair beside the fire, a book open on his lap, and smiled at her. 'Did you enjoy your walk?'

'Yes, thank you. You were quite right. It was just what I needed. It's a lovely evening.'

Uncle Charles peered over his glasses at her. 'You certainly look a great deal better. You have some colour and . . . '

Kate called out their meal was ready.

'Good. I am sharp-set,' Crista said, taking her uncle's arm and walking with him to the small table beneath the window.

She and her uncle ate in near silence. Crista had too much to think about to instigate a conversation, and her uncle seemed preoccupied. She hated what Reece and her father had forced him to become. An honourable man, she could see shame daily eating away at him. If they escaped this situation without being thrown in gaol, Crista knew her uncle's richly deserved retirement would be plagued by unwelcome recollections of their narrow escape.

Her uncle caught her watching him and smiled. But that smile didn't reach his eyes. He looked shrunken and defeated, a thousand times removed from the upright, cheerful man she had known and loved her entire life. She blamed Reece for the transformation. But most of all, she blamed herself.

Perhaps she should have put her uncle's welfare first and confided in Lord Amos after all. With all the power and influence at his disposal, he would be able to help her. But when he knew her shameful secret, would he still want to? His first allegiance was to his family, as evidenced by their recent conversation. The only time he had seemed severe was when he said the duke would not tolerate ne'er-do-wells in the district. He had been referring, she thought, to pick-pockets, or men who prayed on helpless women. God alone knew what his reaction would be if he learned what Reece had brought upon Shawford.

No, she definitely couldn't tell him.

8

The following morning all three brothers accepted Zach's invitation to ride with him towards the furthest reach of the estate. It did not require them all to examine the dairy herd of Friesian cattle Zach was so proud of, but it was a fine morning, and none of them had anything better to do. Zach's dogs, with their long legs, rangy bodies, and lolling tongues, loped along beside the horses, deviating off every so often in pursuit of rabbits.

'The herd is looking good,' Amos said, leaning on the pommel of his saddle as he cast an eye over them.

'I'm thinking of cross-breeding for meat,' Zach replied.

'You could do worse than speak to Lady St. John,' Vince replied, sharing a grin between his brothers when Zach scowled. 'She has two first-class Hereford bulls on her estate.'

'You think Herefords and Friesians would produce decent beef cattle?'

Zach and Vince fell into an animated conversation on the matter. Amos had little to contribute. He knew a great deal more about horses than he did cattle. He drank in the view of the rolling Hampshire countryside, one he would never tire of, and counted his blessings. The verdant fields dotted with livestock and wooded slopes with trees in full leaf were all part of the Sheridan estate as far as the eye could see. Zach prided himself on being fair to his tenants and workers but, even so, it seemed unjust that one family should own so much.

Not that they really owned the land, he thought. They were merely custodians for the next generation. The Sheridan estate might look as though it ran without a hitch, but that was only because the four of them were fully occupied with various aspects of its management. Not a day went by when problems of one sort or another didn't vie for Zach's arbitration.

'What news did Maynard bring you from the Crown?' Zach asked Amos as they turned back towards the house, walking their horses side by side.

'Reece has been at the Crown for a month. He claims to be a merchant looking for a market for his produce.'

'Not a jeweller then?'

'No, and he hasn't made himself popular at the Crown. He struts about the place as though he was a person of consequence, but isn't fooling anyone.'

121

'He hasn't asked all and sundry for advice on whom to contact about his merchandise?' Zach scowled. 'A taproom is the first place any merchant would think to enquire.'

'Precisely,' Amos replied.

'A month is a long time to do nothing but swagger about and annoy people,' Zach said. 'What the devil is he up to? And why did Chesney pretend he's his assistant?'

Nate shrugged. 'Why not call Chesney up to the house and ask him?'

'No!' Amos shook his head decisively. 'Chesney claimed the rogue was his assistant for a reason.'

'Well, of course he did,' Vince said. 'And that reason obviously involves your Miss Brooke.'

'Chesney and Miss Brooke are afraid of Reece,' Amos said. 'We need to find out more about Reece before I confront either one of them.'

'How shall you do that?' Vince asked.

'To begin with, I shall set Martha to work her charm on him.'

'The devil you will!' Nate's scowl caused his brothers to laugh.

'Fear not,' Amos said. 'She doesn't like the man, I gather, but he keeps trying to win her favour. Martha knows how to flirt and extract information from her customers without compromising her . . . er, honour.'

Nate continued to glower at nothing in particular. 'Do you want me to ask her?'

'No, I shall call at the Crown and talk to her later myself,' Amos replied. 'I think it might be as well to have a couple of men follow Reece, if your offer still stands, Zach.'

'I'll see to it.'

'Thank you.'

'Your concern is for Miss Brooke, Amos,' Zach said, sounding unusually serious. 'Mine is for maintaining the status quo between Shawford and Compton. I shall leave you to decide what to do about the situation with Chesney, but if it looks as though it might have an effect upon local politics, then I shall have to intercede.'

'Ah, the joys of being a duke,' Nate said teasingly.

'Little brother, you have no idea.'

'Nor do I wish to find out.'

'Me neither,' Amos agreed with alacrity. 'Speaking of which, hurry up, do your duty and get leg-shackled, Zach. Being your heir apparent holds no appeal for me.'

'Ungrateful coves!'

Grinning, Zach pushed his horse into a canter. The others followed his example, and they raced neck and neck all the way back to the stables.

★ ★ ★

Crista was up at first light, determined to make up for the time she had not spent in the workshop the previous evening. She was equally determined to banish all thoughts of Lord Amos from her head. Her uncle was in the shop, attending to a customer, when the back door opened. Crista tensed, but didn't look up from the complicated filigree she was constructing.

'Good morning,' Reece said politely.

Crista couldn't believe his audacity. He had tried to brutally assault her the previous evening. Crista still felt cold all over whenever she dwelt upon what could have happened. But this morning he was behaving as though nothing untoward had occurred. She remained stubbornly silent, until he moved in front of her, blocking her light.

'I cannot see what I am doing if you stand there.'

'I could think of no other way of gaining your attention.'

'I have nothing to say to you.' She dealt him a chilling glance before immediately returning her attention to her work. 'You disgust me.'

'You seem to forget you work for my masters.'

'I am unlikely ever to forget *that*.' She

carefully heated her filigree arches from a distance so the solder didn't blow off the wire. 'But since you raised the matter, who *are* your masters? Whose tune do you dance to? I would like to know who to blame for my circumstances, aside from you.'

'I cannot tell you that.'

'Because you don't know?'

'Because you certainly don't need to.'

Damnation. That was no help. If she fell on her sword, metaphorically speaking, and disgraced her own reputation as well as her uncle's, she could take Reece down with her. But he would be replaced, and the operation moved elsewhere with some other craftsman coerced into doing their bidding. She must discover who the brains behind the operation was so she could destroy him also.

'You could be well paid for your work,' Reece said. 'If only you were not so stubborn.'

'We have had this discussion before. I am not a criminal and want no monetary gain for being forced to act like one.'

'The streets are full of people with fine principles.' A mirthless chuckle rumbled in Reece's throat. 'However, it's your decision about being paid.'

He was strutting about, emphasising his point by banging his cane on the floor,

125

sounding a little desperate. She glanced at him and was surprised by what she saw. He was no longer quite so well-groomed and looked as though he hadn't slept well. Perhaps he had seen Lord Amos ride to her rescue. Now that she considered the matter, she was sure he must have. It gave her considerable satisfaction to imagine Reece worrying about what she had or had not said to his lordship.

'I will do as I see fit.' Crista tossed her head. 'My advice is not to push me too far, or you might discover I push back harder than you might suppose.'

'And I would strongly advise you not to rebel against the people I represent.' There was a hard edge to Reece's voice. 'Think of what happened to your father.'

'I have agreed to work for you.' Crista put her soldering iron aside and treated him to her most disdainful glare. 'But I think it only fair to warn you, if you lay so much as one finger on me ever again, I *will* have my revenge.' Her hand hovered over the still hot soldering iron. 'Do we understand one another?'

When his eyes narrowed and his face turned puce with rage, Crista wondered if she had pushed him beyond his endurance in much the same way as he had driven her. She received her answer when he took a step towards her and raised his cane.

'That is precisely the reaction I would expect from a bully and tyrant,' Crista said, quelling her anxiety and imbuing her tone with a wealth of disdain. 'I dare say it makes you feel invincible to beat members of the weaker sex.'

She was rewarded by an intensified glower and a tense, oppressive silence. He continued to wave his cane about, and she thought he would actually strike her with it. Part of her hoped he would, then she could retaliate, and this *arrangement* between them would come to an end, leaving the pieces to fall where they may. Crista was almost beyond caring. She was doing this for her sister's sake, but the ungrateful child had not once contacted Crista to see how she was bearing up. She deserved whatever fate befell her, but her uncle most decidedly did not, so she must not allow her temper to overcome common sense.

At the last moment, Reece lowered the stick, breathing heavily, his eyes still shimmering with rage. 'God save me from opinionated females,' he muttered.

'If you don't care for my society,' she replied in a sweetly sarcastic tone, 'that situation can easily be remedied.'

'Don't imagine you can't outgrow your usefulness.'

'My, my, are you reduced to threating me?' She folded her arms across her torso and sent him a teasing smile designed to antagonise. 'How disheartening to be so out of control.'

'I have an engagement,' he said abruptly.

'Then don't let me detain you.'

'Have a care, Miss Brooke,' he said over his shoulder as he departed.

All the fight drained out of her when the door closed behind him. She fell back onto her stool, leaned her elbows on the workbench and dropped her head into her hands, close to tears of despair. Dear God, she couldn't take much more of this. Why were they so determined to use her? It was a rhetorical question. Of course she knew why. Even so, there had to be other jewellers who would willingly participate in their scheme and accept the payment she stubbornly refused to take. A willing worker was worth ten pressed into service, surely?

Giving herself a mental shake, she wiped her moist eyes and returned her attention to the duchess's necklace with a sense of renewed purpose. At least it was honest work, but the pride and pleasure she would normally feel at creating such a beautiful piece was lost beneath concerns for herself and her uncle. She only had four more days before the party, and there was still much to do to complete the suite of jewellery. Her own problems would just have to wait.

Crista reheated her soldering iron and returned to work.

* * *

Reece exchanged a few brief words with Chesney. He was his usual curmudgeonly self, but it was apparent he knew nothing of Reece's interlude with Miss Brooke on the common. Since no avenging Sheridans had descended upon him, it was safe to assume she had not confided in Lord Amos, either. Now, in the cold light of day, far from being relieved not to have been exposed, Reece felt only frustration at having failed to put Miss Brooke firmly in her place. By reminding her who was in charge of their association, he had hoped to see her cower. By fighting with him, she had only succeeded in strengthening his determination to have her. And, one way or another that was precisely what he would do. A mere slip of a girl with an inflated opinion of her own worth would never get the better of Edward Reece.

He walked briskly through the village, looking over his shoulder frequently to ensure he wasn't being followed. That morning at the Crown, he had received a message to attend his master at his home. Usually, they met on the same day each week, always at night. Reece wondered what could have happened to cause alterations to their arrangement. He was confident he had done nothing to give dissatisfaction.

He reached his destination without attracting any particular attention to himself. His knock was answered by Mary, who sent him a cheeky smile as she ushered him into the house.

'The master is expecting you, sir. He said you are to go straight through to his study.'

'Why don't you come down to the Crown when you finish your duties tonight?' he asked her.

She giggled. 'I might just do that.'

'Ah, you little minx.' Reece handed her his hat and cane and grinned for the first time that day. 'You mean to tease me.'

'You'd best not keep them waiting,' Mary replied, fluttering her lashes and giggling harder.

'Them?' Reece's smile abruptly faded. 'There is someone with your master?'

'A gentleman arrived an hour ago in a fine coach. I have never seen him before, but they're waiting for you. Off with you now before you get me into trouble.'

Reece tapped on the library door, curious

and a little apprehensive.

'Ah, Reece, there you are.' His employer looked up from the chair beside the fire.

'Good morning, sir,' he replied evenly, looking towards the gentleman in the other chair, waiting for an introduction that was not forthcoming.

'Matters are moving on faster than we anticipated,' his employer said, leaving Reece standing like a recalcitrant schoolboy summoned to the headmaster's study to answer for his misdemeanours. 'For reasons that need not concern you, we have a special commission we require Miss Brooke to undertake for us.' He paused, presumably for effect. 'Very special indeed.'

'I hear she has been making trouble,' the other gentleman said, curling his upper lip in evident disapproval.

'She will do as she is told, sir.'

'So I should damned well think. How difficult can it be to keep an old man and a slip of a girl in line?'

'I can assure you, sir, that — '

'I don't require your assurances. I require results,' the gentleman snapped. 'Especially now. This is the ultimate commission.'

The man stood up, produced a box from his pocket and spread the contents on a small side table. Reece gasped when some of the biggest diamonds he had ever seen rolled across the black velvet cloth and came to rest in a sparkling display of cut, clarity and crystal-clear colour. Reece knew little about jewellery, but couldn't fail to be impressed. Their value could keep a man in style for the rest of his days.

'We have others working for us, but none as good as Miss Brooke,' the gentleman said in a hushed voice, as though paying homage to the jewels spread before them. 'She can reproduce her father's work without anyone being able to tell the difference, which is why she is so valuable to us and why I wouldn't trust anyone else with these stones.'

'Are you absolutely sure she will not try to sabotage them?' Reece's employer asked.

'She wouldn't dare,' Reece replied with more conviction than he actually felt.

'She had better not,' the other gentleman said, 'or I shall hold you personally responsible.'

'What instructions am I to give her?' Reece asked.

The stranger produced sketches of a necklace, bangles and earrings and spread them across an adjoining table. 'The largest stone is for the centrepiece of the necklace,' he said. 'But I am sure it will be obvious to the girl.'

Reece nodded, hoping that would be the case because the sketches meant nothing to him.

'You can tell her that once she completes the work to our satisfaction we will leave her be. That ought to ensure her co-operation.'

'How quickly do you need this done, sir?' Reece asked.

'Immediately. The gentleman purchasing them is in a hurry. Given the amount he is spending, we can't afford to keep him waiting.'

'She's making a suite of jewellery for the Duchess of Winchester's birthday,' Reece said. 'She won't put that aside for any consideration and frankly, if she does, it might cause the Sheridans to ask awkward questions.'

'Damnation!' The man thumped his fist against the arm of the chair he had resumed sitting in. 'I can't afford any delays.'

'It would be wise to allow her to finish the duchess's commission,' Reece's employer said in a considering tone. 'It will only take four more days.'

'She should not have been permitted to take the commission in the first place.'

'That was . . . er, unfortunate,' Reece said, shuffling his feet when he felt the full force of the gentleman's displeasure focused upon his profile. 'I was unable to prevent it from happening without raising suspicions.'

'All right,' said the stranger with a prolonged sigh. 'Go and see her right now. Take the stones and drawings to her and explain what is needed.' He carefully replaced the stones in their case. Each one had an individual space into which it fit exactly. 'After she has finished the duchess's pieces, she has a week to complete this commission. If she does not, or if she damages or loses the stones, remind her of the consequences.' The man stood up, grasped his lapels, and scowled. 'For all of her family, but especially for her.'

'I am sure I don't need to remind you how important this is for us all,' Reece's master emphasised, standing also. 'There will be a healthy bonus for you, if you can see this through smoothly. But, if you fail us,' he added in a tone of great gravitas, 'you know what to expect. Allow her to see the stones, but keep them with you until she is ready to set them. Never let them out of your sight.'

Reece's hands were shaking as he took the case of stones and sketches from the stranger. His master had not referred to him by name, but he was most definitely a gentleman. He exuded an air of authority that implied he was accustomed to total obedience. He was a little desperate too. Why else would he risk coming here and allowing Reece to see him? All the other commissions had come through his master, and the people behind the scheme had taken pains to remain anonymous. It made no sense to abandon caution just because their operation appeared to be reaching its zenith.

Recognising he was being dismissed, Reece bowed to both gentlemen and was greeted in the hallway by Mary, holding his hat and stick and sporting a cheeky grin.

'Later, Mary my love,' Reece said absently, taking his things and leaving the house at a fast pace. He would enjoy a modicum of revenge by going immediately to Miss Brooke, explaining what was required of her, and putting the fear of God into her just in case she decided to do anything foolhardy.

9

'Magnificent, my dear.' Uncle Charles examined the duchess's completed suite of jewellery closely through a jeweller's loupe. 'The workmanship and the attention to detail is quite exquisite. You have excelled yourself. Your skill now exceeds both your father's and my own.'

'Oh, Uncle Charles, that isn't true.'

'You don't look satisfied with the results, Crista. What is it?'

She sighed. 'I suppose I can no longer take pride in honest work because my conscience isn't clear.'

'I understand very well, but at least we are to be released from further obligation once you have set those wretchedly ostentatious diamonds. That will save us the trouble of finding a way out of this situation, and the rest of the family's safety is guaranteed.'

Crista made an unladylike sound at the back of her throat. 'The rest of the family deserve no such consideration.'

'Perhaps not, but even so, we — '

'Besides, how can we be so sure they will keep their word?' Crista paced the length of the workshop, too anguished to sit still; too tired to think coherently. She had been working fourteen-hour days to finish this jewellery, and now she had to start on the diamonds for Reece. The mere thought of it was exhausting. 'Besides, I had rather set my heart on exposing them, regardless. Were it not for you, then I would certainly find a way to do precisely that.'

'You mustn't worry about me, my dear. Promise me you won't do anything rash. I think we can assume they will let us be after this because those stones are the best they have. I have certainly never seen their like before.'

'No.' Crista shook her head. 'Nor I.'

'They have built up their clientele slowly, teasing them with the distinctive pieces your father made before you took over. They've been careful not to flood the market, but have found someone who wants to flaunt the diamonds. They must know they will be noticed, questions will be asked, and they will be compelled to lie low.'

'Asking questions will not serve since the people behind the scheme are too wily to reveal their identities. It's Reece, or people like us, who will get caught.'

'Yes, but even so — '

'And I still don't trust them to keep their

word. They have given us no reason to believe anything they say.'

'True, but what choice do we have?' Uncle Charles spread his hands. 'Besides, they have promised to return the documents your father signed, and once they do, they will have no further hold over us.'

'Even if they speak the truth, it doesn't seem right they should get away with what they have done. The jewels we have handled are stolen, Uncle. They belong to someone who must be missing them, and by handling them we have become no better than common criminals ourselves.'

'Ah, Crista, don't fret so, my dear. Your principles do you credit, but even supposing you decided to expose the scheme, whom would you tell?'

Crista bit her lip in frustration. 'Well, there must be someone. I'm sure the duke wouldn't be happy if he knew what was happening beneath his nose here in Shawford.'

'That would ruin my reputation, lose me the duke's patronage, and cause more friction between the villages. It is better the duke remains in ignorance. Besides, it will not be for much longer, and then we can go back to the way we were. Or rather I can. You, my dear, will be free to live your life however you see fit.'

Perhaps, Crista thought, expelling a slow, frustrated breath, but she would never be at peace with her conscience. 'Yes,' she replied. 'That is why I haven't said anything.'

'I am so sorry you're having to deal with this at a time when you ought to enjoy being young, my dear. I hold myself responsible.'

'You? Oh, Uncle!' Crista threw her arms around his neck. 'You are not culpable. My father's greed, powered by my mother's ambitions, are at the root of this problem.'

'Yes, well, it does no good to dwell upon that. Your father paid a high price for his misguided actions.' He patted her hand. 'Run along upstairs and rest. It is getting late and you look exhausted. We shall enjoy a quiet dinner and tomorrow afternoon, we have the party to look forward to.'

'I have decided not to go, Uncle. There is too much for me to do here.'

Uncle Charles fixed her with a steely gaze. 'If you do not go, nor shall I.'

Crista threw up her hands. 'You are the most terrible manipulator,' she said, shaking a finger at him. 'You know very well you have just said the only thing to change my mind. My conscience is already quite overburdened enough without adding the curtailment of your pleasures to my tally of misdeeds.'

'It will do us both good to forget our

troubles for a few hours.'

Crista saw no reason to point out she could not forget them, even for a few minutes.

'Yes, perhaps it will, and I am curious to see how the jewels are received. To say nothing of your beautiful chalice.' She ran her fingertips over the finished piece of silver. 'I should like to see the duchess wearing the rubies. Although I don't suppose she will do so for an afternoon garden party. Pity. Even so, if she takes pleasure from them, it might just reignite my pride in a commission well executed,' she added, more in hope than expectation.

The bell over the shop door jangled.

'That will most likely be Lord Amos come to collect these things.'

Crista's foolish heart leapt at the sound of his name, and she was conscious of colour flooding her cheeks. Fortunately, Uncle Charles took himself off to the shop and could not have noticed her reaction. Crista placed herself behind the door, pathetically eager to hear his voice.

'Good day to you, Chesney,' said the voice that haunted her dreams.

'Lord Amos. Your timing could not be better. If you would be so good as to take a seat, I shall pack up the items. I shall be but a moment.'

'Take all the time you need. I am in no particular hurry.'

Crista kept well clear of the door when Uncle Charles returned to the workroom. She passed the jewellery, nestled in a velvet-lined box, to her uncle. He took it with one hand and the chalice with the other. Crista stood behind the door to open it for him, but did not completely close it behind him. She peeped through the gap as Uncle Charles placed the commissions on the counter in front of his lordship and slowly lifted the lid of the box containing her creations.

Crista knew she had done some of her best work, but also experienced a moment's anxiety as Lord Amos bent his dark head over the jewellery, taking an inordinate amount of time to examine it. Even though she could not take public credit, she so wanted him to approve. It would be enough to know he admired what he saw.

After what seemed like an eternity, he lifted his head again.

'Exquisite,' he said, addressing the door behind which she stood, as though talking directly to her. 'You are to be congratulated, Chesney. It is one of your finest creations.'

'I cannot take much of the credit.'

Lord Amos continued to look at her door.

'In that case, you must ensure the credit is directed to the right quarter.'

Crista stifled a gasp. He knew, or at least suspected. But how could he? How had they given themselves away? They had been so cautious. Dear God, what if he said something? That would mean Crista's full history would become public knowledge, which in turn would put paid to Reece's activities. She would be glad about that, of course, but the consequences for her family would be dire. *Can I trust you, Lord Amos?* Strangely enough, her panic subsided, and she intuitively understood he would keep her secret, at least for now. She didn't need him to do so for long. Once she had done this final commission for Reece, Amelia would be safe, and it would no longer matter.

'I sincerely hope the duchess will take pleasure from her gift, my lord,' Uncle Charles replied. 'That will be credit enough for all concerned.'

'I do not see how it could be otherwise,' he replied softly.

The chalice was then admired, both purchases were wrapped, and Lord Amos took his leave. As he did so, he said, 'I look forward to seeing you and your niece at the party tomorrow. I hope Miss Brooke has not forgotten I offered her a tour of the stud.'

★　★　★

By agreement, all six siblings met before the dinner hour that evening. It was a family tradition to present their mother with her new piece of silver on the evening before the garden party, so it could be admired in private and added to the cabinet.

Amos's brothers and sisters were awestruck by the beautiful suite of jewellery.

'I had no idea old Mr. Chesney was quite so talented,' Annalise said, fingering the delicate necklace and holding it up against her own neck.

'Mama will be thrilled,' Portia said. 'She does so enjoy her baubles.'

Zach laughed and tugged at one of his younger sister's curls. 'If these are your idea of baubles, I shall present you with Chesney's account to settle. Trust me, it will make your eyes water.'

'A price beyond rubies,' Portia murmured.

'Chesney's creation has set Portia to quoting the bible,' Nate said, shuddering.

'Portia quotes things all the time,' Annalise reminded them. 'She is far cleverer than all the rest of us. Unlike me, she is not frivolous and always has her nose in a book.'

'That is not the only difference between us, Anna,' Portia replied. 'When I make my debut next year I am hardly likely to be run off my feet by amorous beaux keen to win my favour.'

'Of course you are,' Annalise said. 'Don't make the mistake of underestimating your charms, or you will miss all the fun. Not that there is much fun to be had in a ballroom with four brothers glowering at any gentleman who dares to approach you.'

'That bounder Simpkins was sniffing around your petticoats the entire season, Anna,' Vince said, scowling.

'He's in dun territory and would have compromised you in a heartbeat just to get his hands on your dowry,' Zach added.

Amos nodded. 'Or just to get his hands on you.'

'You see what I mean, Portia. They are totally impossible. They frighten away the gentlemen who interest me as well as those whom they seem to think have ulterior motives.'

'Perhaps if you concentrated on gentlemen who do not enjoy reputations as rakes,' Zach suggested with a long-suffering sigh.

'Where would be the fun in that?' Annalise lifted her shoulders. 'Gentlemen with dark reputations are so much more interesting. You know how easily I become bored.'

'And she wonders why we watch over her,'

Vince said, shuddering.

'I wouldn't mind quite so much if the four of you practised what you preach, but I feel persuaded you are all bent upon committing the same indiscretions you accuse my admirers of contemplating.'

'We are not indiscreet with innocents,' Nate said.

'Ah hah.' Annalise grinned triumphantly. 'So you admit it then?'

'Don't let our mother hear you giggling, Anna,' Nate said, wagging a finger at her. 'You know how vulgar she considers it.'

'Speaking of our mother, are we all agreed the jewellery will be well received?' Zach asked.

'How could it not be?' Vince shrugged. 'Besides, we commissioned it, so it's too late for a change of heart.'

'Oh, Zach could pay for it without noticing the loss,' Portia said airily. 'And then give it to his lady love instead of Mama.'

'Does Lady St. John favour rubies?' Annalise asked with an angelic smile that earned her a frown from the Duke of Winchester and caused his brothers to share a chuckle.

'Quick, I can hear her coming,' Portia said.

Zach whipped away the box containing the rubies. The silver chalice, beautifully studded with emeralds, was left on the table in solitary splendour. Faraday opened the door for the duchess, who gasped when she saw her gift.

'My goodness,' she said. 'Those wicked rumours were clearly not true. Mr. Chesney has definitely not lost his touch.' She picked up the chalice and examined it from all angles. 'It is better than anything he has ever done before and will make a wonderful addition to the collection. Thank you all so very much.'

Faraday took the chalice and carefully placed it in the spot that had been cleared for it at the front of the cabinet. A footman circulated with champagne. When they had all been served, Zach raised his glass.

'Mother,' he said. 'A very happy birthday. I hope tomorrow and all the years to follow will bring you health, happiness, and everything your heart desires.'

'Thank you, Zach. Seeing you all here together makes me happier than you could possibly know.' She paused to sip at her drink, and Amos was sure she had to be thinking about their father. 'Now, if one of you boys were to find himself a suitable wife and make me a grandmother, my happiness would be absolute.'

'I say, Mother,' Vince replied for them all. 'That's asking a lot. What's the rush?'

'I shall refrain from pointing out that Zach

is now thirty,' the duchess said, 'but only because it would fall upon deaf ears.'

The brothers instinctively moved closer together, as though there seeking safety in numbers.

'Given this is a particular milestone in your journey through life, Mother, we, the six of us, thought a more personal gift was called for.' Zach produced the box containing the jewellery from the side table where he had placed it and handed it to her with a flourishing bow. 'I hope this will compensate in some small way for the lack of grandchildren.'

'My goodness, I was not expecting anything. Whatever is this?'

'Open it, Mama,' Annalise said, skipping with impatience.

The duchess placed her glass aside and did precisely that. 'This is exquisite!' She covered her mouth with one hand, a most unusual show of emotion for their habitually composed mother. 'Absolutely exquisite. I have never owned rubies. I wonder how I could have overlooked their brilliance.'

'I knew you did not, and suggested them,' Annalise said. 'But I can take no credit for approving the design. The boys did all that, proving they do have their uses.'

The duchess elevated a brow. 'I knew Mr. Chesney was a skilled craftsman, but I had no idea he was quite so innovative when it came to design.'

'He has a niece who did the design,' Vince replied.

'Really?' Amos could see his mother's curiosity was piqued. 'I had heard something about a young lady staying with him.'

'She will be here tomorrow,' Zach said. 'I dare say you would like to meet her.'

'Certainly, I would.'

'Well then, Amos, you must make sure Miss Brooke is brought to Mother's notice.'

'The rubies are Burmese, which apparently are the best,' Amos said. 'They are supposed to ease transition by providing clarity.'

Their mother's eyes were moist. 'Thank you so very much, all of you. It was a most thoughtful thing to do. I never imagined I would own any more jewellery now that . . . well, your father was the only person who ever purchased any for me, apart from what I inherited from his mama and that will be passed on to your wife, Zach. If you ever settle upon one,' she added, smiling to take the sting out of her words.

'Now you know why I persuaded you to wear the cream silk, Mama,' Annalise said. 'It will make a perfect backdrop for the jewels.'

'So it will, my dear. How clever of you to think of it.' The duchess wiped her eyes and kissed each of them in turn. 'My goodness, I feel terribly spoiled. It is almost worth being a year older.'

'We are very glad you like your surprise,' Amos said.

'Come along, Mother.' Zach proffered his arm. 'Dinner is served.'

10

'I hope you don't intend to be at Winchester Park this afternoon, Miss Brooke,' Reece said, strolling into the workshop on the morning of the party, looking as though he was spoiling for a fight. Well, if he was, he had come to the right place.

'Certainly I do. The duchess wishes to meet me.'

Fleeting alarm crossed Reece's features. 'That would not be wise. I forbid you to go.'

Crista bridled at his arbitrary tone, even if she secretly harboured her own doubts about attending. Unlike Lord Amos's family, who were too well bred to press her with impolite questions about her reasons for being in Shawford, the villagers would feel no such restraint. It would be better to disappoint Uncle Charles than risk more sinister repercussions for the sake of an afternoon's entertainment.

'You can forbid all you like, but I shall still attend.'

Every fibre in Crista's body rebelled when he grabbed her upper arm so tightly it brought tears to her eyes. 'Go if you must, but never forget what will happen if you say

150

one word out of place. I shall be there, and I will be watching your every move.'

'I told you never to touch me again, you odious reptile!'

She reached for the nearest weapon to hand, which happened to be a sharp pair of tweezers. She stabbed the back of the hand touching her arm with as much force as she could manage and pinched. He howled and released her, sucking his hand into his mouth.

'Just remember, you are only useful to us until those diamonds are set.' Something dark and dangerous flashed through his eyes. 'Then my masters will not care what happens to you, and I will have my revenge.'

So saying, he stormed from the shop, leaving Crista to regret her hasty action. She pushed such thoughts aside and ran up the stairs to change. She donned the same gown she had worn for her previous visit to Winchester Park — her only respectable one. She took more trouble than usual with her hair, brushing it until it shone, and asked Kate to help her style it.

'There we are, miss,' Kate said, putting aside her brush. 'You look a picture.'

'Hardly, but at least I won't disgrace the family,' Crista replied, wrinkling her nose at her reflection.

'Here's your bonnet.'

'Thank you, Kate. Now get off yourself and enjoy the party.'

'That I will, miss. It's always such good fun, and the duke is so generous.'

With her straw bonnet containing her wayward curls, Crista had run out of excuses to linger and joined her uncle, waiting for her in their sitting room.

'This is actually the back entrance to Winchester Park,' Uncle Charles explained as he drove his curricle, pulled by a reliable old cob, along the same track they had taken previously. 'There is a similar track that leads from Compton. I have always thought the two paths were deliberately constructed by a previous duke to prevent the two sets of villagers from having to converge.'

Crista smiled. 'Surely, they are not *that* uncivilised.'

'At the beginning of the party they will be on their best behaviour. But once the ale flows . . . well, I dare say you will see for yourself. Someone from one village will make a disparaging remark about the other, offence will be taken, and that will be when things disintegrate.'

'I wonder the duke allows them on his property if they behave so very badly.'

'Oh, they manage to remain civil while they are at the Park. It's when they set off for home the trouble starts, which is when the two tracks become invaluable.'

Crista laughed. 'Separating the warring factions?'

'Precisely. I happen to know the current duke discreetly places some of his strongest footmen along the tracks when the villagers leave, just in case of trouble.'

'I hope you never get involved in these disputes, Uncle,' Crista said with mock severity.

'Not now, but when I was a younger man,' he replied, his rheumy eyes sparkling with mischief, 'there happened to be a very attractive young lady residing in Shawford. When she rejected the advances of one of the coves from Compton, he had the temerity to say some rather unfortunate things about her. Well, I could not allow that situation to pass unchallenged.'

'You formed an attachment to a lady, Uncle?' Crista looked at him with great curiosity.

'I have not always been old, you know.'

'And nor are you now.' But he had never married. Crista had often wondered why, and hated to think he had lived all these years nursing a broken heart. 'What happened to the lady? Did she disappoint you?'

'She had the poor judgement to run off and marry the blacksmith from Compton.'

'Oh dear.'

'Quite. It caused something of a ruckus at

the time. Intermarriage between the two villages is frowned upon. Had she taken up a career as a light-skirt it would have been less shocking.'

'No, Uncle, you are teasing,' Crista said, laughing.

'Indeed I am not.'

'Will the lady be here today?'

'Oh, I am sure she will be. I think she regretted her hasty decision to marry her brawny blacksmith, but there is nothing to be done about that now.'

'Well, it stands to reason she must regret it,' Crista cried loyally. 'She could have had you.'

Uncle Charles sighed. 'It was all a long time ago.'

They drove on for a moment or two in silence. Crista tilted her head backwards so she could enjoy the soft breeze on her face and the sight of a cloudless blue sky on a perfect summer's day.

'Where is the front entrance to Winchester Park precisely?' Crista had been so nervous on her last visit she hadn't taken much interest in the geography.

'About five miles in the other direction, on the main Winchester Road.'

Crista smiled, noticing her uncle's conveyance attracting considerable interest from the occupants of the procession of vehicles they had slowed down to join. He appeared to know everyone, and smiled and waved to those they passed on foot. Crista smiled too but looked directly ahead, thus avoiding the curious questions she could sense the pedestrians formulating as they stared openly at her.

It took another half-hour to cover a distance that should have taken five minutes, but everyone was in high spirits and didn't mind the delay. It was a beautiful day, and they fully intended to make the most of the holiday. Crista felt herself relax, and she vowed she too would enjoy herself. Let tomorrow take care of itself. She was her uncle's niece, come from London to visit him, and would admit as much to anyone who asked.

Freed from the curricle, Crista and her uncle headed for the front lawns. She gasped, barely recognising the place she had seen only a week before. It had been transformed into her idea of a carnival, even though she had never seen one. There were clowns, tumblers, jugglers and even a fire-eater who had attracted a huge crowd of wide-eyed spectators.

'Where did these people come from, Uncle?'

'They are a travelling troupe of gipsies whom the duke invites back each year to entertain us.'

'They certainly do that,' she replied, pausing to watch a juggler whose hands moved so fast she was unable to count the number of balls he kept in the air.

There were people everywhere, all in their Sunday best. Children ran riot, unable to decide which attraction to watch first. Fiddlers played a lively jig that already had people dancing. Long tables groaned beneath the amount of food set upon them, and Crista saw the barmaids from the Crown and Anchor almost run off their feet trying to keep up with the demand for ale. Organised games appeared to be underway already. She recognised pitch-halfpenny and skittles.

'There used to be a tug of war,' Uncle Charles told her. 'And wrestling bouts.'

Crista big her lip. 'But let me guess. The competition between the villages got too intense.'

'I see you begin to understand.' His eyes twinkled. 'There will probably be leaping for gloves.'

'I have never seen that.'

'Then you have a treat in store. And later, there will be a cricket match where the men will show off their prowess and the ladies will admire their physiques.'

'Uncle Charles!'

'Don't pretend to be shocked, my dear,' he replied, chuckling. 'There is no sin in appreciating masculine prowess.'

'But this cricket match, surely that creates just as much rivalry between the villages.'

'Ah, but it does not. The current duke's father instigated it, having run out of entertainments that did not debilitate half the male villagers and prevent them from working for a week after the party. And so, he decided the cricket match would be the gentry against the villagers, forcing the two villages to join forces in their quest for communal glory.'

'How clever. Does Lord Amos play?' she asked, wishing the words back as soon as they slipped past her guard.

Uncle Charles fixed her with a penetrating look. 'I dare say he will.'

'Oh look,' she said hastily. 'What are those girls doing?'

'Practising their dancing,' Uncle Charles replied. 'Each village has its young girls devise a dance in honour of the duchess's birthday.'

'Don't tell me, another source of fierce competition.'

'Quite so.' He steered her towards the food. 'Shall we have something to eat and drink before we move on?'

★ ★ ★

Amos's family mingled with the growing crowds, eating what they ate, drinking whatever was on hand to quench their thirst. A duchess rubbed shoulders with a farmer's wife, a duke chatted on equal terms with an articled clerk. Amos was in debate with a market trader about the possibility of an early harvest and the price of corn. Even so, he knew the moment Crista Brooke set foot on the estate. He sensed her presence and fancied he heard her laughter above all the noise and mayhem caused by Shawford and Compton residents making merry.

She remained with her uncle, not appearing to speak to anyone else, even though Chesney paused frequently to exchange a word or two here and there. Reece was nowhere in sight. Amos watched her wander near some children playing pitch-halfpenny and saw her smile at something one of them said to her. Her uncle's attention was then taken by Mrs. Gower, and Miss Brooke was temporarily alone. Amos seized the opportunity. Excusing himself from the trader, he made his way towards her.

'Miss Brooke,' he said. 'I am so glad you decided to come.'

'Good afternoon, Lord Amos. I told you I would be here.'

'I thought you might have had a change of heart.'

'Even if I had, my uncle would not have

permitted me to remain behind.'

Amos grinned. 'I always knew he was a sensible fellow.'

'Who is that lady he is in such animated conversation with?'

'Oh, that's Mrs. Gower. She was a Shawford girl originally but caused great problems by marrying Compton's blacksmith.'

'Oh, so she's the one.' She looked more closely at Mrs. Gower. 'That explains it then. My uncle was disappointed in love as a young man, you know.' She sent Amos a wistful smile. 'He told me as much on the way over here. I didn't realise he and the lady were still, how shall I put this . . . ' She blushed beneath his amused expression. 'Oh well, you know what I mean.'

'Affairs of the heart have been ever thus.'

'I wouldn't know.'

Amos sent her a teasing smile. 'I find that very hard to believe.'

'I think it says much for my uncle's constancy and the intensity of his feelings that he never looked elsewhere which, obviously, he did not.' She sighed. 'He must have been very much in love. It's so sad.'

'You are very tender-hearted, Miss Brooke.'

'On the contrary, Lord Amos, I am simply very fond of my uncle.'

'He doesn't look disappointed now.'

'No, they certainly seem to have a lot to say to one another.' Miss Brooke smiled. 'She's still a very handsome woman.'

'Talking of which, if it would be convenient, my mother is waiting to thank you for designing her beautiful jewellery. She is quite delighted with it.'

'Oh well then, perhaps my uncle — '

'I don't believe he often gets an opportunity to speak with Mrs. Gower, what with relations between the two villages being the way they are. Let's leave them be.'

She lowered her head, concealing panic-stricken eyes beneath the brim of her bonnet, as though afraid of what Amos might read in her expression. After a moment, she straightened her spine, took a deep breath, and lifted her chin.

'And you accuse me of being romantically inclined,' she said with a wry smile.

He proffered his arm and returned her smile with a heated one of his own. It wasn't entirely appropriate, but appropriate behaviour had a habit of deserting him when he was anywhere near Miss Brooke. 'Your uncle and Mrs. Gower can't get up to much mischief in the middle of this throng.'

'You were about to say at their age.' She shook a finger at him as they commenced walking together towards the house. 'Shame on you, Lord Amos. Love does not discriminate by age.'

'True. My parents seemed as devoted on the day my father died as they must have been on their wedding day.'

'Then they were very fortunate,' she replied, her expression remote.

'What do you make of our little gathering?' he asked.

'Little?' Her eyes widened and she was her lively self again. 'I have never seen anything quite like it. It is remarkably generous of the duke.'

Amos laughed. 'We live in expectation of uniting the villages, being optimists by nature. Not that it will ever happen, but we do our humble best.'

'There is absolutely nothing humble about this establishment,' she said, glancing up at the elegant façade of the enormous building as they climbed the steps to the terrace.

'Mother is waiting inside,' Amos said.

He led her into the drawing room, where his mother sat with Portia. As they entered the room, so too did Annalise.

'Oh good, I haven't missed you. I got cornered by Miss Higgins who wanted to talk some more about that wretched Flemish lace. You must be Miss Brooke. How do you do. I am Amos's sister, Annalise, and we are all in raptures about the beautiful jewellery you designed for Mama. You really are so very clever, I cannot think how — '

'Anna, please!' Amos held up a hand, stopping his sister's cheerful flow of words, aware it might well have gone on for another five minutes otherwise. 'Give Miss Brooke a chance to acknowledge you.'

'Lady Annalise.' Miss Brooke smiled and bobbed a curtsey.

'Oh, I am so sorry. My tongue runs away with me sometimes.'

Amos quirked a brow. 'Sometimes?'

'Never mind about Amos. He doesn't understand the way we women think.' Annalise linked arms with Miss Brooke, and they walked across the room together. 'Mama, here is Miss Brooke, the clever lady who designed your birthday gift. Miss Brooke, this is our mother, the Duchess of Winchester, and my sister Portia.'

'You are very welcome, Miss Brooke,' the duchess said.

'It's an honour to make your acquaintance, Your Grace.' Miss Brooke showed composure as she curtsied to their mother and then turned to repeat the gesture to Portia. 'Lady Portia.'

'Do please come and sit beside me,' their mother said. 'I must know where you learned

162

to design so beautifully.'

Amos would like to know that too and took a seat as soon as Miss Brooke and Annalise had done so.

'I can't say I was taught precisely, Your Grace. It is just something I seem able to do instinctively. My uncle's eyesight is not what it once was, and I offered to help him if I could.'

'Then it is very fortunate for me you happened to be here.'

'I cannot draw to save my life,' Annalise said. 'Portia, on the other hand, shows great talent, but then she is good at everything she does.'

'I couldn't design jewellery,' Portia replied. 'I shouldn't know where to start, although I would probably enjoy the challenge.'

'I have seen my uncle's work often enough to have formed ideas,' Miss Brooke replied.

'And yet I don't recall ever seeing you here before,' the duchess said. 'I am sure I would have remembered, had we met. Do you intend to remain in the district?'

'My plans are not yet finalised. My father died recently, you see, and Uncle Charles invited me here for a change of scenery.'

'I am very sorry to hear that, Miss Brooke,' their mother replied softly. 'I am fully acquainted with the pain of loss.'

Now was the time for Amos to ask where her sister was, and why she had not come to Shawford, too. Before he could do so, their mother spoke again, and what she had to say both surprised and delighted Amos.

'You and your uncle must dine with us before you leave, Miss Brooke. I absolutely insist. I would like you to see me wearing your beautiful designs. I could not do so this afternoon, of course. Rubies in the afternoon would look . . . well, not quite the thing, but I must insist you dine. I shall arrange it very soon.'

'Thank you, Your Grace, I would — '

Miss Brooke looked decidedly relieved when Nate bounded into the room, and all heads turned in his direction instead of hers. His mysterious little vixen didn't like being the centre of attention, or answering questions about herself.

'I say, you must be Miss Brooke.' She stood to curtsey and Nate bowed over her hand. 'How do you do. I am Nathanial, and it's a pleasure to meet you. You are so very clever, but I am sure my family have already told you as much.'

'Thank you, Lord Nathanial,' she replied resuming her seat, looking a little over-whelmed by her reception but otherwise, remarkably poised. Too poised. Miss Brooke was used to good society. The more Amos got to know her, the less he understood her.

'I came to tell you the cricket is about to start. You and I are needed, Amos.'

'Very well.' Amos stood, as did all the ladies. 'Let's go and give them a sound thrashing, little brother.'

'This is the best fun imaginable,' Annalise said. 'It is almost like warfare but without the bloodshed. You must sit with us, Miss Brooke. I absolutely insist. She must, must she not, Mama.'

'Absolutely.'

Satisfied that Miss Brooke would be in the safe hands of her family, Amos excused himself and went off with Nate to join the fray.

11

Crista walked outside with the rest of the ladies. During her absence the ale had cut through inhibitions, as evidenced by noise levels that had increased by several decibels as groups organised themselves around the makeshift cricket pitch immediately below the terrace. Demarcation lines had been drawn up. The majority of Shawford's residents lined one boundary, Compton's the other. The duke's family and friends took the seats in the centre, dividing the two factions in case the fragile truce didn't hold.

'We have to keep the spectators from killing one another somehow,' Lady Annalise whispered to Crista, loud enough for everyone to hear.

'I hadn't realised quite how vicious the feuding actually is,' Crista replied. 'How did it start?'

'It's been going on for so long no one can quite remember.' Lady Annalise flashed an impish smile and Crista instinctively warmed to her. Had circumstances been different . . . but they were not and regrets were pointless. 'Shall we sit here?'

'I wonder what has become of my uncle.'

She scanned the crowd, noticed him in conversation with some tradespeople from Shawford and waved to him. He smiled and waved back. The duchess took a seat in the shade with some of the older ladies. Crista felt rather self-conscious seated in the front row between Lady Portia and Lady Annalise. Her gown was woefully inadequate when compared to theirs, but if they noticed, it didn't seem to bother them. She didn't belong with these elegant ladies, and yet felt perfectly at home in the midst. She thought briefly of her mother, who would have been in seventh heaven to find herself thus situated.

All four Sheridan males suddenly appeared before them, in shirtsleeves, laughing but looking seriously intent. Their beauty took Crista's breath away and it was very difficult for her to hide just how impressed she was by their formidable physiques — all muscle, sinew and raw power.

'Miss Brooke,' the duke said. 'No, please don't get up. I am very pleased you could come.'

'It seems even the weather falls in with your plans, Your Grace,' she replied.

'It wouldn't dare do otherwise,' Lord Vincent said, swinging his right arm in a circle, as though preparing to bowl the cricket ball.

'Who is that gentleman?' Lady Annalise asked, looking directly at a tall, imposing figure who was striding towards her brothers.

'That's my good friend Clarence Vaughan, Earl of Romsey.'

The duke introduced them all by name as soon as the earl joined them, including Crista. The earl was very handsome, with a relaxed attitude and easy charm. Crista could quite see why Lady Annalise seemed impressed, blushing when the earl took her hand. According to the rumour mill in Shawford, which her uncle assured her was seldom wrong, Lady Annalise had caused quite a stir during her first season and rejected several eligible offers. That was hardly to be wondered at. She was very beautiful, so lively and full of fun, as well as being handsomely dowered. Crista felt dull and uninteresting by comparison.

'Good heavens, Clarence, I had no idea you were back in England.'

Lord Romsey looked towards the speaker, as did the entire party. Crista barely suppressed a gasp. One of the most beautiful women she had ever seen joined the party, dressed in the height of fashion — just not English fashion. The lady's cream cambric-muslin gown was tight-fitting, with plain long sleeves finished with exquisite blue lace that fell over her hands. Two rows of similar lace adorned the hem. Her pelisse was sky-blue kerseymore and fit tight to her svelte form. Her bonnet, perched on top of a cascade of golden curls, was velvet, the same colour as her pelisse, with a high crown and full ostrich plume.

'Frankie, how delightful.'

The two shook hands like old friends. Crista noticed Lady Annalise frown at their intimacy. So, too, did the duke.

'You two are acquainted,' the duke drawled.

'Indeed,' the earl replied. 'Frankie and her rogue of a husband lived in Paris at the same time as me.'

Ah, Crista thought, that explained her distinctive fashion sense. Parisians knew the meaning of style. Lady Annalise looked as though she wanted to ask a question, but was unable to formulate the words. Crista felt a moment's sympathy for her. She was similarly afflicted when attempting to say something amusing to Lord Amos but being anywhere near him appeared to suck her mind dry and glued her tongue to the roof of her mouth. It was most vexatious.

'Come along, Zach,' Lord Nate said. 'They're waiting for us.'

'Do come and sit with us, Lady St. John,'

Lady Annalise said as the gentlemen moved towards the pitch. 'This is Miss Brooke.'

'You must be the lady who designed the duchess's jewellery. I have just been admiring it. You are so very clever.'

Crista smiled. 'Thank you.'

'Such talent is a rare gift. Don't allow anyone to talk you out of doing what you do so well.'

Crista thought of her precarious finances and assured her there was little chance of that happening.

'Now then,' Lady St. John said. 'Who shall win this silly game, do you suppose?'

'Which brave soul acts as umpire?' Crista asked.

'Oh, the vicars from each village take it turn and turn about,' Lady Portia replied.

'That *is* brave,' Lady St. John said with an animated smile as she put up her parasol. Crista didn't possess one, but since her face was already blighted by unsightly freckles it didn't make much difference if the sun had its way with her complexion.

The duke's team was to bat first, and the openers walked out to a smattering of applause.

'Oh my goodness,' Lady St. John said. 'Look at the size of the man about to bowl. I shouldn't like to face him.'

'That is the son of Compton's blacksmith,' Lady Portia replied.

'Ah, that would account for all those muscles.'

'Lady St. John!' Lady Annalise sounded shocked but looked decidedly amused.

'Well, my dear, if they didn't wish us to admire them, they would not run about in their shirtsleeves, showing themselves off. In France, I learned there is nothing wrong with open admiration for anything of beauty, albeit human or inanimate.'

'How very sensible of the French,' Crista replied. 'Were you living there during the fighting?'

'We weren't in any danger. My husband was something frightfully important in the government, our English government, that is, and we were always one step ahead of the skirmishes.'

And yet Lady St. John was a widow, so something had to have gone wrong.

'What did Lord Romsey do in France?' Lady Annalise asked.

'Oh, good shot!' The ball sailed over the boundary rope for six. 'He did, and I believe still does, fill a vital role in His Majesty's government. It's all terribly hush-hush. You can never get them to talk about what they do. I gave up trying a long time ago.' Lady St.

John shrugged. 'I probably wouldn't understand it even if they attempted to explain.'

Crista couldn't recall a time when she had enjoyed herself more, or a time when she had felt more relaxed. She had forgotten *how* to relax, she realised now, because she had been living for so long under such very great strain. But these ladies, who treated her as an equal and sought her opinion on every conceivable subject, were lively and engaging company.

As the game went on, Crista felt rather sorry for the beleaguered clergyman acting as umpire. All his decisions were met with loud protests by either one side or the other, but at least it didn't come to blows. Lord Amos had just gone in to bat. He stood at the crease, looking around at the field placements, and Crista was sure his gaze briefly came to rest upon her, as though he wanted to be sure she was watching him. How could she not be? In his billowing shirt and tight breeches, his hair blowing in the breeze, hard, unyielding muscles at work beneath that shirt, she couldn't have dragged her eyes away from him if her life had depended upon it. The massively-built blacksmith's son thundered down his run and let the ball fly at a terrifying rate. Crista felt the urge to duck and couldn't understand why Lord Amos didn't take evasive action. Instead, he swung his bat in a graceful arc, timed it beautifully, and sent the ball crashing to the boundary for four runs.

'Oh, well done!' Crista clapped louder than anyone else.

'The contest seems rather even,' Lady Portia remarked a short time later when another wicket had fallen, and Lord Amos was joined at the crease by the duke. Crista noticed a marked increase in the deployment of fans as the females watched the two brothers, standing in the middle of the wicket, conferring about tactics. Lady St. John appeared especially transfixed.

'They have better bowlers,' her sister replied. 'I think we shall lose this year.'

'Does it really matter?' Crista asked.

'My dear, we are talking about a male sporting event.' Lady St. John's scandalised expression made them all laugh. 'They are such little boys, and *nothing* matters more. Absolutely nothing.'

'She's right,' Lady Portia said, raising both brows. 'My brothers pretend it's a massive bore, but they actually look forward to it for weeks in advance.'

'Is anyone thirsty?' Lady Annalise asked. 'We shall have to serve ourselves. Almost all the servants have been given the afternoon off to join in the fun.'

A loud roar went up as the last wicket for

the duke's team fell. There was a brief respite, then the villagers took their turn to bat.

'They really are like little boys,' Lady Annalise said. 'You're quite right about that, Lady St. John.'

'Oh, do call me Frankie. And I hope I may call you Anna.'

'Please do. Just look as them throwing themselves around the field.'

Lady Portia grinned. 'Family honour is at stake.'

'Now let me see if I am following this right,' Lady St. John said. 'The villagers need four more runs to win. Is that correct?'

'Yes,' Lady Portia replied. 'And they have two more balls from which to score those runs.'

Lord Vincent was bowling. Crista ought to be supporting the villagers, but instead she willed his lordship to clean bowl the blacksmith's son, now wielding his bat in massive fists, making it look like a flimsy stick of wood. All the ladies fell silent as the first ball hurled down the wicket and flew past the blacksmith's bat. No run.

'One ball left,' Crista said to no one in particular, chewing the inside of her lip in her anxiety. 'The blacksmith must hit a boundary.'

He squared up, looking as if he had every

intention of doing precisely that. When the ball was delivered, he caught it squarely in the centre of his bat and sent it hurtling over the bowler's head, directly towards the ladies' position. It travelled at a ferocious rate, causing Lady Annalise and her sister to instinctively take evasive action. Crista, on the other hand, felt unable to move. The ball came closer, and she heard voices shouting her name. A ball hit as hard as this one had been, picking up speed as it shot through the air, could kill her. Crista knew that, but if she moved, the villagers would win. It was a ridiculous thought to have, but . . .

She looked up and saw the red orb still heading directly for her. Getting closer. Her occupation had given her very good hand-eye co-ordination. She stared at the ball as it fell towards her, and suddenly leapt from her seat. She stepped inside the boundary, reached up and caught it one-handed.

'Oh my goodness!' Lady Annalise's voice barely registered.

The stultifying silence was broken by a roar of voices, including the entire duke's team shouting *How was that?* at the umpire. The clergyman considered the matter and slowly raised his finger, indicating the blacksmith had been dismissed. Pandemonium broke out. The duke's team had won because Crista caught the final ball of the innings.

Crista clapped a hand to her mouth when it looked as if the entire spectacle was about to degenerate into a massive brawl. 'What on earth have I done?' she muttered.

★   ★   ★

Lord Amos was still chuckling to himself as he dressed in a clean shirt and stood in front of the glass to tie his neckcloth. He was anxious to find Miss Brooke and offer his congratulations. That was one of the best catches he had ever witnessed. Anarchy had been saved by the game being declared an honourable draw, but everyone knew the duke's team had won on a technicality. There was nothing in the rules to preclude a spectator from taking a catch, although the villagers had declared increasingly volubly as they quenched their collective thirst with copious amounts of Jeggins's ale that in future years there ought to be. Being beaten was hard enough to swallow. Having a female take the winning catch spelt total humiliation.

Whistling to himself, Amos descended the stairs and walked past Zach's library. Voices came from within but didn't slow him down. Zach's voice however did.

'Spare me a moment, Amos,' the duke said,

leaning through the open door. 'You need to hear this.'

Amos turned into the library, and Zach shut the door behind him. Romsey, Zach's friend from his Oxford days, was also in the room. The gentlemen were drinking whisky, and Zach poured one for Amos without bothering to ask if he would like one.

'Thank you,' Amos said, taking a sip of his drink, wondering why the mood was so sombre, and what it had to do with him.

'You are probably not aware that Romsey here is part of His Majesty's Diplomatic Corps,' Zach said.

'No, I didn't know that,' Amos replied. 'That would explain why you've been living abroad, I suppose. Must have been a lot for you to do following the end of the war.'

'Quite,' Romsey replied. 'I came back to England about a year ago, after the pater died, and I assumed the title, but I'm still actively involved at the foreign office. I've also just taken over responsibility for the new police office in Southampton and wanted to speak to Winchester here about criminal activity in the area.'

'Romsey has his hands full. There is plenty for him to sort out on this side of the channel regarding his diplomatic efforts in Europe,' Zach said, his expression sombre.

'Something I can help with?' Amos asked politely.

'Very possibly, but I'll let Romsey explain.'

'Looting,' Romsey said succinctly, handing his glass to Zach for a refill. 'You would not believe me if I told you the amount of treasure Napoleon and the French forces looted from the countries they conquered. Suffice it to say, it was on an unprecedented scale.'

'I'm not condoning it,' Amos replied. 'But it happens in wars, we all know that.'

'To the best of our knowledge, he got the taste for it in '98 when he supposedly liberated the Maltese from the Knights of St. John.' Romsey paused to sip his drink. 'He also liberated seven million francs' worth of treasures from the island's monasteries, churches and residences while he was about it. Then he moved his thieving ways on to Egypt, and while doing more liberating, this time from the Ottoman Turks, the state treasury was emptied. Our sources suggest that at least half of it went directly into Napoleon's own purse.'

Amos let out a low whistle. 'Much good it did him.'

'Quite, but part of my assignment in the peace dealings is to force the French to send back what they stole.' Romsey lifted his shoulders. 'Hardly surprisingly, many works still remain in French hands, impossible to track down, or have been *lost* by the soldiers assigned to transport them.'

Amos and Zach exchanged a glance. 'There's human nature for you,' Amos said.

'Our troops managed to discover a large part of Napoleon's personal loot. We weren't taking any chances and decided to remove it to safety until we could identify its rightful owners. Before we did that, we had the sense to have the whole lot catalogued. I oversaw that myself, thinking light fingers were less likely to purloin it if we had a full account of what was there.'

'I'm guessing that didn't work,' Amos said. 'Or we wouldn't be having this conversation.'

'I handpicked the squad of soldiers who were to accompany the wagons to a safe and secret location.' He grimaced. 'Not so very secret as it transpired. The entire squad was ambushed, annihilated, and the loot stolen.'

Amos grimaced. 'Presumably, very few people knew of this, so you suspect involvement from someone on the inside.'

'Right, and now some of the stolen pieces have shown up on this side of the channel.'

'Increasing your suspicions of English involvement?'

'Absolutely, and I have been charged with

179

finding out who was actually behind it all.' Romsey paced the length of the room in some agitation, obviously feeling responsible for the lost treasure and the needless deaths of the men sent to protect it. 'At first I didn't take much notice, thinking one or two pieces would be bound to find their way into the hands of unscrupulous collectors.' He paused to fix Amos with a steady gaze. 'Part of the haul was exquisite gemstones.'

Amos's entire body jerked. Surely he didn't think Miss Brooke could be involved.

'Some of the stones were very rare and distinctive, and turned up in specially-commissioned jewellery, made by one of the top designers in the country,' Romsey added. 'His work is greatly sought-after and commands top prices. We were closing in on him when he died — was brutally murdered, in fact — a few months ago.'

'What was his name?' Amos asked with a sinking heart, already knowing what the answer would be. It had been niggling in the back of his mind since making Crista's acquaintance. The connection between the name Brooke and jewellery.

'David Brooke,' Romsey said.

12

'Sorry, Amos,' Zach said, grimacing. 'I was hoping it wouldn't come to this.'

Amos felt a virulent rage surge through him and moved away from the hand Zach tried to place on his shoulder. 'You knew about this and didn't warn me?'

'Romsey just told me, and I immediately called you in. He had no idea about Miss Brooke being here before today. I didn't want to jump to conclusions, and still do not, but my first loyalty is to King and country. My second is for the welfare of this district. You said yourself something isn't right about Miss Brooke. She never told you who her father was, and allowed us all to think she learned what she knows about jewellery from her uncle.'

Amos managed a curt nod. 'If she knew her father was doing something like this, she had good reason not to reveal the connection.'

'Good point,' Zach agreed. 'And an equally good question we ought to ask ourselves is, why was he murdered if he was in league with the thieves? You said yourself, Romsey, if Brooke made the pieces, they were worth a lot more than if any other jeweller fashioned them.'

'That's true, and as to why he was murdered, I cannot say,' Romsey replied. 'Maybe he had a fit of conscience and said he would no longer play along.'

'We need to talk to Miss Brooke,' Zach said, flexing his jaw. 'Find out what, if anything, she knows. I thought you would want to be included, Amos, since you know the lady best.'

Amos walked towards the mantelpiece and leaned one arm against it, his back to the room. 'She made the jewellery for our mother herself,' he said after a moment's contemplation. 'I would stake my fortune on that. But,' he added, turning to face his brother and the earl, 'that doesn't mean she has anything to do with this mess.'

'When Winchester told me she was here, and you suspected her of making jewellery and being involved with a cove by the name of Reece, it rang alarm bells. You see, the new pieces made by Brooke necessarily dried up after his death.' Romsey paused, his expression sombre. 'Then, about a month ago, a few more appeared.'

'How do you know?' Amos challenged. 'They could have been made by Brooke before he was killed.'

'Oh, I have a network of spies in all sorts of places, and know for a fact the pieces in question were commissioned after Brooke died. I spoke to a lady who owns an emerald bangle. She has no idea the gems were stolen, and I didn't enlighten her. I don't want the rogues to know we're on to them. Once Brooke died, his designs became even more sought after, which could be another reason why he was killed. Anyway, the woman's husband was told when he made enquiries about a Brooke emerald bangle, it was one of the last items the designer made before his death.'

'Making it that much more valuable,' Zach said with a sardonic smile.

'Quite, but we happen to know it was made after his demise. We checked his workshop and there were no finished pieces there.' Romsey sighed. 'If it was just this one piece, I might accept it was genuine, but others have appeared since then. To the uneducated eye they appear to be Brooke's handiwork, but experts tell me they were not made by him.'

'Whom did the man commission the emerald bangle from?' Amos asked. 'Surely, you can pressure him to say where it came from.'

'A respectably established jeweller, who readily gave me particulars of the man who sold it to him.' Romsey shrugged. 'That left us chasing shadows, of course. The seller was nowhere to be found, and his name meant nothing to me.' He thumped the arm of his chair with his clenched fist. 'It's damned frustrating. These people are well-organised, ruthless, and very good at covering their tracks. I still don't know the name of the traitor who stole the loot and had all those good men killed, but I won't rest until I find out.'

'All right, Zach,' Amos said, shaking his head. 'Send for Miss Brooke. Let's hear what she has to say for herself.'

★ ★ ★

Following Crista's unfortunate involvement in the outcome of the cricket match, the ladies moved into the house to take tea. They hadn't been there for long when a footman appeared in the doorway and cleared his throat.

'The duke's compliments, Miss Brooke. His Grace requests you attend him in his study at your convenience.'

'You mean he told you to fetch Miss Brooke without delay,' Lady Annalise said, grinning. 'Zach never requests, he demands.'

The footman's lips quirked. 'Quite so, my lady.'

'Good heavens.' Lady St. John raised a speculative brow. 'Don't allow His Grace to

184

ring a peel over you, Miss Brooke. It was a matter of self-preservation.'

'Zach is more likely to reward Miss Brooke for giving our side the victory,' Lady Portia said with a wry smile.

'Excuse me, ladies.' Crista stood up, wondering what the duke could possibly want with her.

'If you don't reappear soon, we shall come and rescue you,' Lady Annalise assured her.

Crista managed a nervous smile and followed the footman along several corridors, quelling the urge to flee in the opposite direction. Her guide stopped in front of a door before she could act upon that impulse and stood back to allow Crista to walk through it. She straightened her spine as she entered a magnificent library, expecting to find the duke waiting to receive her alone. She stopped in her tracks when she saw Lord Amos and Lord Romsey there, too. All three gentlemen stood up, looking exceedingly sombre.

'What is it?' she asked, conscious of her heart racing. 'Has something happened to my uncle?'

'Please take a seat, Miss Brooke,' the duke replied calmly. 'To the best of my knowledge your uncle is perfectly well.'

Relieved on that score, Crista perched on

the edge of a chair, wondering why Lord Amos seemed so determined not to look at her. She was not left in ignorance for long and listened, with growing despair, to Lord Romsey's reasons for being there.

'Ah, so you know.'

'You.' Lord Amos looked horrified. 'You really are involved in all this?'

'No. Yes.' She shook her head, feeling giddy, relieved, horrified — a whole maelstrom of conflicting emotions.

'Perhaps you should start at the beginning, Miss Brooke,' the duke said, not unkindly. 'Explain everything you know.'

'Well, my father and Uncle Charles are brothers — '

'Excuse me interrupting, Miss Brooke,' Lord Romsey said. 'But I assumed Chesney was your mother's brother.'

'No, their mama, my paternal grand-mother, married twice, first to a Mr. Chesney, then Mr. Brooke. Technically Mr. Chesney is my half-uncle, I suppose.'

'I see. Pray continue.'

'My grandfather Brooke was a jeweller by trade and apprenticed both my father and Uncle Charles to that same trade.' She paused. 'To Matthew Boulton in Soho.'

The duke and Lord Romsey obviously knew the name and appeared impressed.

Lord Amos stood statue-like, and could not have made his disappointment more evident.

'Both men excelled, but my father showed exceptional ability. His reputation grew, and he set up his own business, first in small premises in Soho, then in Bond Street. He became quite well known. Very well known. There was hardly a society lady who did not crave a Brooke original, and as his reputation grew so too did his fortune. His company was craved in all sorts of elevated circles he might not ordinarily have frequented.' She paused to moisten her lips. 'That is how he met my mother. Her father commissioned a pendant for her birthday. She was so delighted with it that she insisted upon meeting Papa and thanking him in person.'

'Would you like some water, Miss Brooke?' the duke asked politely.

'No, I would prefer to talk about this. I *want* to talk about this. It needs to be spoken about.' She addressed the comment to Lord Amos, but might as well have saved her breath for all the reaction she got from him. 'My mother, unlike me, is very beautiful. If you listen to her on the subject, she will tell you she was feted by lords and heirs to great fortunes when she was a girl, but she chose my father, causing her family to disinherit her.'

'Her family?' the duke clarified.

'Oh, she is the youngest child of Viscount Woolford of Hertfordshire. The youngest and the only girl out of six. She was spoiled, allowed to have her way in everything, and so did not believe her father was sincere in his intention to disinherit her. Besides, she was in love with my father, and love would conquer all.' She rolled her eyes. 'Of course, it did not, and when she found her father *was* in earnest, and society's doors were closed to her as a consequence, she missed what she had once taken for granted.'

The duke grunted. 'I can well imagine.'

'To begin with, the marriage went well. Papa was feted by society and Mama basked in reflected glory, enjoying all the parties and entertainments they were invited to. Mama still expected to live in style, ever hopeful she would be granted a reprieve by her family, especially if she and Papa, the golden couple of the moment, were seen in all the right places.'

'But the viscount held firm?' the earl suggested.

'Yes, I have never met him, but I understand he is known for his stubbornness. Mama had brought his family's name into disrepute by marrying a tradesman and could not be forgiven.' Crista sighed. 'Anyway, I was born, and my sister Amelia arrived four years later. We had the best of everything, including a good education, but I spent every spare second in my father's workshop, fascinated by what he did, learning at his knee. My mother didn't approve, of course. She considered it no place for a lady of quality, but did not mind living off the proceeds and had Amelia to pamper, offsetting her disappointment in me. Amelia is every bit as beautiful and, excuse me, as self-centred as my mother.'

'The life of a famous jeweller's wife lost its appeal?' Lord Romsey suggested.

'She bankrupted him,' Crista replied starkly. 'Nothing he supplied her with was good enough, and she always demanded more. My mother was my father's one weakness. He never fell out of love with her, and never stopped trying to live up to her expectations. I lost all respect for him in that regard, but loved what we managed to create together in his workshop.'

'You inherited his skill?' the duke asked.

'So I've been told but, of course, a female making a mark for herself in a man's world is out of the question.'

'Your father ran out of money,' Lord Romsey said. 'What happened then?'

'He lost the Bond Street shop through an unfortunate misunderstanding about three years ago. Someone he did a commission for claimed he had used a fake stone. He had not, of course, the idea was preposterous. I subsequently discovered . . . ' Feeling embarrassed, Crista paused to clear her throat. 'I subsequently discovered the commission had been for the daughter of a widower who was enamoured of my mother. I don't care to think about what she got up to in private, but I do know she would never go so far as to leave my father for another man. She could not withstand the scandal, especially as she still lived in hope of being reunited with her family. Anyway, I have always believed the gentleman made that false claim, and ensured society knew of it, to ruin my father and increase his chances of persuading my mother to leave him. Mind you, Papa was ruined anyway. Mama had seen to that with her extravagant ways.' She looked up at the duke. 'May I have that water now, please?'

The duke poured her a glass, handed it to her, and she took several sips, taking a moment to calm her turbulent emotions.

'Thank you,' she said, placing the glass aside. 'About a year ago, he was approached by someone who suggested he carry out private commissions using gemstones provided by that person. I advised him against it most forcibly because it sounded highly suspect, but Papa was desperate. Mama became involved, recognised the monetary rewards and persuaded him to do it. Mind you, he knew his own worth. Anyone could make the sorts of items they required, but if they were marked with the distinctive Brooke insignia their value increased exponentially. He drove a hard bargain and forced the people to draw up a written agreement.'

'The devil he did! Excuse me, Miss Brooke, but do you have a copy of that agreement?' the earl asked.

'Unfortunately not.' Crista lifted her shoulders. 'If I did, I would not be in this farrago.'

'They are forcing you to help them?' Lord Amos asked, turning to look at her and speaking for the first time.

'Well, of course they are! I hope you don't think I would do so of my own volition.'

When he made no reply, Crista surmised he very likely did.

'Do you know the names of the other parties involved?' Lord Romsey asked.

'No. Papa told me he had signed the document, and I believe him; but I never saw it, or anyone involved. Papa tried to protect me. Much good it did him.'

'But now he is dead,' the duke said. 'Murdered.'

'Now he is murdered,' Crista agreed.

'Why did they kill him if they needed you to replace him, Miss Brooke?' Lord Romsey asked.

'Because he could no longer live with what he had become,' Crista replied bleakly, fighting back tears. 'He told them he was not willing to do anything else for them, and the agreement he had signed gave him leave to cancel whenever he wished. They laughed in his face, of course, and told him what I already suspected. That contract was not worth the parchment it was written on. He was involved in the wretched business, they had his signature to prove it, and he would do as he was told or pay the consequences.' She pleated her fingers nervously in her lap. 'He thought that would mean public exposure, and my mother told him he couldn't risk that.'

'Your mother is still alive?' Lord Amos asked.

'Yes.' The question surprised Crista. 'Why would you think otherwise?'

'Oh, I just assumed . . . I thought you came to live here with your uncle because you had nowhere else to go.'

'No, my mother and Amelia live in Chelsea.'

'I see.' It was the duke who replied. 'You were telling us about your father's decision to distance himself from his illegal activities.'

Crista winced at the harsh words. 'I heard Mama and Papa arguing about it. I remember quite vividly, because they never argued. My father always gave in before it reached that point. Anyway,' she added, staring at the rug beneath her feet, 'for once Papa stuck to his guns, never imagining they would follow through with their threats. I mean, how could they without exposing themselves?'

'And so they murdered him instead,' the duke said softly.

'Yes, they murdered him in a very public, very gruesome fashion, as though they knew they could get away with it. Which, of course, they did.' She impatiently dashed aside an errant tear. 'Everyone supposes Papa was set upon by cutthroats and was killed when he wouldn't give up his purse. The real perpetrators will never answer for their crime.'

'How did you become involved, Miss Brooke?' Lord Romsey asked.

'That was unfortunate. Papa had a legitimate commission half-finished when he died. I felt I owed it to his memory to complete it.' She emitted a mirthless chuckle. 'They say a good deed never goes unpunished, with good reason. By the purest of bad luck, you see, someone involved with the stolen gems found out about it and discovered I had made it.' Crista frowned. 'That is the part I don't understand. No one, or almost no one, knew what I was capable of. Mama insisted upon that. God forbid that her father should hear of it. So how did they know?' She spread her hands. 'Anyway, they confronted me and forced me into the situation you now find me in.'

'You could have refused,' Lord Amos barked.

'Oh yes, of course I could!' She sent him a damning glance, wondering how she could ever have been attracted to someone so unfeeling, so unwilling to acknowledge the impossible situation she had found herself in. 'And finished up like Papa.'

'They would not — '

'That is what Papa thought. Besides, they have that document Papa signed and threatened to make it public. That would ruin his reputation and ruin my sister too. She is on the brink of making an highly advantageous marriage.' She scoffed. 'Mama is in alt, but her intended's mother is far from happy about her son's determination to have Amelia, the daughter of a jeweller who was careless enough to allow himself to be murdered. The slightest whiff of further scandal would give her an excuse to insist her son does not go through with it.'

194

'I take it you came to Shawford in an effort to evade the rogues,' the duke said.

'Yes, and that was another miscalculation. I *did* refuse to work with them at first and came here for the precise reason you suggest, Your Grace.' Crista glowered at Lord Amos as she spoke. 'They didn't know about Uncle Charles, since he and my father have different names, and because Uncle Charles has lived quietly in this part of the world for several decades. I thought I could hide away here until they gave up on me. If they couldn't find me, there would be no reason for them to expose Papa's activities and ruin Amelia. But they followed me here, threatened Uncle Charles and left me with no choice.'

'I am terribly sorry,' the duke said.

'That is very generous of you.' Crista turned towards Lord Amos, anxious to hear what he had to say. He remained stonily silent and Crista died a little inside. She had lost his good opinion and his reaction cut to the quick. 'Now Uncle Charles has been dragged into this sorry business, and I see it eating away at him a little more each day.'

'The man Reece is your only contact?' Lord Romsey asked.

'Yes.' She shook off her self-loathing and faced the earl. 'He is the only one I have ever seen. But he knows I've reached the end of

195

my tether, much as my father did. I think that is why they have promised to leave me alone if I perform one last service for them.'

'What service?' asked the duke and Lord Romsey together.

'They have some enormous diamonds. One of them is over twenty carats.'

'From the Turkish Empire,' Lord Romsey said, his face alight with interest. 'We were wondering what had become of those.'

'They require me to make up a suite of jewellery to their specification using the stones. After that, they have assured me I will never hear from them again. I'm not sure if I believe them but the stones are magnificent. They have obviously been holding them back, waiting for the right buyer prepared to pay the king's ransom they are worth.'

'Do you have the stones in your possession?' Lord Romsey asked.

'No, I have seen them briefly, but Reece will keep them until I have made up the settings.'

The duke and Lord Romsey shared a glance. 'Then if you wish to revenge yourself on them for your father's murder, and for what they have done to you and your uncle, perhaps we can use that against them.'

Lord Amos sent her a condemning glance. 'Zach, how can you be so sure — '

'You don't believe me?'

That he could think she *chose* to be dishonest caused pangs of disillusionment to rip through her, twisting and tearing at her insides until the pain threatened to overwhelm her. His attitude of aloof disbelief should not matter to her, nor should it surprise her. The upper classes had a way of conducting themselves that didn't allow for human frailty. His opinion was of no consequence, and yet the crushing disappointment she felt threatened to suffocate her. Crista knew she could get angry, sob her heart out and beg him to believe her, or absent herself from the fray with what dignity she still retained, intact.

She chose the third option.

'Excuse me, Your Grace,' she said tersely. 'I have great need for fresh air.'

13

Reece arrived late at the Park, mingling with the throng when they had all consumed a few libations and were too intent upon enjoying themselves to take much notice of him. He had not originally intended to come at all given the responsibility he bore for the priceless diamonds entrusted to his care. But since there was not a living soul left in Shawford that afternoon, a compelling need to keep a watchful eye on Miss Brooke caused him to decide the stones would be safe where he had hidden them.

He felt very uneasy about the changes in Crista Brooke since his attempts to become better acquainted with her had ended so badly. She was now openly scathing in his company, which only made Reece want her more. He wondered where she had found the confidence to defy him quite so obviously. Perhaps Lord Amos had offered her his protection, damn the man! Just because he was rich and titled, he seemed to think he could move in on Reece's property.

Never mind, there was plenty of Miss Brooke to go around. Sheridan would tire of

198

her once he got what he wanted. Then it would be Reece's turn. Once the diamond jewellery had been made, his masters would have no further use for her, but Reece most certainly would. He felt himself hardening at the prospect. There was just something about her, about the way in which she deliberately flouted his authority that fired his blood.

He strolled around the periphery of the cricket game, wondering where she could be. He couldn't see her with her uncle, or any of the other Shawford residents. Why would she be? She had gone out of her way to keep herself apart from everyone except Chesney since her arrival here. He glanced towards the ladies seated between the two sets of villagers and growled loudly enough to attract attention to himself. What the devil! He shaded his eyes against the sun, convinced the light must be playing tricks on him. But there was no mistake. Miss Cristobel Brooke was seated with the ladies of the house as though she was their equal, and looking entirely at her ease.

A frisson of concern halted Reece in his tracks. Lifting her skirts for Lord Amos was one thing, but being accepted by his family was altogether another. Surely, she hadn't been stupid enough to say anything? No, she was too concerned about her family to take the risk.

Reece scratched his head, relieved his employer had not attended today. He would not be pleased by Miss Brooke's public exhibitionism. Reece was downright worried about it. As soon as the cricket was over and he could get anywhere near her, he would make sure she remembered what responsibilities rested with her. It wouldn't be much longer now. They were in the last over. Now it was the last ball. Reece smirked. It looked as though the gentry were in for a thrashing. Reece joined in the good-natured jeers from the villagers as Lord Vince ran in to bowl the final ball. The jeers turned to wild cheering when the ball sailed towards the boundary.

What the devil did she think she was doing? All the other ladies took evasive action, but Miss Brooke remained sitting precisely where she was, oblivious to the warnings shouted at her. At the last moment, when Reece had been sure the ball would strike her head, she stood up, crossed the boundary onto the playing field and caught the ball one-handed.

The silence that greeted her action was followed by applause and loud cheering but Reece was too stunned to react in any way. His employer would hear about this, and Reece would be in trouble for permitting the incident to occur. How in the world he was supposed to keep control over one as independently-minded as Miss Brooke was a conundrum Reece had been struggling with this past month. Perdition, if he had thought she flaunted herself before, it was nothing to the attention she had drawn to herself with that catch. He heard people asking who she was, and it wasn't long before both sets of villagers learned she was Chesney's niece.

With people now swarming all over the pitch, it was an age before Reece could force his way through to the place where Miss Brooke had been sitting. He did so just in time to see her disappear into the house with the other ladies. Reece would never gain admittance and felt impotent with rage as he waited for her to reappear, not wishing to think what she and Lord Amos might be doing. Thinking about it anyway, he passed the time plotting increasingly violent ways to extract revenge on the chit for leading him such a merry dance.

She was gone for an eternity, and there was no saying which door she might leave the house by. She could already have done so, and Reece would be none the wiser. On the point of giving up, he saw her emerge from a doorway and step out onto the terrace directly above Reece's position.

'That's it, my beauty. Come to Reece,' he

muttered, smacking his lips in anticipation.

She hugged her torso, looking angry and upset. Sheridan had probably used her and then sent her away. Reece grinned. What else could she have expected? He was about to climb the wall that divided it from the lawns below it and join her when the door behind her opened and Lord Amos stepped out.

Reece swore violently. On the point of walking away in search of a tankard of ale, he changed his mind and moved as close to the terrace as he could, curious to know what they were in such deep conversation about.

★ ★ ★

Amos watched helplessly as Miss Brooke whirled through the doors to the terrace. She held her head high, but was trembling with emotion, and pangs of disillusionment haunted her eyes.

'You could have handled that better, Amos,' Zach said mildly.

'I'm not angry at her.'

'Nor should you be.'

'She's devilish brave, if you ask me,' Romsey remarked.

Zach slapped his shoulder. 'Go after her, make sure she's all right. Romsey and I will discuss ways to use this situation to her advantage as well as our own. I think your Miss Brooke would welcome an opportunity to right quite a few wrongs and salve her conscience. We'd best get Chesney in here as well, let him know we're aware of the situation. Bring Miss Brooke back when she's more composed.'

Amos went slowly, incensed by all she'd been forced to endure; angry with himself for not making his feelings more apparent. He had failed her when she needed him the most and needed to right that situation, if he possibly could. He found her standing in an alcove that virtually concealed her from the people roaming the lawns below them. Tears flowed down her face, wild and unchecked. She tensed when she heard his footsteps, looked up and sent him a damning glance.

'Leave me be.'

'Lending you my handkerchiefs is becoming a habit.' His attempt at levity fell flat when she snatched his proffered linen and turned her back on him.

'What are you doing here?'

'I was concerned about you.'

'Don't worry, Lord Amos. I shall not steal the family silver.'

'Don't be ridiculous.'

'Ridiculous, am I?' She swirled around to

face him, anger radiating through her tears. 'You didn't believe what I just said, even though you've seen direct evidence of how Reece treats me. Or did you think that was simply a falling out amongst thieves?'

'You can't possibly think — '

'Presumably you imagine I became involved willingly.'

Tears glistened on her thick lashes. Amos yearned to wipe them away, fold her in his arms, and assure her he believed every word she had said, even if his reaction had led her to think otherwise. He placed his hands on her shoulders and forced her to turn and face him.

'I believed you,' he said softly.

'No you did not. If you had you would not have been so appalled, so accusatory, so . . . oh, so everything.' She threw her hands in the air. 'It was very hard to tell the truth for fear of what you . . . yes you, might think of me.' She poked him in the chest for added emphasis. 'You looked as though you wanted to kill someone, and I thought that someone was most likely me.'

'My violent thoughts were directed at the cowardly people who forced you into this position. With your mother, and your father even.'

'Thank you, at least for believing me,' she

said stiffly, all the fight appearing to drain out of her. She mopped her eyes with his handkerchief. 'I should go and find my uncle.'

'Are you so very anxious to leave me?'

'I have lost your respect,' she said so quietly he could barely hear her. 'I didn't deserve to have it. Even so, I didn't expect the loss to hurt quite so much.'

She glanced up at him through eyes swamped with fresh tears. The sight moved Amos in unimaginable ways. He knew how brave she was and suspected she seldom gave way to such a firestorm of emotion.

'You are quite wrong, you know. I have never respected you more. How you have worked against your instincts, morals, and better judgement in your determination to protect your ungrateful sister, is truly admirable.'

He held her captive with his gaze, watching her reaction as realisation slowly dawned. 'You really don't blame me?' she asked.

'All I blame you for is not confiding in me before now. You must have sensed I only wished to be of service to you.'

'I had my uncle's welfare to consider. He ought to have sent me packing when he realised what problems I have visited upon him. Instead, he stood beside me every step of the way, never once admonishing me.' Renewed tears spilled down her cheeks. 'He can no longer do close work and had planned to retire very soon. He has a house on the edge of the village all picked out. Now, thanks to me, he cannot stay in the district and hold his head up.'

'Nonsense! Zach has just sent for him. He will tell him he knows and does not blame him.'

She gasped. 'The duke would do that?'

Her eyes widened. Dry now, albeit red-rimmed and puffy from crying, they smouldered with luminescence, sapping Amos's rapidly dwindling willpower. He captured one of her escaped curls between his fingers and twirled it around them. She watched him, her breathing becoming increasingly ragged as he slid his other arm around her waist and pulled her against him.

'The duke doesn't blame either of you, and nor do I.'

'You don't?' She eyes widened even more. 'You really don't?'

He could sense the rapid beating of her heart and an overwhelming torrent of fiercely protective feelings gripped him. Cristobel Brooke had been made to feel inconsequential her entire life. She had been compared unfavourably to her sister, her mother had no time for her, and now she was being exploited by tyrants who worked against the interests of England. Amos was damned if he would allow that situation to continue.

'I really don't,' he said, lowering his head until his lips hovered so close to hers that her breath peppered his face. 'Zach and Romsey are devising a means for you to get even with these blaggards and be free of them forever. But I won't allow you to be part of their scheme if there is the slightest danger to you.'

She moistened her lips with the tip of her tongue. 'Surely that's for me to decide?'

'Oh no! The decision is mine.' He traced the line of freckles across her nose with the tip of his index finger. 'I like these. They give your face character.'

She managed a wry smile. 'That's hardly a compliment.'

'I know your mother and sister have made you feel second best, but you — '

'Lord Amos, I — '

'Amos. You must call me Amos.'

Her lips quirked. 'I can't do that.'

'Certainly you can, and I shall call you Cristobel.'

'Crista suits me better.'

The fingers of one hand softly touched the back of her neck, pulling her face even closer to his. 'So it does, sweet Crista.'

Amos smothered an oath as he pulled her body tighter against his and claimed her lips in a drugging kiss. Those soft lips parted beneath his in an unspoken invitation she probably didn't know she had issued: one he was powerless to ignore. He plundered her mouth with seductive strokes of his tongue as he deepened the kiss and inexorable need gripped him. He was conscious of her enticing curves as one hand ran down the length of her back, drawing her closer. However close, it would never be close enough to satisfy Amos's growing need for her. He was even more conscious of the soft swell of her breasts pressed against his chest.

The appealing mewling sound that forced its way past their fused lips brought Amos to his senses. They were out in the open, with a potential audience of several hundred people strolling the lawns below them. Much as he would like to explore her quite remarkable sensuality, now was neither the time nor the place.

'I'm sorry,' he said, breaking the kiss. 'I ought not to have done that, even if I've wanted to since first setting eyes on you.'

She stumbled when he released her, and he reached out a hand to steady her. 'I know that can't be true. I don't need false assurances.'

'You must learn to accept a compliment,

Crista,' he replied, stroking the curve of her face.

'I am a realist, Lord Amos, and — '

'Now that I have kissed you, you absolutely must use my name. I insist.'

'No matter what I call you, we can't ignore the circumstances.'

'I better understand now why you're so determined not to marry. You only have your mother and father's example to guide you. I, on the other hand, saw a very different aspect of marital bliss while growing up and fully intend to persuade you that you are wrong.'

'Why should you care what I think?'

Amos shook his head. 'Come,' he said, taking her elbow. 'Zach will wonder what has become of us.'

'Lord Amos . . . Amos, I wanted to — ' She broke off, her face flooding with colour. Amos paused, very much wanting to know what she was too embarrassed to ask him.

'Yes. What is it?'

'Oh, nothing. I was being fanciful. Ignore me.'

'There is obviously something on your mind. I need to hear what it is.'

'This is not the time.'

'There will probably never be a right time. Just ask me.'

'All right.' Her face still flamed with colour

but she inverted her chin and met his gaze. 'Since you brought the subject of marriage up, I want you to know that I'm perfectly serious in my intention never to marry. I am well able to earn my own living, even if I can't take public credit for the pieces I create.'

Amos ground his jaw. 'That seems unfair.'

'However, I . . . ' She broke off, plucking her lower lip absently with her index finger. Amos was now even more intrigued by her acute embarrassment. 'However, I am filled with curiosity about . . . well, about what happens between a man and a woman, and I was rather hoping you might satisfy that curiosity.'

'What!'

'Am I so very repellent to you?' She dropped her gaze, blushing even more furiously.

Amos tilted her chin with his fingers until she was obliged to look at him. 'You know very well you are not. But I can't do what you ask.'

'Oh, excuse me. You obviously fear I have ulterior motives. I can assure you that is not the case. I simply have an enquiring mind.'

'There are things we can do to answer some of your questions, but I will not take matters to their natural conclusion, and there's an end to the matter.'

Her embarrassment gave way to a capricious smile. The vixen was starting to discover the depths of her feminine powers. It was a joy for Amos to behold, even if it did create difficulties of a very different nature for him.

'I can't believe we're having this conversation, but am glad that we are. It helps to have something other than Reece and his vile demands to think about.'

'Speaking of which, we ought to return inside.' He took her hand and secured it in the crook of his arm. 'By the way, where did you learn to catch a cricket ball?'

14

Reece's jaw fell open.

'What the devil!' His body shook with a combination of rage and jealousy as he observed Sheridan hold Crista Brooke in his arms and kiss her like he had every right in the world to take such liberties. 'Damn the man, does he have no shame?'

The fact that Reece had similar plans for Crista was neither here nor there. He was not an aristocrat amusing himself with a woman from the lower classes. Nor had there been hundreds of people on the common to observe their activities when he attempted it. Not that anyone else seemed to notice Sheridan's outrageously arrogant behaviour. Reece probably would not have seen it either if he hadn't been watching them so closely. They were almost entirely concealed by the alcove they occupied, only Sheridan's back in view, and the villagers were having much too good a time to be concerned about the activities at the big house.

Reece was surprised by the compulsion he felt to go to Crista's rescue, even though she didn't appear to require rescuing. He was not normally inclined to interfere in other people's business, and certainly shouldn't do anything to draw attention to himself now. Nor should Crista, he thought, grinding his jaw as he watched the kiss continue.

And continue.

Perdition, it should be him kissing her, Reece thought, emitting a frustrated growl that caused people to stare at him and then give him a wide berth. It should be him igniting her passions. He had known since first making her acquaintance there was something special about her, and he wasn't just referring to her tempting body. With her skill as a jeweller and his connections they could be set for life, if only she wasn't too stubborn to see what a fine team they would make.

He snarled as he watched Sheridan man-handling the woman he had now convinced himself was intended for his wife. Damnation, he had hardly been able to hear a word that passed between them, but it was obvious Lord Amos and Crista were on far better terms than Reece had supposed. What to do about it? Reece watched them go back inside and walked slowly away, now badly in need of ale. He ought to inform his master about this development. But if he did so, the blame might fall upon him for not keeping her under better control.

It *would* fall upon him.

He knew what had happened to her father when he ceased to be of use to his employers, and he had no desire to become their next victim.

Reece reached the table where the ale was being served. It was swamped with thirsty customers, and it was a considerable time before Martha slapped a half-full tankard in front of him. Reece was too preoccupied to complain about the short measure, especially since he didn't have to pay. Another week and this damnable business would be over. He would be handsomely recompensed and could get on with his life. As he calmed down, he was able to convince himself Crista would never risk admitting what she had done for him and his employers. She wasn't stupid and must realise the Sheridans would never hold with such behaviour. Ergo, she would lose her rich admirer.

As the ale slipped down his throat and the power of rational thought gradually returned to him, he ceased panicking. He had control of the diamonds, and they would never leave his sight. When he was with Crista, he would ensure he was always armed, and be on the alert for problems. Then, when this was all over, he would show Miss Crista Brooke what it was like to know a real man.

As she returned to the library on Amos's arm, Crista was a conflicting mass of elation, nerves, and confusion. She didn't know precisely what had just occurred between them. Had they reached an understanding? He had refused to take her as his mistress when she so brazenly made the request. Crista felt her face flame as she relived that humiliation. But Amos had said there were things they could do to satisfy her curiosity, so he wasn't rejecting her precisely. But what things? She ran the tip of her tongue across lips that felt pleasantly swollen and still tasted of him. She glanced up at him and encountered the dark weight of his gaze focused on her face, heavy-lidded and seductive.

'Shush, it will be all right,' he said softly, as though he understood her turmoil, and she felt the muscles in his arm flex and tighten beneath her fingers. 'I will take care of you.'

'Yes, I believe you will.'

And she did believe it. His words, heartfelt and persuasive, were all that was necessary to convince her. With Amos and his powerful family fighting for her cause, she no longer felt quite so isolated, or impotent.

Her new-found confidence faltered when they walked into the library and she saw her

215

uncle there with the duke and Lord Romsey. But he smiled at her, which was all it took for her to fly across the room and throw her arms around his neck.

'Uncle, the duke knows everything, but it will be all right,' she said, the words tumbling past her lips in a breathless rush. 'We are going to — '

'There, there, child, don't fret.' He patted her hand and gently detached her arms from around his neck. 'The duke graciously does not blame us.'

'I can still scarce believe it.' Crista shook her head. 'I would never have imagined — '

'Please have a seat, Miss Brooke,' the duke said. 'Lord Romsey and I have been discussing the matter and have come up with a plan.'

'Then let's hear it,' Amos said amiably, standing directly behind her chair with a proprietorial hand resting on its back.

'You don't have the diamonds in your possession?' Lord Romsey affirmed.

'Quite so,' Crista replied. 'I haven't even touched them. Reece merely showed them to us and then whipped them away again.'

The duke nodded. 'But you have the designs and know the precise dimensions of the stones?'

'Yes, Your Grace. I can't make the settings without that information.'

'How long will it take you to make up those settings?'

'Would it serve you better if I was swift, or if I took my time?' Crista asked.

It was Lord Romsey who answered her. 'Such delicate work must require precision.'

Crista bit her lip, feeling an inappropriate smile bubbling to the surface. 'In that case, at least five days.'

'Five days will be perfect. I ought to be able to put arrangements in place in that time.' He went on to explain the precise nature of their plan. 'There is negligible danger from your perspective, Miss Brooke. Little is required of you, other than to do as Reece has asked.' He sent her a conspiratorial smile. 'With one major adjustment, of course.'

'Oh, of course.' Crista's smile probably reflected the relief she felt at being able to fight back, at last. 'Indeed there is not the least possibility of my being caught. Reece doesn't watch me *that* closely.' She turned to her uncle. 'Do you agree?'

Her uncle's beaming smile was a joy to behold. Crista realised now that she had not once seen that smile since Reece came into their lives.

'There is just one difficulty,' Crista said, sobering. 'My mother and sister will be in danger.'

Amos nodded. 'I agree. Which means they

will have to be removed from London.'

Amos made it sound like the easiest thing in the world to achieve. Indeed, in the case of Crista's mother, it would be, simply because Amos was a duke's brother. As soon as Mama realised who he was, she wouldn't make the slightest difficulty.

'They cannot stay with us, Uncle. It's the first place they would be looked for.'

'They could stay here,' Amos said.

'No.' The duke shook his head. 'I won't risk exposing our mother and sisters to this business.'

'Ah, quite right.' Amos nodded. 'I had not stopped to consider.'

The room fell silent as its occupants contemplated this unforeseen difficulty.

'You could apprehend Reece with the stones in his possession, and he will most likely give up whoever he works for to save his own miserable skin,' Crista said contemptuously.

'He probably doesn't know more than one other person involved,' Lord Romsey replied. 'And I want the person at the very top. The one responsible for all those soldiers being slaughtered.'

'Yes.' Crista nodded emphatically. 'I understand perfectly.'

'And so, the problem remains,' Amos said.

'What are we to do with Miss Brooke's mother and sister?'

'Frankie would probably agree to house them,' Lord Romsey said.

'Lady St. John?' The duke frowned. 'If I will not involve the ladies in this house, why would I ask her?'

'She was married to a diplomat,' Lord Romsey replied. 'She's used to unusual circumstances, is discreet and entirely reliable. She only lives ten miles from here, and so Miss Brooke can visit her mother and sister without too much inconvenience if she so wishes.'

Crista did not particularly wish, but refrained from saying so. 'It seems an awful lot to ask of a stranger,' she said dubiously.

'Frankie would adore the opportunity to be of assistance, I expect,' Lord Romsey answered. 'But it will mean explaining all the particulars to her, Winchester. She can't be asked to help without knowing what she's becoming involved with.'

The duke rubbed his jaw for a moment or two before nodding somewhat reluctantly. 'Very well. We will tell her everything, with your permission, Chesney, and see if she agrees.'

'By all means, Your Grace,' Uncle Charles replied.

Amos rang the bell; a footman answered it and was despatched to find Lady St. John.

She appeared a short time later and blinked when she saw so many people assembled in the library.

'Gosh, this looks serious,' she said. 'I do hope, Your Grace, you have not been chastising this poor child for her life-preserving catch.'

The duke fixed Lady St. John with a penetrating look, and Crista was perfectly sure his lips twitched. 'I wouldn't think of it. She actually saved the day.'

'Then how can I be of service to you?'

'Please have a seat, Lady St. John.' The duke himself conducted her to a vacant chair and waited until she had arranged her skirts to her satisfaction before moving away from her. 'We have a favour to ask of you. Romsey here thinks you will agree to help, but I don't want you to feel under any obligation.'

To Crista, the atmosphere felt rife with anticipation as the duke's and Lady St. John's gazes clashed. There again, perhaps Crista's overactive imagination was running away with her. Be that as it may, she was sure there was an attraction between them. Indeed, the duke would have had to be blind and infirm for that not to be the case. Lady St. John was beautiful, elegant, lively and witty. She was also not afraid of the duke and appeared to enjoy verbally sparring with him. Crista allowed herself to wonder.

'Then perhaps you had better tell me what this is all about.'

'Certainly, but first, excuse me, I don't think you are acquainted with Miss Brooke's uncle.'

The time had come to reveal what she had been forced to do to yet another person. Crista felt her heart sink. She enjoyed Lady St. John's society. Not that they were friends precisely, and their paths were unlikely to cross very much in the future . . . but still.

'Oh, you poor thing!' Lady St. John leapt from her chair the moment the duke finished his explanation and rushed across to take the seat beside Crista. She reached for her hand and squeezed it. 'How infamous! I shall gladly have your mother and sister stay with me for as long as necessary. They will be perfectly safe at Farrington House.'

Crista was overcome by her generosity. 'Thank you, Lady St. John, but before you enter into that commitment, I ought to warn you that you may feel differently once you become acquainted with my mother. She can be rather . . . er, overpowering.'

Lady St. John elevated her chin. 'You just worry about your part in all of this and leave your mother and sister to me.'

Crista smiled, thinking perhaps her mother

was about to meet her match. 'Thank you so very much.'

'When can I expect the pleasure of their company, Clarence?'

'Well now, let me see.' Lord Romsey fell into momentary contemplation. 'It is about seventy miles from here to London.'

'It can be covered in one day with a fast conveyance if one doesn't mind the inconvenience. I shall go and collect them,' Amos said, 'and take your new barouche, Zach, and a team of four. If I leave at first light, I can be in our townhouse by nightfall, collect your relations first thing in the morning, Miss Brooke, and be at Lady St. John's by dusk the day after that.'

'You will need to give my mother advance warning so she can pack,' Crista said.

'No,' the duke said. 'No warning. No one must know where she has gone, or why.'

'Quite so.' Amos nodded. 'I will allow her half an hour to throw a few things in a valise. Then we shall leave.'

'Ah, that will not serve,' Crista said. 'My mother is seldom about before noon, and you wish to leave at first light. You will have to call upon her the moment you arrive in town and warn her of your intention if you wish to get back here in one day.'

'Quite so, but that will make it possible for

her to tell people where she's going.'

'I am fairly sure once she knows who you are, Lord Amos, and you demand her secrecy she will say nothing.'

Crista could see everyone understood what she meant by that remark, saving her from the embarrassment of explaining her mother's social ambitions.

'Surely if you tell her Miss Brooke is in danger, that is all it will take to ensure her secrecy,' Lord Romsey said, looking mystified. Crista smiled and didn't bother to set him straight.

'Are we agreed then?' the duke asked.

They discussed the arrangements for some additional time, until they ran out of things to say. Amos strode about in front of the fireplace, stating several times he thought Crista's part in it all was too dangerous, and there had to be another way. Crista and her uncle jointly put him right on that score. Their desire to clear their names, see the villains apprehended, and be able to live with their consciences again was too pressing to concern themselves with the slight dangers.

'I ought to return to the party before the alarm is raised,' the duke said. 'Lady St. John. May I escort you?'

'By all means.' She stood up and placed her hand on the duke's proffered arm. 'It has been a pleasure making your acquaintance, Miss Brooke, and I shall take very good care of your relations. Do not concern yourself about them.'

'Thank you, Lady St. John,' Crista said, standing up to offer her a brief curtsey.

'Until later, Miss Brooke.' The duke inclined his head in her direction. 'Gentlemen.'

The duke opened the door, and he and Lady St. John walked through it, the lady leaving a pleasant floral fragrance in her wake. A smile flirted with Crista's lips when she heard the duke remark to Lady St. John he suspected she was enjoying herself.

'Immensely,' she replied without hesitation. 'Life has been so very dull since I returned to England. This is just what I need to alleviate my boredom.'

Crista sent a glance Amos's way and found he was looking directly at her.

'Thank you for going to fetch my family,' she said softly. 'I am sorry you are being put to such inconvenience.'

'It is entirely my pleasure.'

'I shall remind you of that after you have spent an entire day in a carriage with my mother.'

'I think Lord Amos will be able to manage your mother,' Uncle Charles said. 'And I also think we ought to take ourselves off home, my dear. It has been a long day.'

Crista nodded, aware that any opportunity for a moment alone with Amos would be denied to her. Perhaps that was just as well. Having distance between them for a few days, while she contrived to make sense of what had passed between them, would not be such a bad thing.

'I shall call upon you when your family is installed at Farrington House,' Amos said, walking to the door with her and her uncle. Taking her hand, he rather recklessly, she thought, kissed the back of it. 'I dare say you would like to visit them and reassure them about your welfare.'

Crista was perfectly sure her welfare would be of no pressing concern to her mother or sister. Then she saw dark desire reflected in his eyes and thought perhaps he had an ulterior motive in making the suggestion. Suddenly the urge to see her mother again became a matter of the greatest urgency.

'Thank you, Lord Amos. That would be very kind of you.'

15

Amos set off at first light, the barouche drawn by four prime-goers keen to stretch their legs. Zach was there to see him on his way.

'Are you sure you don't want to take a man with you?'

'I'm perfectly capable of driving myself to London.'

'I wasn't suggesting otherwise,' Zach replied calmly.

'Just keep a careful eye on Chesney while I am gone.'

Zach quirked a brow. 'Chesney?'

'I don't like this business, Zach.' Amos settled himself on the box seat and took the ribbons from the groom holding the horses' heads. 'These people are ruthless. Look what they did to Miss Brooke's father. If they even suspect she plans to cross them, the consequences don't bear thinking about.'

'Nothing will happen to Miss Brooke,' Zach replied in a reassuring tone that failed to quell Amos's growing unease. Romsey's plan seemed straightforward, but his main objective was to catch the mastermind. Amos couldn't shake the disquieting feeling that in

226

his haste to achieve that objective, Romsey had overlooked something which could place Crista in danger. 'You have my word. Now go, and we shall see you again in two days' time.'

The brothers shook hands, and Amos set his team to a brisk trot down the long, winding driveway that led to the main Winchester Road. Traffic was light, and he made good speed with his own horses pulling the conveyance for the first leg of the journey. He paused just long enough at the first staging inn to change his team, tapping his foot impatiently when the grooms worked frustratingly slowly to harness the fresh team.

Finally, back on the road with nothing to do but drive, Amos was at leisure to cogitate, his mind occupied with thoughts of Crista and the quite remarkable impression she had made upon him. Her fiery determination to restore her uncle's reputation gave him much to admire. And even more to think about. He ought not to have given into temptation and kissed her. He definitely should not have offered to show her a little more of what she would be missing if she really meant never to marry. It had been a reckless and foolhardy commitment to enter into, but then her request was not something a man expected to hear spilling from an innocent lady's lips.

Amos slowed to pass through a toll gate on the outskirts of London, aware that it would be foolish to keep his word but surprised by the strength of his determination to do so. It would be sheer folly. Not because he was afraid Crista would be unable to control her passions, but because he might well not be able to harness his own.

By the time he drove into London that evening, he still had not sorted his thoughts or intentions regarding Crista Brooke into any sort coherent order. He reached Sheridan House in Berkeley Square when it was still full light. Zach's grooms came running from the mews, showing no great surprise at Amos's unexpected arrival. He jumped down from the box seat, surrendered the barouche to them, and stretched to ease the aches he had acquired during the long drive. He entered the house through the side door, tired, dusty and in serious need of a drink.

'Good evening, my lord,' Paddock, the head footman in charge of the house in the family's absence, said politely.

'Evening, Paddock,' Amos replied. 'I need something to eat and drink and a change of clothes. Then I need to go out again, immediately.'

'I shall make the necessary arrangements, my lord.'

One hour later, fed and impeccably attired, Amos headed for Chelsea astride a sturdy hunter. It was not a district he was well acquainted with. He took two wrong turns and asked directions twice before he found the street, and then the small house Crista's mother occupied. He tethered his horse to the gatepost, ascended the steps and knocked. The door was answered by a middle-aged maid. She appeared rather awed when Amos gave her his card, sent his compliments to her mistress.

'Please come in, my lord. I will see if she's at home.'

The maid showed him into a tiny dining parlour set with a table that could seat six at the very most. He glanced around, but the room offered up no clues about the residents of the establishment. Before he could decide if that was significant, he heard what had to be Mrs. Brooke's voice quite clearly coming from the adjoining room.

'Lord Amos Sheridan. Good heavens, Amelia, I wonder what brings such a gentleman to our door, and at this time of night, too.'

Amos didn't hear what Crista's sister said in response.

'Show him in at once, Meg. Don't leave his lordship waiting about. Oh, how desperate he must think us to be living in such a hovel.

Does my hair look all right? Sit up straight, Amelia. Don't let his lordship catch you slouching.'

'Please to come this way, my lord,' Meg said deferentially.

Amos stepped into an equally small drawing room and was confronted by a starkly beautiful woman in her middle years. He could see a resemblance to Crista in the shape of her mouth but for all her beauty, Mrs. Brooke lacked Crista's expressive eyes. She was dressed in a fashionable evening gown that showed off her figure but had nothing of half-mourning about it. Amos noticed these things in a few seconds before turning his attention to Amelia Brooke. She was also strikingly pretty, and her dove-grey gown more closely reflected the recent loss of her father. Both ladies curtsied low to Amos, who offered them a slight bow in return.

'Thank you for receiving me, Mrs. Brooke.'

'You are very welcome, Lord Amos, although I am quite unable to account for the honour of seeing you here. This is my daughter, Amelia.'

Again Amos inclined his head.

'Please take a seat, my lord. You are come from Winchester?'

Amos confirmed that was the case, waiting for Mrs. Brooke to remember she had another daughter and enquire after her health. She did not do so.

'You must excuse these lodgings. They are temporary. Very temporary,' she said, wrinkling her nose. 'Will you take refreshment, my lord?'

'I didn't come here to drink your wine, or concern myself with your living arrangements,' Amos replied curtly. 'I came because Miss Brooke has urgent need of you.'

'Miss Brooke.' She glanced at Amelia. 'But she is here, and perfectly safe. My daughter is soon to be advantageously married.' Mrs. Brooke seemed confused. 'I fail to understand.'

'I was referring to *the* Miss Brooke. Miss Cristobel Brooke.'

'Crista.' A shadow of suspicion passed across Mrs. Brooke's face. 'I don't know how she came to be noticed by you, my lord, but I can assure you Crista is very independently minded and constantly rejects any advice I offered her. She would never seek my help.'

'Then I seek it on her behalf.' Amos fixed Mrs. Brooke with a look of determination. 'You and Miss Amelia will oblige me by returning to Winchester with me at first light.'

'First light!' Mrs. Brooke shook her head. 'I'm sorry, Lord Amos, but I have no idea why you would come all this way and make such an extraordinary request.'

'Then let me speak plain. Your daughter is

putting herself in danger by carrying on with the work your husband started.'

Amelia gasped. 'Mama!'

All colour drained from Mrs. Brooke's face. She flapped a hand at Amelia, silencing her. When she spoke again, her voice took on a hard edge. 'I cannot imagine what you mean.'

'And I don't have time to bandy words with you.' Amos stood and paced the length of the small room, his progress impeded by an excess of furniture. 'Your daughter does not need you, you're quite right about that, but if you remain in London, you could both be in danger. Miss Brooke asked me to take you to safety, and that is precisely what I plan to do.'

'My husband never should have involved himself with those vulgar people. I told him so quite forcefully, but he wouldn't listen to my advice. Thanks to him, we are reduced to living like paupers.'

'Your husband paid a very high price for his mistakes,' Amos replied in a glacial tone.

'Oh, he only did what he did to please me. We were quite devoted you know.' She lifted a tiny square of lace-edged cambric to her face and wiped away a non-existent tear. 'I gave up so much to marry him and never had cause to regret it until . . . well, until — '

'Don't distress yourself, Mama. It will only bring on one of your headaches.'

Amelia Brooke laid a gentle hand on her mother's shoulder. Neither woman had, as yet, asked what difficulties Crista had encountered that placed them both in danger. If fact, neither of them had enquired after Crista at all.

'My husband's reputation was ruined by a false accusation, which forced him to do what he did. And now Crista is following in his footsteps.'

Amos had heard enough. 'Please be ready to leave at first light.'

'Mama, what if Mr. Devonshire returns early?'

Amos fixed Amelia with a probing glance. 'Devonshire is the man you are to marry?'

'Yes. He has gone to the country and we don't expect to see him for another week, but he is so devoted to Amelia, we would not be surprised if he found a reason to return early. We were just now talking about that very possibility. What will he think if he finds us not here?'

'You cannot under any circumstances tell him, or anyone else, where you have gone.' Amos quelled his anger and turned on the charm. 'I feel persuaded you are both patriots.'

Mrs. Brooke blossomed beneath the

devastating smile Amos bestowed upon her. 'I flatter myself we both put the affairs of our country before our own concerns.'

'Then you will oblige me by writing to Devonshire, inventing a reason for a trip to . . . oh, I don't know. Your relations, perhaps?'

'Alas, my family and I are not on the best of terms, Lord Amos. An unfortunate misunderstanding.'

'Then we shall think of something else. How many servants live on the premises?'

'This house is so small that only Meg lives in. We have a cook who comes in daily.'

'Then Meg will have to come with you. Leave a note for the cook to say you have been called away, and be ready to leave at first light.'

'The duke is very generous to invite us to Winchester Park, my lord.'

Crista had been quite right about her mother. She clearly thought she would be a guest of the duke's and was preening at the thought. Amos did not set her straight.

'You ought to assume you will be away from London for a week,' he said. 'Pack sufficient clothes for that amount of time.'

'We shall set about it right away.'

Satisfied they would do so, Amos pressed upon them the importance of being ready when he arrived in the morning.

'I would like to make the journey in one day without having to stay on the road overnight.'

'Oh, I so agree,' Mrs. Brooke said. 'Posting inns are shockingly uncomfortable places.'

'Until tomorrow then.'

Amos took his leave but lingered in the hallway, taking his time donning his hat and gloves.

'Amelia, this is the very best of good fortune,' he heard Mrs. Brooke exclaim. 'Lord Amos's brother is the Duke of Winchester. Only imagine that! There are four brothers, all as good-looking as Lord Amos, and all of them single. I could see at once Lord Amos was taken with your beauty, my dear. You must make yourself agreeable to him tomorrow. You will have an entire day in a carriage with him. Only imagine, you might finish up doing much better than Mr. Devonshire.'

'But I *like* Mr. Devonshire.'

'Surely you would like to be the next Duchess of Winchester even more?'

'Well, I suppose — '

Amos had heard quite enough. Mrs. Brooke was everything Crista had warned him to expect and worse. Tomorrow would be a long day.

★ ★ ★

Crista settled at her workbench at first light on the day following the party, still reeling from Lord Romsey's revelations. She wondered if Amos had yet set out on his journey to London, and if he had spared her a passing thought. Her own mind was consumed with memories of *that* kiss. Amos had caused dormant feelings inside of her to spring to life, filling her with an acute longing that, even in the cold light of day, refused to subside. She blushed when she recalled how she had brazenly responded to his advances and then asked him to show her more.

Dear God, how could she have been so bold?

Whatever must he think of her? Well, it was all his fault. He was the one with all the experience and made her forget who she was supposed to be. She blamed her unmitigated relief at being able to restore her uncle's reputation and ease her own conscience for her temporary lapse. In fact, she placed the blame everywhere except where it belonged, which was squarely on her own shoulders. Lord Amos should not have kissed her, it was true, but she most assuredly should not have kissed him back.

Now that she was again firmly in control of her common sense, she would not repeat her request; but if he instigated the promised tuition, she would not claim a change of heart either. She was no coward, and remained as curious as she had ever been. Even more so. But she would not lose sight of the fact Lord Amos was a duke's brother, and she was the daughter of a disgraced jeweller, and the gap between their respective social situations was an unbridgeable chasm.

She was lost in thought when the back door opened. She shuddered, knowing it would be Reece come to annoy her. He did not usually show himself at such an early hour. Presumably, she would have to endure his presence indefinitely until this final commission was complete.

'Good morning,' he said.

Crista continued to work upon the repair to a delicate seed pearl necklace she was undertaking for an old lady in the village and made no reply.

'What are you doing?' he demanded to know, moving close to peer over her shoulder.

'You are in my light.'

'And you did not answer my question.'

He sounded short-tempered. She glanced up at features pinched with anger. What had she done to overset him this time? Not that she especially cared, and certainly didn't intend to ask.

'A repair,' she said shortly.

'You have not started the settings for the diamonds?'

'I shall commence them when this is done. Not before.'

He grasped her shoulder so hard she cried out and dropped the necklace. 'Enough! You will not play games with me. You're not with your fancy friends now.'

Ah, so that what this was about, Crista thought. He had seen her at the Park yesterday sitting with the ladies.

'Remove your hand,' she said in a mordant tone. 'I warned you once before, never to touch me again.'

Before she could reach for a weapon, he released her.

'You turn your pert little nose up at me, yet flaunt yourself in front of the Sheridans.' He sneered at her. 'They will use you and cast you aside.'

'And you will not?'

'I have already told you. Throw your lot in with me, and we'll make a killing.'

Crista tossed her head, put the finishing touches to her repair, and wearily reached for the drawings for the diamond jewellery.

'I do not like you, Mr. Reece. I don't approve of what you stand for or the people you work for. I want nothing from you, other than never to see you again.'

'You will change your tune once your rich lover passes you over.'

Crista spread the drawings over her bench, completely ignoring Reece.

'Do you need the diamonds yet?' he asked.

'No, not for several days. I've no wish to handle those ostentatious stones before it's absolutely necessary.'

'In that case, don't let me prevent you from starting work on the settings.' He settled himself on a bench by the window and crossed his arms over his chest.

'You are preventing me by blocking the light. Go and find something else to do. I can't concentrate with you looming over me.'

'I am perfectly comfortable here. I don't trust you, Miss Brooke, and intend to keep a close eye on you until this commission is finished.'

16

Amos was heartily relieved he had chosen to drive the barouche himself, making it impossible for Mrs. Brooke and her ambitious daughter to plague him with questions and flattery while they were on the road. The moment they stopped at posting inns that situation altered. When driving up to London alone, he felt no necessity to linger at those establishments. With two ladies in his care, he was obliged to offer them refreshment at each stop, and they always accepted, which necessitated hiring a private room.

'Are all of your brothers at Winchester Park, Lord Amos?' Mrs. Brooke asked during their final stop.

Amos confirmed that they were.

'Do you entertain much?' Amelia asked.

'We just had a large party to celebrate the duchess's birthday. We have no further entertainments planned. We live quietly when in the country.'

'Ah, so we will become a part of your family circle.' Mrs. Brooke's eyes gleamed at the prospect. 'That will give us all an opportunity to become better acquainted.'

'I regret to disappoint you, but you and Miss Brooke will not be staying at the Park.'

Mrs. Brooke looked horrified. 'I hope you don't expect us to stay with Mr. Chesney. He and I do not see eye to eye.'

Amos wasn't surprised. 'Alternative arrangements have been made for your comfort.'

'What arrangements?'

'Come, the horses are ready,' Amos replied. Glancing through the window he was pleased to see the team he had left at this inn the previous day again harnessed to the barouche, impatient to be off. 'I don't want them to get cold.'

The sun was low in the sky when Amos drove the carriage to the door of Farrington House. He wasn't surprised to see Zach emerge from the house at Lady St. John's side, laughing at something she had just said to him. Zach was very tight-lipped about his amorous ambitions, even with his brothers. He was especially careful not to put himself into situations that could be misinterpreted — such as this one, and that gave Amos pause. Lady St. John was a widow, so he supposed that put a different complexion upon matters, but even so . . .

Amos raised a hand in greeting, which Zach acknowledged in similar fashion. He halted his team, jumped down from the box seat, and helped his passengers to alight. Mrs. Brooke looked up at the façade of the pretty manor house, shown to its best advantage by the backdrop of the lowering sun. It was a fraction of the size of Winchester Park but a great deal finer than her previous lodgings in Chelsea. Even so, Amos was sure he noticed her wrinkle her nose in disappointment.

'Come,' Amos said. 'Let me introduce you to your hostess.'

'Is that gentleman His Grace?' Mrs. Brooke asked, reviving at the sight of Zach.

'Indeed.'

'Oh my goodness! Stand up straight, Amelia, and prepare to meet a duke.'

With the introductions made, Lady St. John fell effortlessly into the role of hostess.

'You must be exhausted, Mrs. Brooke,' she said sympathetically. 'Travelling these days quite takes it out of one. However, I am so very glad you were able to accept my invitation. Now come inside, I will have you shown to your rooms, and when you have revived your-selves we shall have a light supper.'

'You ought to marry that woman, Zach,' Amos said as they stood together and watched Lady St. John effortlessly organise Mrs. Brooke and her daughter. 'You could do a lot worse.'

'I don't aim to marry anyone,' Zach replied. 'I shall leave the marrying and begetting of heirs to you and my other brothers.'

'Sounds like dereliction of duty to me,' Amos grunted, circling his arms to restore some feeling into them after hours of controlling four lively horses.

Zach laughed. 'Very likely.'

They walked into the drawing room, where Lady St. John soon joined them.

'If I had realised quite what we were asking you to take on,' Amos told her, 'I would not have allowed you to be inconvenienced.'

Lady St. John laughed. 'Don't worry. I have met women like Mrs. Brooke before. Besides, having her here makes me feel useful. I dare say she is anxious to see her older daughter.'

'Actually,' Amos replied, grinding his jaw as he accepted with a nod of thanks the snifter of brandy Lady St. John handed to him, 'she hasn't once mentioned her name all day.'

'Hmm, I suppose that shouldn't surprise me.'

'Well, they're here now, out of harm's way, which ought to relieve Miss Brooke's anxiety.' Zach turned his attention to Lady St. John. 'Don't forget, under no circumstances can your guests be seen in either village.'

She sent Zach a teasing smile. 'I am a very efficient gaoler. If I take an interest in a person, he or she does not easily escape.'

'I can't imagine anyone being foolish

enough to want to,' Zach replied, holding her gaze for longer than was strictly necessary. Amos grinned. His brother, for all his denials, was definitely interested in their lively new neighbour.

'That is because I seldom settle my interest upon anyone who is foolish.'

'I'm glad to hear it.' Zach laughed. 'Come along, Amos. Let's escape while we can.'

'How cruel!' Lady St. John's eyes gleamed with mischief. 'I heard Mrs. Brooke telling her daughter to change into her best gown, and to make haste about it. I am sure it is not *me* she hopes to impress.'

'God save us!'

Zach swallowed down his drink, Amos followed his example, and they took their leave.

'If Mrs. Brooke remembers that she actually has another daughter,' Amos said as they did so, 'please tell her I shall bring Crista to see her tomorrow evening.'

★　★　★

Christa massaged the small of her back and sighed with pleasure when an expansive stretch eased her aching muscles.

'Is something amiss?'

Reece simply would not let her be. Every time she looked up, she felt the heavy weight of his gaze monitoring every move she made. She was surprised how difficult she found it to work slowly, giving Lord Romsey time to put his part of the plan into effect. She laboured over every precise shape and dimension, frequently referring to the drawings, even though she had already committed the design to memory. Her uncle came and went between the workshop and the shop itself, sharing her frustration over Reece's constant presence.

'You make him nervous,' Uncle Charles had told her the night before. 'He senses your growing rebelliousness and worries you will sabotage the design.'

Crista flashed an impish smile. 'If only he knew.'

'He is being vigilant because of the value of the gems, or possibly our attitude is more defiant.' The sparkle had returned to Uncle Charles's eyes. 'Just remain steadfast, my love. This will soon all be over, once and for all.'

Yes, Crista thought, that would be a cause for rejoicing, if she knew who she was supposed to be. She had no idea what she planned to do with her life without her father in it to guide her. She had always assumed she would work beside him. Now, she would have to make her way alone; as far away from the Sheridans as possible because, against every vestige of good sense, she had fallen passionately in love with Amos.

She shook her head, unable to comprehend her foolishness. She had a little money of her own saved and she would return to London the moment she was free to do so and establish herself in lodgings. Then she would trawl around the jewellers she knew, find honest work for herself, lose herself in it, and soon forget her moment's madness.

Yes, that was absolutely what she would do.

Amos might be back by now, Crista thought as she packed away her things at the end of the third day and thankfully watched Reece disappear out the back door. She took herself upstairs, changed into a gown and took trouble with her hair.

'I must face Mama,' she said by way of explanation when she joined her uncle at the dinner table and he raised a brow in surprise. She seldom took much trouble over her appearance at the end of her long days and her uncle didn't stand on ceremony.

'Ah, of course.'

She could see her uncle wasn't deceived about the true reason for the effort she had taken with her appearance but, mercifully, he changed the subject.

As soon as their meal was over, Crista

excused herself, grabbed a shawl and almost ran to the spot where she had agreed to meet Amos. He was already there, leaning against a tree, and she took a moment to drink in the sight of him before he observed her. He was dressed casually in shirtsleeves and tight-fitting inexpressibles. He wore no hat and a soft breeze stirred his hair away from his head. He stared off into the distance, looking remote, severe, and she suddenly felt apprehensive about interrupting him.

A twig snapped beneath her foot and he turned in her direction. He saw her and his severe expression gave way to a glorious smile that made Crista's uncertainties evaporate. She would defy any woman who was the recipient of such a riotous smile to remain immune to it.

'There you are,' he said.

'I hope I have not kept you waiting,' she said at the same time.

'How was your journey?' she asked.

'It went much as you predicted.'

'Oh dear. As bad as that?'

He chuckled. 'Your mother and sister are now guests at Farrington House. I shall take you over there now.'

'Is it safe for us to be seen together?' She glanced at the curricle pulled up beneath a stand of trees, the bit jangling in the horse's mouth as it cropped at the grass. 'Reece has not left me alone throughout my work days. Odious man!'

'He's unlikely to leave the Crown. He has the diamonds to protect.'

'Yes, the responsibility seems to be making his nervous.'

'Come.'

He took her hand and helped her into the curricle. She felt a searing warmth as his fingers closed around her palm. He held her gaze for a protracted moment, and Crista felt herself slowly drowning in the depths of fathomless eyes that darkened with desire. He opened his mouth, and she thought he was about to speak; but he abruptly snapped it closed again and walked around to the opposite side of the conveyance.

He didn't say a word as he drove them at a smart trot towards Farrington House, avoiding the village. She sensed his glance frequently resting upon her profile, but didn't trust herself to look at him in case her expression gave her away. If he could remain detached and not refer to the last occasion when they had been alone together so, too, could she.

'I have not told your mother the entire truth about why she needed to come to Winchester,' he said, breaking the silence as

Farrington House came into view. 'Nor did she ask.'

Crista rolled her eyes. 'That doesn't surprise me.'

'I told her only that she might be in danger. Whenever I referred to the work that caused your father's death, she changed the subject.'

'Mama is very good at ignoring that which she does not wish to face.'

'I have left it for you to tell her as much or as little as you think wise.'

'I'm sorry my family is such a trial,' she said, turning her face into the breeze instead of looking at him.

He removed one hand from the reins and placed it on both of hers. '*You* could never be a trial to me, Crista.'

'I don't expect you to . . . I mean . . . ' *Stop being so considerate. It confuses me and isn't helping.*

He stopped the curricle at the front steps, where a groom rushed up to take the horse.

'Are you ready for this?'

Crista grimaced. 'You had to endure an entire day of my mother and sister. I dare say I shall survive a half-hour.'

Amos laughed as he jumped down and came round to help her alight. He placed her hand on his sleeve and led her to the front door, which opened before they reached it.

'Good evening, my lord.' The butler inclined his head to Amos and then to her. 'Lady St. John and her guests are in the drawing room. Please follow me.'

'Ah, Lord Amos.' Lady St. John stood when they entered the room. 'And Miss Brooke. How delightful to see you again.'

'Lady St. John.'

Crista curtsied and was astonished when Lady St. John waved the gesture aside and enveloped Crista in a fierce hug instead.

'I have been taking good care of your relations, as you can see.'

'Thank you.' Crista took a deep breath and then turned to her mother and sister. They had watched her walk in on Amos's arm, and then be embraced by Lady St. John, with identical expressions of incredulity. 'Mama, Amelia. How are you both?'

'You look well, my dear,' Mama said, recovering quickly. 'How have you been?'

'Lady St. John,' Amos said. 'I apologise for my attire. I'm not fit to be seen in your drawing room. Shall we take a turn in the gardens and leave Miss Brooke to become reacquainted with her family?'

'By all means, Lord Amos.'

'Oh, there is no occasion for you to leave,' Mama said breezily. 'We do not in the least mind that you are not formally attired, Lord

Amos. Goodness, Crista is not fit to be seen either. She didn't even trouble to put on a bonnet, although I suppose things are done different in the country.'

'Please excuse us.'

Amos sent Crista a warm smile and left with Lady St. John. It was very quiet in the room once Amos quit it, but Mama quickly broke the silence.

'What on earth is going on here, Crista?' she demanded to know.

'I apologise if sending for you has caused you inconvenience.'

'Remember to whom you are speaking and keep a civil tongue in your head.'

Crista swallowed and did her level best to calm down. Her mother, for all her many faults, was still her mother and deserved a modicum of respect.

'I apologise, Mama.' Crista took a seat beside Amelia. 'I came here because the people Papa was working for needed me to continue with that work.'

'Then you ought to have refused,' Mama replied briskly.

'Do you not imagine I would have done so if I could? It was you who encouraged Papa to take the business in the first place.'

'I didn't know it would end so badly. I can't be held responsible for that.'

Of course you cannot! 'They threatened to destroy what was left of Papa's reputation if I didn't work for them.' Crista cleared her throat. 'Failing that, they threatened the two of you.'

'Mama!' Amelia clutched her throat. 'Are we safe? Are we to be murdered in our beds? What would Mr. Devonshire say if he knew?'

'That is another reason why I agreed to help them, Amelia. But now, the duke and his brothers have found out about the deception.'

Mama made a strangled noise and looked as though she was about to faint. 'And yet you seem to be intimate with Lord Amos.'

'He and his associates are planning to trap the rogues. Lord Romsey works for the government and wants to catch the man behind the scheme, which is why we brought you two to safety.'

'And so the Sheridan family do not think ill of you?' Mama sounded pathetically hopeful. 'They realise you were coerced?'

'They know I was. I have told them the complete truth.' Crista fixed her mother with a determined gaze. 'They know why Papa did what he did and who persuaded him to do so.'

Mama's body stiffened. 'I suppose you told them it was my doing, when it was no such thing.'

'What's done is done, Mama,' Crista said with a weary sigh. 'This all will be over in a day or two, and it will be safe for you to return to London. I shall find work somewhere or other and we need never see one another again.'

'Don't be so hasty, Crista.' Mama straightened her spine. 'Your father didn't leave us well provided for and my own Papa is still being incredibly stubborn. He continues to refuse to see me, even though your papa is dead and that chapter of my life has come to an end. I shall . . . er — ' She glanced at her hands, swallowed twice and then looked up at Crista. 'I shall need your help to survive.'

'I am sure Amelia and Mr. Devonshire will provide you with a home. You will be more comfortable with your favourite daughter.'

'Ungrateful child! After all I have done for you.'

Crista sighed. To her precise recollection, her mother had never done anything except complain about her conduct. They had not been together for more than five minutes and already the atmosphere was rife with tension and accusation. She thought of Winchester Hall and how the family there interacted with such casual affection towards one another. Money did not create that sort of ambience. She knew that very well since her maternal grandfather had never laid eyes on her, holding on to a grudge for all these years because his favourite child, his only daughter, had married against his wishes.

'Tell us about Winchester Hall,' Amelia said, her eyes coming alight with interest. 'Mama says all four brothers are as handsome as the duke and Lord Amos. It is quite shocking that none of them are married. I should like to meet all of them.'

'You are engaged to Mr. Devonshire,' Crista reminded her sister.

'It does not hurt to play the field, at least until one has a ring on one's finger.'

Predictably, Mama sprang to Amelia's defence. 'Mrs. Devonshire is still averse to the match, and if she has her way it will not go ahead.'

'What did Lord Amos talk to you about while he drove you over here?' Amelia asked, standing to admire her reflection in a nearby mirror and patting a stray curl into place. 'I think he is quite the most handsome gentleman I have ever seen, and I should like to know what subjects engage his interest.'

It clearly did not occur to Amelia that Crista represented any sort of competition. 'I believe he enjoys blood sports,' Crista replied, biting her lip to prevent a smiling from escaping. 'He abhors ballrooms, as do all his brothers, and they avoid them whenever they can. They love to play cards and are very good at cricket.'

'Oh.' Amelia wrinkled her nose.

'It probably explains how they have managed to avoid marriage for so long,' Mama added. 'But now we have been thrown into their company here in the country, it is an excellent opportunity for you to shine, Amelia.'

Mercifully, the questions thrown at her about the Sheridan family were brought to an end by the return of Amos and Lady St. John. Crista stood up with alacrity.

'I shall see you again when this is all over, Mama.'

She didn't kiss her mother or sister, but gladly returned Lady St. John's embrace. She was conscious of her relations watching from the drawing room window as Amos helped her into his curricle and drove away at a brisk trot.

'Are you all right?' he asked.

17

'It was foolish of me to expect my mother to care about anything other than her own comfort,' Crista said, impatiently brushing away tears with the back of her hand. 'I shouldn't allow it to overset me.'

'I entirely agree.'

Amos was too angry by what he had overheard of Crista's interview with her family to say anything more. He concentrated on driving instead, giving her a moment to recover her composure. He seethed when he thought of the obstacles she still had to overcome to aid Romsey and free herself from the villains controlling her. Her wretched mother's social aspirations were the underlying cause of Crista's problems and yet the woman had not offered one iota of support to her elder child.

Amos cast frequent sideways glances at her as he put distance between them and Farrington House as quickly as he could. The desire to offer her comfort and consolation had never been stronger — hence the destination he had in mind. Besides, she was in no state to return to her uncle's apartment quite yet, or so he told himself.

'Where are you taking me?' she asked, when he turned the curricle off the main path and into the woods on the edge of the Sheridan estate.

'Somewhere we can be alone, unless you would like me to take you home immediately.'

She hesitated for a long time before responding. Amos was surprised by just how ardently he hoped she would not ask to be taken back to Chesney's establishment, even though it would be the safer course of action. But safe, sensible actions had never been his forte.

'No,' she said eventually. 'The woods are peaceful at this time of night.'

'Quite.' He halted the curricle and helped Crista down from it. 'If you enjoy woods, see what you make of this,' he said, proffering his arm.

They walked along in silence, Amos acutely aware of her every nuance. He remained as silent as she was, allowing the peace and tranquillity of the woods to work their magic. Gradually, the shadow of disillusionment left her eyes, she exclaimed with pleasure at her surroundings and she even laughed at a squirrel's antics.

He guided her along the track, turned the final corner, and there it was — the Sheridans' hidden trout lake, situated in a clearing between the trees. Shafts of lowering sun reflected a dozen different shades of turquoise on the torpid water, its surface barely stirred by the gentle breeze.

'I had no idea this was here,' she said, her eyes now alight with pleasure as she watched aquatic birds dive for their supper. Verdant green reeds rustled as a beautiful kingfisher, disturbed by their arrival, soared gracefully above them.

'Not many people do. As I understand it, in times gone by we were plagued by poachers, so a clever ancestor ordered the planting of the trees you now see around you.'

'Making it impossible to reach the lake by any means other than tracks like the one we just followed.' She nodded. 'That must make life so much easier for your keepers.'

'Very likely.'

They stood in silence for a while, appreciating the beauty of the scene, and Amos sensed the tension slowly drain out of her.

'Would you like to walk a little more?' he asked.

'Certainly I would. I want to see the lake from all aspects.'

They followed the path that skirted the water, watching dragonflies skimming its surface, admiring the water lilies in full bloom, and listening to frogs croaking in disharmony. A heron stood statue-like in the shallows, eyes piercing the surface of the lake, patiently waiting for its dinner to obligingly swim past.

'It really is remarkably serene,' Crista said. 'Thank you for bringing me here. It's just want I needed.'

'Hmm, I'm not so sure about that.'

She shot him a curious glance. 'What do you mean?'

'You'll see.' He took her elbow. 'Come and see the boathouse.'

She shook her head when she observed the veranda and adjacent room furnished as a conservatory. 'Your idea of a boathouse is larger than a lot of residences I visited in London.'

Amos shrugged. 'We enjoy our comforts.'

He guided her to a settee in front of a full-length window overlooking the lake. She sat down and he took the place beside her.

'Are you really all right?' he asked, taking her hand and slowly running his fingers down the length of hers. 'The strain of having Reece constantly looking over your shoulder must have played havoc with your nerves.'

'I am relieved to have my uncle looking more like his old self.' She looked away from him but didn't extract her hand from his grasp. 'I hadn't realised quite how comprehensively the strain of dishonesty had worn him down.'

'And what of you?' Amos released her hand and transferred his attention to her hair, grasping a random curl and winding it around his finger. 'It is you who will be taking all the risks.'

'Me? Oh, I feel a great sense of relief. Uncle and I have practised our parts and know what we must do. I'm sure Lord Romsey's plan will work perfectly.'

'Romsey expects a lot of you.' He fixed her with an ardent expression. 'But if you have second thoughts about taking the risk, you have but to say the word.'

'Oh no, there is no question of my not doing this.' She jutted her chin in a gesture of stubborn determination. 'Lord Romsey has offered me an opportunity to regain my self-esteem. It is I who should be grateful to him.'

'You're trembling.'

'Not because of what I must do for Lord Romsey.' She shrugged. 'I am still angry with my mother. She makes no secret of the fact that she dislikes me and yet expects me to support her once Amelia is married.'

'The devil she does!' Amos glowered at the lake. 'How does she suppose you will do that?'

'I shall find employment with a jeweller somewhere. That has always been my intention. Mama doesn't approve but that won't prevent her from taking advantage.'

Not if I have any say in the matter. 'What else did she have to say for herself?'

'Oh, the usual. She has been badly used. Nothing is her fault. Amelia's interests must come first.' A mischievous smile lit up her features. 'Oh, and one of you Sheridan gentleman is bound to fall desperately in love with Amelia, in which case my support will not be required.'

Amos snorted. 'She is deluded.'

'That is what I wanted to tell Mama.'

They fell into momentary silence. Amos abandoned the curl he was still agitating and slid his arm around her slender shoulders instead. She leaned her head against his torso and emitted a prolonged sigh. To sit here with the woman who occupied so many of his thoughts — conscious or otherwise — seemed like the most natural thing in the world. Amos suspected his timing, to say nothing of the lascivious thoughts currently filling his head, was inappropriate. Even so, he was gripped with the most urgent desire to . . . well, to distract her in the method that sprang spontaneously to mind. In the way she had asked him to distract her. But first he needed to assure himself she hadn't undergone a change of heart.

'Look at me, Crista,' he said softly.

She slowly lifted her head, looking up at him through eyes filled with a combination of desire, curiosity, and a modicum of insecurity. She moistened her lips with the tip of her tongue and his vision hazed. He absolutely had to taste those lips again. The desire to do so suddenly overcame all reason, all common sense; all thoughts for anything other than the raging need that ripped through him.

'I am going to kiss you,' he said. 'If you would prefer me not to, say so at once. I would never force you to do anything against your will. Always remember that.'

She remained mute, but her sparkling eyes gave her away. She wanted this as much as he did. He pulled her onto his lap and into his arms. She came willingly and wrapped her own arms around his neck, playing him at his own game by tangling her fingers in his hair. Her breathing became fractured as their gazes clashed, her cheeks flushed a becoming shade of pink. How anyone could possibly prefer her vapid, self-centred sister to this gloriously diverse, spirited, brave, and highly intelligent female Amos could not begin to imagine, but he was glad for it, nonetheless. The mere thought of another man laying so much as one inappropriate finger upon her filled him with a murderous rage.

Amos lowered his head and claimed her

sweet mouth, forcing her lips apart and exploring with his tongue. His arms closed more firmly about her as he deepened the kiss, savouring the taste of her. God's beard, she was more tempting than she had any right to be, and already Amos felt his control slipping. She murmured something past their fused lips, igniting his desire. His escalated passion manifested itself in the natural way. Seated on his lap, she must be able to feel it. Damnation, of course she could, and the minx was moving against him, instinctively riding his hard length, probably not aware what it actually was. He had suspected she would be proactive, unafraid to follow her body's demands, but so far her reactions had exceeded his wildest expectations. When a series of violent tremors rocked her, he was powerless to prevent his hands from wandering to her breasts. He cupped one through the fabric of her gown, and tweaked the nipple. She cried out and rode his cock harder, pulling her mouth free from his and looking at him through enormous eyes that glowed like molten lava.

'You wanted to know more,' he said, still playing with her breast.

'I had absolutely no idea.'

Amos chuckled. 'I am very glad to hear it.'

'Don't make fun of me.'

'The very last thing I'm doing is laughing at you. I adore your innocence, your willingness to follow your instincts, everything about you.' His hands moved from her breasts and ran the length of her back, introducing themselves to every glorious curve and crevice. Ye gods, if ever a body was designed for mortal sin, it was hers. She shuddered beneath his touch and continued to torture his swollen cock by refusing to sit still. 'I revel in your responsiveness.'

She flashed the sensuous smile of a woman only just starting to appreciate the power of her femininity. 'Responsiveness or brazenness?' she asked.

'Never apologise for your natural instincts, sweetheart.' He sent a line of scorching kisses down the length of her neck. She threw her head back, giving him easier access, and made a cute mewling noise. 'I think I always knew you would be this way. It was one of the many things that attracted me to you.'

'There's nothing special about me.'

Amos suppressed a groan when she moved her bottom harder against his groin. He raised a hand to the back of her neck and pulled her head down until he could again kiss her as thoroughly as she deserved to be kissed. He was burning with need, but knew he couldn't take matters to their natural conclusion. He shouldn't even have taken them this far, but having done so, it hardly seemed fair to leave Crista in a state of such heightened awareness. She needed to be calm and in control in order to face the dangers ahead of her. That was his only reason for continuing with this dangerous game.

Of course it was.

He would ignore his own agony and concentrate upon giving her pleasure by sating her endless need. He found the ties to her gown and loosened her bodice. She was wearing a thin chemise that left little to the imagination, and it was the work of a minute to slip that from her shoulders also. Bare to the waist, her magnificent breasts with their pert nipples, rosy pink and hard to the touch, were displayed for his inspection. He examined her face for signs of distress but could discern only increased passion and incandescent desire in her expression.

Thus encouraged, Amos lowered his head and feasted upon a fat nipple, grasping the fullness of her breast between his fingers and pushing it more firmly into his mouth. When she cried out, he increased the pressure and nipped gently at her swollen flesh.

'You find that pleasurable?' he asked, briefly lifting his head.

Crista was gripped by selfish longing;

breathless with yearning for that which she did not fully comprehend. Well, she understood the theory well enough, but what she had so far experienced was beyond her wildest imaginings. She threw her head back, bold and abandoned, revelling in the feel of Amos's skilled lips teasing her breasts.

Her breasts!

She was sitting in a boathouse, half-naked, on a gentleman's lap while he did these remarkable things to her. And he was still fully clothed. She ought to be ashamed of her behaviour. Instead, she felt the tight knots inside of her loosening and her mind flying free, unhindered by thoughts of how she *ought* to behave. All of her life she had been sensible, choosing to learn her father's trade and help him retain his reputation, until it was irredeemably lost. Never had she taken a moment to think about her own pleasures, perhaps because on a visceral level she had known life had been building up to this blissful moment. Now it had arrived, she would enjoy it and hang the consequences.

Guilt would come later when she had time to reflect upon what she had done.

'Yes,' she replied, her voice sounding bruised, earthy, like it didn't belong to her. 'I find it very pleasurable.'

His shirt rubbed against her sensitised skin

but she didn't suggest he remove it. If he released her, he might reconsider his actions. Crista wasn't prepared to take that chance. Boldly she looked into his face, swept the hair away from it with both hands and placed a soft, open-mouthed kiss on his lips. He groaned and immediately took control by drawing on her lower lip until her body shuddered. His tongue, velvety and sensuous, worked its way into her mouth again, tangling with hers until it felt as though her body would explode with need.

'Amos!' She stared wide-eyed into his face when he broke the kiss. She was panting, totally abandoned, in desperate need of something that hovered annoyingly just out of her reach.

'It's getting late,' he said brusquely. 'I ought to take you home.'

'Don't you dare!' Still on his lap, she planted her fists on her bare hips. 'You can't leave me like this.'

'Like what, angel?' he asked, a glamorous smile flirting with his lips.

'You would know more about that than I do, which is precisely my difficulty.'

'This is as far as we can go.'

'There must be something else. I'm not completely ignorant. I read books, you know.'

'Ah books, that would explain it.'

When his lips quirked she thumped the

solid wall of his chest in frustration. 'Don't laugh at me!'

'Books are a very poor substitute.'

'Precisely my point,' she replied with a triumphant smile. 'And I need to know what you intend to do about it.'

'Hmm, what indeed?' He flicked his fingers across one of her nipples and she felt the most extreme reaction swirl through her, settling very agreeably in the pit of her belly. 'There's something very erotic about having a half-dressed wanton draped over my lap in the open air.'

'Don't try and pretend the situation doesn't excite you, my lord, or that it's not one you have experienced before, because I know differently.'

He flexed his brows. 'You think I make a habit out of this sort of thing?'

She tossed her head. 'I'm perfectly sure you do. According to my mother, gentlemen in your position don't stint on their pleasures.'

'I dare say she's in a position to know,' Amos said, so quietly she barely heard him.

'You are not nearly so in control as you make yourself out to be,' she said, wishing she hadn't mentioned her mother and made him scowl. 'You are a passionate man, and right now your passions are inflamed.'

Amos's expression underwent a fractional

alteration and, thank the lord, he returned one of his hands to her breasts. 'You clearly studied your books well.'

'I do everything well.'

She felt his deep, throaty chuckle vibrate through his chest. 'Perhaps a little too well.'

'Thank you,' she replied primly.

Amos groaned. 'All right, minx. Let's see what we can do about your plight. Sit across my lap. Put one knee on either side of my thighs.'

'Are you not going to . . . er — ' She blushed furiously as she pointed to his breeches.

'I already told you I wouldn't take your virginity.' He kissed her brow, almost chastely. 'Just trust me.'

She lifted her skirts clear and did as he asked, wondering what he could possibly do to her while still fully clothed. The moment she was in position, her bare breasts squashed against his shirt, he slid his arms around her again and pulled her into another of his bruising kisses. His skilled lips reignited her desire, sending dizzying waves of sensation spiralling through her. It was almost too much for Crista to withstand. Her senses fragmented when one of his hands reached between them and played with a nipple. At the same time, he lifted his hips and thrust them against her hard, holding her in position with one strong arm so she was compelled to meet his thrust in her most sensitive spot. She gasped past their fused lips as rushing, soaring excitement gripped her and the odd sensation in her midsection intensified, igniting in a fireburst of pleasure.

'Amos!'

She tore her lips from his, unable to get sufficient air into her lungs when he repeated the process. Her skin was slick with dewy perspiration, her heart raced, and her spirits soared. This was what she had waited so long to discover. The feelings that sometimes came to her in the dead of night, keeping her awake with longing, were about to be explored to their ultimate limit. He watched her intently as feelings of sharp, tangible need stunned her senses. She rolled her head from side to side, gasping.

'You like that, my fiery little vixen?'

'Yes! Don't stop. Do it again.'

When Amos groaned, Crista sensed she was asking too much of him. His control was not *that* strong. He ought to release himself from the confinement of his breeches and do this properly. There was no reason why he should not. Gentlemen often made free with females from the lower classes, especially when, like her, they were more than willing. But she knew he wouldn't go that far, and her disappointment was intense. She wanted to lay with him, just once. It would be enough for her, and she would make no further demands on him. She ought to explain that to him but was too lost in an erotic daze to think about anything other than the extraordinary way he made her feel.

The hand playing with her breast squeezed hard, his groin thrust against her with additional force, tugging at her on a level she could not control, and her world imploded. She cried out his name as fire lanced through her veins and exquisite shards of intense sensation flooded her bloodstream. On and on it went, wild and uncoordinated. Crista's head spun in delirium until the surging tide of pleasure gradually ebbed and she forced her eyes open again.

'Amos,' she said softly, blinking until his features ceased to be blurred by her passion.

He smiled, kissed the end of her nose, and stood up, sweeping her into his arms. Seeming to realise her legs would not support her quite yet, he sat her down again and fastidiously replaced her clothing.

'Thank you.' Aware she ought to be embarrassed, she felt only a deep sense of fulfilment.

'It was entirely my pleasure.'

She laughed. 'That is patently not the case. It hardly seems fair. There must be . . . er, something I can do for you in return.'

'You have done more than you could possibly know,' he said, taking her hand and leading her from the boathouse. 'Come, I must take you home before your uncle wonders what has become of you.'

The silence between them as he drove the short distance was very different to the tension that had prevailed when they left Farrington House. Perhaps that was because Crista was a very different person, more mature, more aware. She ran her tongue across her bruised lips and lifted her face to the breeze in an effort to cool it down.

'Romsey could return as early as tomorrow,' Amos told her when they neared the village. 'Are you prepared?'

'Yes, I am ready.'

He was warning her they couldn't be alone again, Crista supposed. Warning her not to have expectations. As if she would! Her name was not Amelia.

'When he returns we will send someone to the shop. He will ask if Mrs. Willow's necklace is ready for collection and give you what you need.'

'I know that,' she chided gently. 'We have been over it a dozen times.'

Amos stopped the curricle just short of the rear entrance to her uncle's premises and jumped down to help her alight. He could do nothing more than briefly take her hand and caress her with his eyes before he let her go.

For Crista, it would have to be enough to sustain her through the coming days.

18

'How was your mother?' Uncle Charles asked over the breakfast table the following morning.

Crista rolled her eyes. 'Nothing is her fault and Amelia is bound to marry one of the Sheridan brothers.'

Uncle Charles's lips quirked. 'Whatever happened to Mr. Devonshire?'

'What indeed?'

'Are you all right, my dear?' Uncle Charles fixed her with a probing gaze. 'There is something different about you. Are you worried? Today could well be the day, you know.'

Crista bit her lip, conscious of her face heating, wondering what Uncle Charles had seen in her expression that gave her away. She hoped he wouldn't guess the true reasons for the changes in her. 'Let's hope so,' she replied briskly. 'I have had quite enough of Reece dogging my footsteps.'

'We shall soon see the last of him.'

'Yes,' Crista agreed, putting aside her napkin and standing up. 'Excuse me, Uncle, I ought to start work. I don't wish to fall behind with our legitimate business.'

'Quite so, my dear. You go on through. I

shall be there directly.'

Reece didn't look quite so suave as usual when he appeared in the workshop shortly after Crista. His clothing was rumpled, he was unshaven, and there were dark circles beneath his eyes. Perhaps the waiting, or having responsibility for the diamonds, was wearing on his nerves.

She busied herself with dragging out work on the settings that could have been done in half the time she had pretended it took. Now she awaited word from Lord Romsey so they could put their plan into action. All Reece's attempts at conversation were met with silence, and he eventually gave up trying to engage her attention. Instead, he seated himself at the back of the workshop and disappeared behind a newspaper.

Crista tried not to tense each time she heard the bell ring over the shop's door. She tried just as hard not to think of her liaison with Amos. Those precious memories must be put aside until she was at leisure to give them the complete attention they deserved.

Uncle Charles was kept unusually busy with customers. Even so, when the bell sounded again in the early afternoon, she instinctively knew it was the call she had been anticipating. She wasn't surprised when Uncle Charles came into the workshop and asked if Mrs. Willow's necklace was ready.

At last!

'Yes, here it is, Uncle,' she replied, reaching beneath the workbench and handing him a box. 'I hope it will give satisfaction.'

'I'm sure it will.'

Crista's palms were damp as she met her uncle's gaze and deftly took the fake diamond he passed to her in return for the necklace box. She very much hoped the stone was precisely the right size, in accordance with the dimensions she had passed to Lord Romsey. He had not had much time to make the arrangements, but she supposed when one had the might of the government behind one, most things were possible. She would soon find out. If it didn't fit snugly into the appropriate space in the velvet-lined box which Reece carried with him then the plan would fail and her part in the deception would be exposed.

Keeping the stone tightly snuggled in one fist, Crista wiped her other hand down the outside of her breeches. Reece had picked up his newspaper again once Uncle Charles left the workshop and was showing her no particular attention.

'I must finish the ring for Mr. Stormer,' Uncle Charles said, returning to the workshop and setting himself up on the bench beside Crista.

'I promised it for this afternoon.'

'So you did, Uncle.'

Crista spent the next half-hour putting the final touches to the settings, sent her uncle a probing look, and then turned to Reece.

'I am ready for the stones now,' she said coldly.

'Ah, at last.' He stood up, extracted the box from his coat pocket and handed it to her with great ceremony. 'Take care with those stones. They're worth a fortune.'

'I know how to handle diamonds.' Crista felt perspiration bathe her body as she opened the box, willing her hands not to shake. Uncle Charles stopped his work and leaned over to admire them. Crista picked up the largest stone, applied her loupe to her eye, and examined it closely. 'This, however, is not a diamond.'

'I beg your pardon.' Reece sent her a disbelieving glare. 'What the devil are you talking about?'

'What do you think, Uncle?'

This was the difficult part. One slip and all would be revealed. Confident Reece was watching her uncle in anticipation of him handling the stone, she passed the fake diamond to him and slipped the real stone inside her shirt. She had a pouch attached inside her chemise for that purpose, the only place she could think of where Reece wouldn't dare to look, even if he did become suspicious. The possibility of his examining her sleeves could not be discounted, hence the need for a more intimate, less obvious, hiding place.

'Good heavens, Crista.' Uncle Charles elevated his bushy eyebrows. 'You're absolutely right. Someone's played you for a fool, Reece.'

'What game do you two think you are playing?' Reece demanded. 'That's the same stone as I showed you before. You didn't say anything then.'

'I didn't handle it then,' Crista replied with commendable calm, given her heart was pounding and the real diamond was cutting painfully into the side of her breast.

'Diamonds have a sharp bend that light passes directly through, giving them their brilliance,' Uncle Charles explained, holding the fake stone up to the light. 'This one doesn't sparkle because it has less of a bend, even though it's been cut well.'

Reece sneered. 'That means nothing.'

'Lend me your newspaper, Mr. Reece,' Crista said. When he handed it to her, she turned the stone upside down and placed it on a sheet of the paper. 'If we can read the print through the stone, or even see distorted black smudges, then it probably isn't a diamond.' Three heads peered down at the stone. 'There, you see, I can read the words quite clearly through it.'

Crista met Reece's gaze, trying not to give away quite how much she was enjoying herself. 'Someone has swindled you, Mr. Reece. There's no question about it.'

Reece looked alarmingly pale. 'That's not possible. The stone hasn't left my possession.'

'Then someone has given you a fake.' Crista picked up one of the smaller stones and examined it. 'This one is genuine. I can tell immediately.'

'How?' Reece snapped.

'It doesn't show any sign of double refraction, whereas this bigger one does. See for yourself. If you look at the facet junctions from the top side of this smaller stone, you see no signs of double vision. Now look at the bigger one.' She handed Reece her loupe and he fixed it awkwardly to his eye. 'Do you see? It is very clear.'

'A real diamond's reflections usually manifest in various shades of gray. This one has rainbow reflections, which indicate a fake,' Uncle Charles said.

'You two have done something to the real stone,' Reece said, his hands shaking with anger, or fear — Crista couldn't be certain which.

'How?' Crista responded. 'You said yourself, they haven't left your person.'

'I don't know, yet, but you must have done something.'

'Why not weigh the stone if you still doubt my word. Fake stones weigh about fifty per cent more than real diamonds.'

'Since I only have your word for how much a real stone of this size ought to weigh, that won't help.'

'All right, since you still appear to doubt us, you can do the ultimate test. Put the stone we have agreed is genuine up to your mouth and breathe over it until it fogs like a mirror. A real diamond disperses the heat instantaneously so by the time you look at it, it has already cleared up.' He did so and it cleared immediately. 'Now try the same thing with the fake.'

Reece fell into the nearest chair when the large stone remained cloudy, dropping his head into his splayed hand and shaking it from side to side.

'Someone has played your masters for fools,' Uncle Charles said softly.

'And it better have not been either of you.' Reece lifted his head, scowling in a manner that was probably supposed to intimidate. All Crista could see was Reece's fear for his own skin. He would be held responsible for this farrago, but she was unable to feel sorry for him.

'I fail to see how it can have anything to do with us,' Uncle Charles said, the voice of calm reason. 'We have done everything you have asked of us, much as it went against our consciences. We were to be rid of you after this. Why would we risk anything going amiss?'

'Someone has put you up to this.' Reece jutted his chin. 'And I shall find out who, never you fear. No one cuts a sham over Edward Reece.'

'What do you wish us to do now?' Crista asked, ignoring the shiver of fear that crept through her when Reece fixed her with a suspicious glare, as though he could see through her clothing to the diamond nestled between her breasts. She suspected at any moment for him to pounce upon her and strip her bare in search of the stone. 'I will set the stones, if you ask me to, but anyone paying the amount this buyer is likely to pay will know a false stone when he sees one.'

'I need to take advice.' Reece scooped up the stones, returned them to their box, and placed it in his pocket. 'Remain here. I won't be long.'

Crista and her uncle waited until the door had closed behind Reece and they were sure he had strode away before turning to face one another.

'We did it!' Crista said, feeling euphoric.

'That we did, my love, thanks to your bravery. But quickly now, we must get rid of the real stone before he comes back and thinks to search us.'

Crista retrieved it from its hiding place, carefully wrapped it in a velvet cloth and slipped it into a pouch. Uncle Charles opened the back door and glanced cautiously up and down the lane. Several people loitered there, including one of Lord Romsey's men dressed as a street trader. He walked across to the door when he saw it open, and Crista slipped the stone to him.

'It all went smoothly,' she assured him.

'Aye, we knew that when Reece tore out of here. We have people following him and will soon know where he goes.'

'Take good care of that stone. It is worth a king's ransom.'

'Don't you worry none, miss. You just get yourself back inside and leave the rest to us.' He doffed his cap and disappeared into the crowd.

'So, Uncle,' Crista said, hugging the old man but feeling strangely deflated now it was all over. 'Our part is done.'

★ ★ ★

Reece's anger quickly gave way to fear as he strode down the main street. It was the busiest time of day, stallholders doing a brisk

282

trade, and it was impossible to tell if he was being followed. How the devil had this happened? He hadn't once left the stone unprotected, so the original stone must have been a fake. But the people his master dealt with were experts. They wouldn't have been misled. His step faltered when he recalled hiding the stones in his room at the Crown when he went to the Park on the day of the party. But he would stake his life that when he returned, they were exactly as he'd left them and hadn't been interfered with. Still, he better not let on to his master they'd been unattended at all.

Images of Crista Brooke kept flashing through his mind. He would bet what few possessions he owned she was involved in some way. But how? She hadn't touched the stones before today. Even so, there was something different about her. A newfound confidence that made him feel disadvantaged. He had become tired of trying to engage her in conversation when he sat in her workshop and so pretended to read his newspaper. In fact, he kept looking around its sides, directly at her, and she appeared to be constantly smiling today, as though she knew something he did not. He had supposed some man had put that knowing smile on her lips. The thought had filled him with jealousy, but that was nothing compared to the way he felt now. He knew what had happened to her father when he had been foolish enough to cross Reece's masters. God forbid they should accuse Reece of somehow switching the stones and consign him to a similar fate.

Switching the stones! He stopped dead in his tracks. God's beard, that's what they must have done, and he'd marched out of there without even searching them, and the entire place. What a numbskull! He didn't know how they had managed it, but Crista had known the size of the stones. She could, with her contacts, have somehow contrived to obtain a fake. Although, he supposed, she would have to go somewhere like London to find someone willing to make it for her. He relaxed when he realised she'd had no time to do so. Besides, he'd been keeping a constant watch on her and the old man. They had not left Shawford.

Relieved on that score, Reece decided to tell his master he had made a thorough search of them and the workshop. He would never know otherwise, and the deception might just save Reece's neck. He reached his destination, glanced over his shoulder, and couldn't see anyone paying any particular attention to him. Taking a deep, calming breath, be wielded the door knocker. He brushed past

Mary when she answered the door, for once not pausing to flirt with her.

'Is he home? I need to speak with him, and it can't wait.'

Mary shrugged. 'I'll tell him you're here.'

★ ★ ★

'Reece went to a house on the edge of the village owned by a man named Mayfield,' Romsey told Amos and Zach. 'What can you tell me about him?'

'Not much,' Zach replied. 'Do you know him, Amos?'

'Moved here a year or two ago, if memory serves. He's a middle-aged nabob who made some money in the Indies, according to talk at the Crown. He is a bit of a recluse, by all accounts, and seldom leaves his house.'

'Well, he left it this afternoon shortly after Reece visited him, in a tearing hurry. Took off in his carriage, heading for the Winchester Road. It's safe to assume he's heading for London. Shame, I was hoping he'd send an express, which we could have intercepted and seen who it was addressed to.' Romsey stood up and stretched. 'Never mind, he can't make it all the way to London today. He'll have to break his journey, and we'll be on his tail the entire way.'

285

'What about Reece?' Amos asked. 'I don't want him causing problems for Miss Brooke. By now, he might suspect her of switching the stones. I won't have her put in danger, not after all the risks she has taken to help you.'

Zach grinned. 'Don't worry, little brother. I predict Reece's ale will be tainted with something that will unsettle his belly and see him confined to his bed for the rest of the night.'

'Ah, that's what you despatched Nate to the Crown to put in hand.'

Zach shrugged. 'Doesn't hurt to be thorough.'

'Provided he doesn't get caught up with Martha and forget what you sent him there to do.'

'Have a little faith,' Zach said, standing to pour whisky for the three of them.

'You must stay away from Miss Brooke until this is all over,' Lord Romsey told Amos.

Amos bridled at his arbitrary tone. 'Who the devil do you think you're talking to?'

'Romsey is right,' Zach said mildly as he handed Amos his glass, defusing the tension with his calm yet authoritative manner. 'We can't risk the two of you being seen together. It would be extraordinary enough to attract attention, and you know how the villagers like to gossip, especially in the taproom, where

Reece might easily overhear what was being said. You don't wish to endanger Miss Brooke, I'm sure.'

'No, of course not.' Amos slumped in his chair and moodily sipped at his drink. 'But I don't like the thought of her being exposed to danger.'

'She won't be,' Romsey replied. 'We have Reece under constant watch and the only other person in the village connected with this business is Mayfield, who is now on the road to London.'

'What do you think will happen next?' Zach asked.

'One of two things,' Romsey replied. 'First of all, Mayfield will lead us to the person behind all of this. We have to assume he has taken the diamonds with him. He will take them to whoever authenticated them for him. Once he confirms the large stone is a fake, he will assume the switch was made here in Shawford, either by Reece or Chesney. Hopefully, he will return with Mayfield to discover which. We know how important this final transaction is to him, so I'm guessing he will take that chance. If he doesn't, we will arrest him in London.'

'You ought to do that anyway,' Amos said morosely, 'and save Miss Brooke from further danger.'

'No one will get near her,' Romsey said, enunciating each word clearly. 'But it's better for us if the ringleader comes down here, then there can be no doubt about his culpability, and no opportunity for him to slip the net. He's a well-connected cove, and if he realises he's been rumbled, there's no telling what plans he has in place for a quick exit from the country.'

'The day after tomorrow, Amos,' Zach said. 'That will see an end to this business.'

Unable to fault their logic, Amos nodded, wondering why he couldn't shake the feeling of unease that gripped him whenever he thought of Crista with only an old man inside the house to protect her.

19

Reece, it transpired, had underestimated many things about Mayfield, especially the violence of his temper. Stern yet mild-mannered, Reece had always respected his guile but had never felt afraid of him. Reece was a good twenty years younger and considerably stronger than Mayfield. Since Mayfield trusted him, Reece had no reason to fear him because what had happened with the diamond was beyond his control. He went to his home, knowing he must be told at once. He felt apprehensive but unafraid to admit to the truth, only to see a very different side to Mayfield when he did so.

'What's this you tell me?'

Mayfield leapt to his feet, knocking his chair over without appearing to notice. His face drained of all colour, except for the network of ugly protruding blue veins decorating his nose. His breath came out in short, angry hisses, and he actually backhanded Reece's face so viciously he cut his lip and left a bruise on his cheek.

'You fool!' he said. 'I told you never to leave the diamonds unattended. Someone got to them and made a switch.'

'They can't have,' Reece replied, staunching the flow of blood from his lip with his handkerchief. 'I've had them with me all the time.'

'Are you sure you didn't get insensible with ale, or allowed some floosy to distract you?'

'Perfectly sure.'

'Then it must have been you who pulled a fast one.'

'Me!' Reece shook his head. 'I wouldn't know how to begin. Besides, why would I be so stupid? I am being well paid for serving you — '

'Huh, if you still expect payment after making such a mull out of a simple assignment, then you're deluded.' Mayfield snarled the words, his face now stained a deep, ugly red, a nerve working beneath his left eye. 'You will be fortunate to escape with your life.'

'The mistake must have been made in London, sir,' Reece said, feeling suddenly very afraid. 'The switch must have been made there, accidentally or deliberately.'

'How do we know a mistake has actually been made?' Mayfield drummed his fingers on the surface of his desk and glowered at Reece. 'Can you tell a real diamond from a fake?'

'No, sir, but the girl and her uncle can. Why would they lie when they know this is the last commission we require from them?'

Mayfield snorted. 'Perhaps they are not as gullible as you appear to be and realise we would never give up on such a prime and lucrative source of workmanship.'

'Even so, I don't see how they could have obtained a fake stone. Besides, I searched them and the workshop and was watching them the entire time when I gave them the stones. If they had made a switch, I would have noticed.'

'You had better hope, for the sake of your own neck, that's the case.' Mayfield lumbered to his feet and grabbed the box containing the diamonds. 'Stay here at the Crown and keep a close eye on the girl and her uncle. I must go to London and report to our masters.' He looked less than enamoured at the prospect. 'Your fate is in the hands of others, but if I have any say in the matter, your inefficiency will be dealt with swiftly and ruthlessly.'

'But, sir, I've done nothing wrong.'

'Get out! Get back to the Crown and await instructions.'

That had been several hours ago. Now Reece was sitting in the taproom, nursing his grievances and a tankard of ale. Whichever way he came at the problem, things didn't look good for Reece, and it was time to consider his own skin. What concerned him most was Mayfield's obvious anxiety about facing his master in London. The man was always composed, always so sure of himself. If he was scared, Reece had good reason to be even more so because the ultimate blame would be placed squarely on his shoulders.

He took a sip of his ale, not as enthusiastic about the local brew as was usually the case. Besides, it had a bitter taste to it tonight. It wasn't the best barrel, but Reece was too preoccupied to complain. The handsome payday he had been anticipating would not now happen, that much was abundantly clear, and it was all the Brooke girl's fault. What a fool he had been to accept her explanation at face value and not more closely examine the possibility of their having switched the diamond. In actual fact, he hadn't under-stood one word in ten about the means of telling a fake stone from the genuine article. Miss Brooke had a happy knack for making him feel stupid at the best of times, and so he hadn't asked for a clearer explanation, or paused to properly consider the alternatives.

Damn it, he was a fool! She and her uncle had worked in tandem to deliberately confuse him. Now he was thinking more rationally, that much was obvious. The little slut could easily have slipped the real stone inside her clothing. Reece bashed his tankard against the table, causing several people to glance in his direction. He glowered at them, discouraging them from approaching him. Not that many people tried to engage him in conversation. He had nothing to say to them, did not desire company and the local populace had long since given up on attempting to befriend him.

It was as clear as day to him now, and he called himself all sorts of a fool for not being more suspicious. They had bamboozled him with talk about how to tell a real diamond from a fake, taken him by surprise, and made it hard for him to think straight. But he was thinking straight enough now. The girl and her uncle had somehow contrived this business, probably with the help of her fancy lover.

Jealousy and rage gripped Reece in a vicious hold. He had assumed she would not confide in Lord Amos, but if she had done so, then the game was definitely up. He needed to leave Shawford, and he needed to do so tonight so he could get well away from the district before Mayfield returned. But he was damned if he would leave without revenging himself against the Brooke girl. He would help himself to a few baubles from that workshop of her uncle's, to compensate for his lost payday, and would help himself to a few other things from Miss Brooke while he was about it. If she was so free with her favours with Sheridan, she could damned well show him the same consideration.

Leaving his ale unfinished, Reece pushed himself to his feet, shoving bodies out of his way so he could reach the stairs. He felt a bit light-headed, and once he reached his room he was obliged to lean against the wall until his head stopped spinning. When he felt a little better, he threw his few possessions into a valise, wondering why he felt so woozy. He had consumed less than half his usual quota of ale, and it didn't normally affect him very much. Putting his reaction down to the strain of his circumstances, Reece slipped down the servants' stairway and out the back door. No point in wasting blunt by settling his account, since he had no intention of ever returning to this rat-infested hovel. He patted his pocket, double checking he had everything he would require close at hand, waited until the coast was clear and then let himself out of the back door that led directly to the mews.

There was a livery stable across the street, at which Reece hired a saddle horse, arranged to leave it at the first posting inn on the

Winchester Road, and mounted up. Anyone asking questions about him would assume that was where he had gone. Not that he anticipated being missed, but it paid to be cautious. Indeed, he had every intention of riding to that inn and catching the next public coach to London, but he had unfinished business to attend to in Shawford first.

He rode to the end of the village and left the horse in Mayfield's stable. As expected, it was empty, Mayfield having taken his carriage and horses to London, and no permanent grooms lived on the premises. The cool evening air helped to clear his befuddled head, and by the time he had walked back to the village, he felt a great deal better. More importantly, he was in control of his anger, ready to make it work in his favour.

He came to a halt at the rear of Chesney's shop without encountering another living soul. They had closed for the day, but Reece could see lights coming from the apartment above. The door leading directly to the living quarters was locked, but that was no impediment to a man of Reece's skill. It took him less than a minute to fix a long implement into the lock, carefully turn the tumblers from the outside, and slip into the entrance vestibule. The hinges squeaked as he opened the door, sounding unnaturally loud. Cursing, Reece concealed himself in the shadows, clutching the cosh he had brought with him tightly in case anyone came to see what the noise was about.

After several minutes, no one had come down the stairs, and Reece considered it safe to make his next move. He could hear voices coming from above. Damnation, he had forgotten Chesney employed a maid-of-all-work, and she would still be on duty at this hour. Well, there was no help for that. In his uncompromising mood, Reece could handle an old man and two helpless women, especially since he didn't especially mind if they lived or died. He took the stairs cautiously, expecting at any moment to be challenged — almost hoping he would be, because he needed an outlet for his growing rage.

Luck was with him. When he reached the top of the stairs, he found the maid with her back to him, carrying dishes from the parlour to the scullery. He followed behind her on silent feet, waited for her to put the dishes down, and then grabbed her from behind, clapping a hand over her mouth to prevent her from crying out.

'Make a sound, and you won't see another day,' he whispered. 'Nod if you understand.'

The girl nodded, her eyes round with fear

as her struggles subsided. Satisfied she was too frightened to move a muscle, Reece produced a kerchief from his pocket and tied it securely around her mouth. He found a length of rope, one of several he had placed in another pocket, and tied her hands behind her back.

'Good girl.'

He patted her ample rear, opened the door to the pantry, threw her roughly inside, and locked the door on her.

Buoyed by his success, Reece crept towards the parlour and peered around the open door. Chesney was seated in a chair beside the fire, smoking a pipe. Crista was sitting across from him, a book open on her lap. It would be impossible for him to reach either of them without being seen, but that hardly signified. He only needed to subdue the old man, threaten him, and the girl would do whatever he asked of her.

'Good evening,' he said, straightening his shoulders and strolling casually into the room.

'You!' Crista leapt from her chair.

'How the devil did you get in here?' Chesney asked, blinking up at him like an owl from behind his glasses.

'Sit down!' Reece bellowed at Crista. At the same time he grabbed the old man and pulled him from his chair. Chesney was stronger than he appeared and fought back, but Reece was easily able to subdue him. 'Move a muscle, Miss Brooke, and it will be the worse for your uncle. Do as I say, and you will both survive.'

Storm clouds gathered behind her eyes. She was clearly about to launch an attack of her own, but thought better of it and backed off.

'What do you want?' she asked instead, her voice insolent, scathing. She ought to be scared, show him some respect. Instead, she looked at him as though he was something she had just scraped from the bottom of her shoe. Well, that situation would change before this night was out. Any thoughts of treating her gently had been eradicated by her attitude, and she only had herself to blame for what she was about to experience. Thoughts of her begging him for mercy fired his lust. 'You will never get away with this, you oaf.'

'It seems I already have.' Reece was surprised at how calm, how in control he felt, as he pushed the old man back into his chair and bound his arms firmly to it with more of his rope. 'Come along, Miss Brooke,' he said politely. 'You and I have matters to attend to.'

She tossed her head and sent him another damning look. 'If you think I will go anywhere with you then you really are deluded.'

He raked her body with a hard, merciless gaze. 'I don't think you fully appreciate your situation. Thanks to your deception with the diamonds, I really have nothing to lose. The people I work for don't tolerate failure, you see, but then, given what happened to your father, you already know that.'

'You . . . ' She pointed a finger at him, no longer quite so composed. 'You killed him?'

'Unfortunately, that privilege didn't fall to my lot.' He fixed her with an indolent smile. 'But, just so we're clear, I would have done so without a second's regret.'

'You are despicable!'

'I'm a survivor and have no intention of remaining here, waiting to be blamed for what you two did. But first, I need to understand how you managed it.'

'Did what?' she replied insolently.

'Come along, my dear, I don't have all night. I know you swapped the real diamond for a fake, and I would like to know how you did it.'

'We did not,' Chesney replied. He looked pale yet defiant, as though he didn't believe Reece would actually resort to violence. Reece curled his upper lip, thinking if he didn't soon talk he would have occasion to know otherwise. Unfortunately, Reece couldn't afford the luxury of dallying all night with the delectable Miss Brooke. There was no telling how quickly Mayfield and his master might return, and Reece needed to be well away before they did. He lifted his cosh above the old man's head, but it had no discernable effect. 'You may beat me to death, if you like, but it will change nothing.'

'You may not mind dying, but I think Miss Brooke's conscience would be troubled if she allowed that to happen.'

Reece glanced at her as he spoke and noticed her chewing the inside of her lip with indecision. It was then that he knew he was right. They really *had* duped him. In which case, perhaps all was not lost. If they swapped the diamonds, they could return the real one and he could, just possibly, regain favour with his masters. He noticed uncle and niece exchange a speaking look, and Chesney shake his head.

'If you have the real stone, it might very well keep you alive,' Reece told them casually. 'Without it, you are no use to me or my masters.'

'But we don't have it,' Crista said, spreading her hands.

'Your rich lover engineered all of this.' Reece pointed an accusing finger at Crista.

'Sheridan said pretty words to you, pretended to admire you, kissed you a time or two, and you did everything he asked of you,' Reece snarled. 'Just as you will for me before the night is out. It no longer matters how you swapped the diamond. It was simply a matter of idle curiosity, because I have decided not to wait for my masters to return.'

'Then don't let us keep you,' Crista replied with an arrogant toss of her head.

'Nor do I intend to leave empty-handed. I must be compensated for the income I've lost, thanks to you two.' He beckoned to Crista. 'Come along, Miss Brooke, you and I have an engagement to keep in private.'

'Never!' she spat at him.

'Oh, I think you'll do as you're told.' He slapped his cosh against his palm and sent a significant look her uncle's way. 'As I keep trying to tell you, I have absolutely nothing to lose now, and desperate men are unpredictable. You and I are going to go down to the shop, and I shall help myself to a few trinkets.'

'Fine,' Chesney said. 'Take whatever you want. Just leave Crista alone.'

'I'm sorry to disappoint you but I have a score to settle with your meddlesome niece.'

He reached out to grab her arm. She responded by bringing a poker down across his hand with considerable force. Reece howled, swore voraciously, and let her go. How the devil had she picked up the poker without him noticing? First a seamless swap of diamonds, and now this. The wretched girl had broken his hand, or so it felt. No matter. He ignored the pain, determined to control her before she inflicted further damage on him, and to make her pay an even higher price for her rebelliousness. She raised the poker a second time, a murderous look in her eye.

'Drop it!'

He raised the cosh over her uncle's head, gave him a tap with it, and she immediately let the poker go. It clattered against the marble hearth and rolled to a halt. Her eyes shot daggers at him, her breath coming in short, angry spurts. But when blood gushed from her uncle's temple she gasped and tried to run to him.

'Now see what you have made me do,' Reece said, smiling as he admired his handiwork.

'Are you all right, Uncle?' Crista asked anxiously.

'Yes, my dear. I have a very hard head. It's nothing but a scratch.' Blood trickled into one of his eyes and he blinked it away. 'Just have a care for yourself.'

Reece picked up a cloak that was draped across a chair and threw it at Crista. 'Put that on.'

She took her time, throwing him looks of intense dislike, but eventually did as he asked.

'Now come over here. Hold your hands out in front of you where I can see them.'

She hesitated, but eventually complied. As soon as she was close, Reece bound her hands tighter than was strictly necessary, just to teach her a lesson. He was clumsy because the fingers of one hand were swollen where she had struck them with the poker, but finally he got it done to his satisfaction.

'Now, downstairs we go. If you're a good girl and are nice to me, then you will see your uncle again. If not . . . well, I shall have no use for either of you.'

'You cowardly blaggard!' Chesney struggled against his bonds. 'Leave her and take me instead.'

Reece laughed. 'You can't give me the things I need.' He grabbed Crista's arm and pushed her towards the stairs. 'Come along, my dear. Time is a'wasting.'

20

'This will make me sound like a most disobliging neighbour.' Lady St. John's eyes sparkled as she shared a glance between Amos and Zach. 'However, if you require a temporary home for Mrs. Brooke and her younger daughter on another occasion, please look elsewhere.'

'So you have met your match.' Zach elevated one brow in idle amusement and sent their guest a teasing smile.

'I thought I had met my share of social climbers in my time, to say nothing of self-obsessed young ladies, but my guests have proven themselves to be in a class of their own. Oh, excuse me, Lord Amos.' Lady St. John covered her mouth with one hand, her eyes still brimming with infectious mirth. 'There I go again, speaking without thinking. I don't include the elder Miss Brooke in my criticism. She is a delight, and I'm very glad to know her.'

Amos, who doubted whether Lady St. John had uttered an indiscreet word in her life, smiled. 'I'm sorry about Mrs. Brooke. Another two days should see you rid of them.'

'Oh, I don't mind for myself. I can easily find an occupation that keeps me out of their way. It is you gentlemen I fear for.'

'Us?' Zach flexed both brows this time. 'Why should we be in danger?'

'If you had spent the past day listening to Mrs. Brooke singing her younger daughter's praises, you wouldn't have asked that question. No one is prettier, kinder, better read, more accomplished, or would make a better wife . . . need I go on?'

'Most assuredly not,' Zach replied, shuddering.

'Mrs. Brooke is quite determined to meet you all, because naturally you will be charmed by her Amelia. She sweeps aside all my objections as though I don't know what I am talking about. Really, if there is something that woman doesn't wish to hear, she's blind to all reason.' Amos nodded, and avoided looking at Zach for fear of laughing. Lady St. John's account of Mrs. Brooke's determination perfectly coincided with Crista's description of her mother's ambitions, so there was really nothing to laugh about. 'Honestly, were the distance between here and Farrington House shorter, I would not put it past them to cover it on foot.'

'Thankfully that's not possible,' Amos said, finally giving way to laughter.

'Mrs. Brooke hasn't once asked about

Crista's situation,' Lady St. John said, her smile abruptly fading.

Amos ground his jaw. 'That doesn't surprise.'

'I, on the other hand, called this evening with the express purpose of asking how it went.'

'We understand the stones were swapped without difficulty,' Zach replied.

'We don't actually know if there were difficulties,' Amos pointed out, 'since we have not been permitted to — '

The door flew open, causing Amos's words to stall and for fear to grip him like a vice when he saw Nate standing there, looking uncharacteristically flustered.

'What is it?' he and Zach asked together.

'Zach, you won't believe what . . . oh, good evening, Lady St. John.' Nate offered their guest a brief, a very brief, bow. 'It's Reece,' he said breathlessly, returning his attention to Zach and Amos. 'He's disappeared.'

'How the devil did that happen?' Amos asked, springing to his feet. 'You were supposed to doctor his ale.'

'I did.' Nate threw up his hands, as though warding up a physical attack. 'One minute he was in the taproom, brooding over his ale, the next he lumbered from the room. I assumed, excuse me, Lady St. John, but I assumed he had gone to answer a call of nature. When he didn't return after ten minutes, I became anxious and went in search of him. He was nowhere to be found so I ran up the stairs to his room and found it stripped of all his possessions.'

'Crista,' Amos said, clenching his fists. 'He will go after her.'

'Romsey has someone watching her place,' Zach replied calmly. 'Let's hear what else Nate has to tell us before we go charging off on a wild goose chase.'

'I deduced he must have run off before his masters come back and put the blame on him. To do that he would need a horse, so I checked the livery stable. Sure enough, he hired a saddle horse ten minutes before I got there and rode off in the direction of the Winchester Road, having agreed to leave the horse at the first posting inn.'

'He's for London then,' Zach said.

'I don't trust him,' Amos said, his voice tight with barely controlled anger. 'I've had a bad feeling about this whole business since Romsey took himself off to London, blithely assuring us everyone would sit tight at his convenience.'

'What of the man Romsey left in the tap-room to keep an eye on Reece?' Zach asked.

'Hmm, funny you should ask, because he

was nowhere to be seen,' Nate replied, rubbing his chin. 'I looked for him when I couldn't find Reece, which is when it occurred to me I hadn't seen him all the evening. I assume he was called off because I was there.'

'Come on,' Amos said, his gut churning with worry. 'If that man had been recalled, we can't be sure the rest of them haven't been as well. We need to ride to Shawford and ensure Miss Brooke is safe and well.'

Zach sprang into action, issuing orders that saw footmen scurrying to obey them, making things happen as only a duke could. In short order, he had men sent to the Winchester Road to look out for Reece and two burly footmen were detailed to accompany them to Shawford. 'The next coach won't leave until the morning,' he assured Amos. 'If he's there, we will catch him before he boards it.'

'He isn't there. He won't leave Shawford until he's had his revenge,' Amos replied with firm assurance. 'Come, Zach, we're wasting time.'

'I shall come with you,' Lady St. John said. 'Don't worry. I won't slow you down and might be of some help.'

The three brothers shared a brief look and then nodded. Zach took Lady St. John's arm and the party headed for the stables. It would only have taken the grooms a minute to saddle all the horses, but Amos couldn't wait that long. He threw Warrior's bridle on himself, leapt onto him bareback and cantered from the yard. The others would either catch up with him, or they would not. Amos didn't have time to wait.

★   ★   ★

Crista received a sharp shove in the small of the back that sent her tumbling off balance in the direction of the stairs. She had no choice but to walk, otherwise Reece would probably push her down them. It was awkward progress with bound hands and a head full of worry for her uncle. Reece, the snivelling coward, had hit Uncle Charles very hard and the wound bled copiously. Unless he could manage to untie his hands and call for help, she didn't care to think about the consequences. Dear lord, where was Kate? Crista had only just remembered their maid. Presumably Reece had overpowered her before he tackled them. She offered up a silent prayer for the girl to be unharmed. If she was not, it would be another tragedy to burden Crista's conscience.

She was more angry than afraid when they reached the ground floor and Reece forced her to unlock the back door to the shop.

'Show me where the best items are kept,' he said abruptly. 'I want small, valuable things, easy to carry and to hock. Nothing that's recognisable, but don't try palming me off with no rubbish.'

As though he will know the difference. Crista showed him a display cabinet with some of their best work inside. She didn't care if he took the lot. All she cared about was getting out of this situation and saving her poor uncle. She took some satisfaction from the fact Reece had virtually no use of the fingers on the hand she had struck with the poker. Crista only regretted not hitting him harder, or managing a second blow before he disarmed her.

Having stuffed a sack full of jewellery, Reece jerked his thumb towards the back door.

'Come along, Miss Brooke,' he said with a sneering grin. 'It's time you and I became better acquainted.'

Crista greedily eyed the various tools she used to make her jewellery, a lot of them small and exceedingly sharp, neatly lined up on her workbench. If she could just pick one of them up. But with her hands tied and Reece watching her so closely, it was impossible. Finally, fear kicked in as the seriousness of her situation struck her. She dragged her feet, but

Reece kept a vicelike grip on her upper arm with his good hand as they left the shop, and he pulled her along at a cracking pace. She almost had to run to keep up with him, or risk being tugged from her feet.

They soon left the village behind them, and it was obvious he had a particular destination in mind. But where? Dear God, surely not a barn or a field. She needed to be near people if she was to have a chance of attracting attention to her plight.

'Cry out or try to alert anyone, and it's your uncle who will suffer,' Reece said, appearing to read her mind when she opened her mouth to call for help from a passer-by who gave them an odd look.

Reece had admitted being desperate and Crista knew he meant what he said. She didn't give him the satisfaction of an answer, instead turning her mind to the best method of escape. She had absolutely no intention of submitting to Reece's vile advances, but had no weapon with which to defend herself and even with an injured hand he was still far stronger than she was. If only she could untie the rope that bound her hands, then she would feel more in control. At least, she was still wearing boy's clothing, which would make it that much harder for Reece to take liberties. She swallowed as she mulled that tiny advantage over in her head. If he wanted to undress her, he would find it awkward with his injured hand. She could see the fingers had swollen, and he was having trouble carrying the sack stuffed with the stolen jewellery. Good! She hope it hurt like the devil.

So, she reasoned, if he couldn't disrobe her, he would have to untie her hands so she could do it herself. Hmm, what would Amos do in this situation? No, she mustn't think about him now. He wasn't here, and she most likely would never see him again, even if she did survive this ordeal. She was on her own and there was no one to fight this particular battle for her. Even so, thoughts of the bliss she had experienced beneath Amos's skilled hands spurred her on. She would never allow another man to lay so much as one finger on her and spoil that recollection. Never! She would bide her time and find a way out of this for herself, and for her uncle.

She absolutely would.

They reached a large house on the outskirts of the village, set on its own grounds. Surely, he wasn't taking her in there. Well, if he was, he was exceedingly foolish because there must be servants, someone who would help her. Hope flared, only to be dashed when he let himself in by a side door that led directly to the kitchen. A maid and a cook sat at the table, drinking tea. Both looked surprised to see Reece with a captive woman in his grasp.

'Hey,' the maid said, standing. 'What's all this?'

'Stay where you are,' Reece replied in a calmly authoritative tone. 'I am about your master's business.'

'Hmm, well he didn't say anything to me about letting you in.'

'Be quiet, Mary!'

The maid sent Crista an odd look. Crista replied with an expressively eloquent expression; one that begged for help, but it quickly became apparent that none would be forthcoming. Reece was clearly no stranger to this house. Presumably, it was the property of his master, the person he colluded with in the theft of the jewellery. The man would have gone to London to consult with people there about the fake diamond, leaving this house vacant.

Damnation!

The maid and cook stared, open-mouthed, as Reece marched through the kitchen, still tugging Crista behind him, and into the hallway. Once there, he shot the bolt across, effectively trapping the servants in the kitchen. Presumably there were no other live-in staff, and even if there were, judging by the reaction of the two in the kitchen, the chances of them defying Reece and coming to her aid were practically none.

She was on her own.

Once again, she was confronted by stairs that Reece pulled her up. She had lost all feeling in her upper arm where he gripped it so tightly, but there was nothing wrong with her cognitive powers. Her mind continued to whirl with ever more fanciful ways of extricating herself from this farrago, disabling Reece, and rushing back to her uncle's aid before it was too late for him.

Reece opened several doors along the upper corridor, grunting with the effort it took him with his damaged hand, the added burden of the sack full of stolen jewellery clutched awkwardly in it. Then he had the bright idea of having her open the doors for him.

'This one,' he said, pointing to the door at the end of the corridor.

She had no choice but to open it. Her heart sank when she found herself in what had to be the master bedroom, dominated by a huge, curtained bed. It was now full dark outside, but it was mid-summer, and a full moon cast plenty of light through the windows. Reece grunted with satisfaction and kicked the door shut behind them.

'I wouldn't wish you to do this in anything other than style,' he said sarcastically, giving her a hefty shove that saw her tumble backwards onto the bed.

★ ★ ★

Amos slid from Warrior's back, his heart sinking when he saw the back door to Chesney's premises swinging wide open. He bounded up the stairs to the living accommodation and found Chesney, semi-conscious, tied to a chair, blood pouring from a wound on his head. Amos ran across to him.

'Crista!' Chesney said in a breathless whisper. 'He has her.'

'Let me help you out of these bonds.'

'No, don't mind me. You must get her back.'

By the time Amos untied the ropes, the rest of the party had spilled into the room. Lady St. John calmly took charge of Chesney, asking one of the footmen to fetch her water and a cloth.

'He'll be all right,' she said, feeling for Chesney's pulse and nodding to assure the rest of them that it was steady.

The footman returned quickly. 'I found her bound in a cupboard.'

Kate fell to her knees in front of the fire, sobbing loud enough to wake the dead. Apart from being scared witless, she appeared unharmed.

'Do you have any idea where he took Crista?' Amos asked, doing his best not to shout with frustration when Chesney gingerly shook his head.

'He said he was going to help himself from the shop and then . . . well, I'm sure you can imagine what he intends.' Chesney sat forward, seemingly oblivious to an injury that must hurt like the devil. 'You have to stop him. He'll take what he wants but won't allow her to live afterwards. I never should have agreed to cross these people.'

'Where would he have taken her, Zach?' Amos asked, pacing the length of the room in growing agitation.

'Not to the Crown,' Nate replied.

'Somewhere he's familiar with, and where he's confident he won't be disturbed,' Zach added.

'Mayfield's establishment.' Amos thumped his fist against the mantelpiece. 'It's the only place he knows, apart from here and the Crown.'

'Stay with Lady St. John,' Zach said to one of the footmen. 'Don't let her out of your sight, or you will have me to answer to.'

The three brothers and the remaining footman left the premises at a run. They remounted but Zach waved them to a halt again a short time later, before they reached Mayfield's house. There was a dim light coming from what had to be the kitchen, but nothing more. They tied their horses to trees on the periphery of the garden and climbed the fence. Zach led them to the stables, where a lone horse stood.

'It must be the one Reece hired,' Amos said. 'Which means he's here. Let's hope to God we're not too late.'

They rounded the side of the house and found the kitchen door unlocked. A maid and cook, seated together at the table, looked up with expressions of alarm. Zach placed a finger to his lips.

'Where is he?' he asked in a whisper.

'We don't know. He dragged a young woman in here a short time ago and locked us in. He said it was the master's business, and we weren't to interfere,' the maid said.

'I told Mary I didn't think it was right, but it's not our place to say so. Besides, what could we do?'

A thump, followed by a loud yell from upstairs rendered further explanations unnecessary. Zach and Amos shared a look and then put their shoulders to the kitchen door.

It gave way on the second attempt with a loud crack and splintering of wood. They ran up the stairs, taking them three at a time. The noises came from the room at the end, and Amos was beyond worrying himself about stealth. Every second could make a difference to the fate of the woman he had fallen helplessly in love with. He thrust the door open and, thanks to the light from a full moon pouring through the windows, he saw Crista quite clearly. Her shirt was torn, her hands bound tight enough for there to be blood on her wrists, but her eyes glinted with the light of conquest. She was alive, and it was not her who had cried out, but Reece. He was prostrate on the floor and she stood over him, systematically grinding the heel of her shoe into the fingers of one hand.

'Crista!' Amos ran to her. 'Are you all right?'

'My uncle?' she asked at the same time.

'Lady St. John is with him,' Zach said. 'You can let him go now,' he added, supressing a smile as he looked down at Reece, either howling with pain or spitting with rage. Amos was unsure which, and didn't especially care. 'We thought you needed rescuing, but clearly we underestimated you.'

'What happened?' Nate asked.

'He tried to . . . well, you know, but I

smashed his hand with a poker when he broke into our apartment. When he pushed me onto the bed I pretended to lose consciousness. I couldn't think what else to do, but you might as well know I have never fainted in my life. I leave that sort of thing to Mama and Amelia. Anyway, I remembered their example, how they use that ruse to get their way, and decided there had never been a better time to attempt it myself.'

Amos shook his head in frank admiration. 'Inspired!' he said softly.

'More like desperate,' she replied. 'The moment I sensed Reece get on the bed beside me I brought my knee up into his groin and knocked him to the floor. Before he could recover, I stamped on his bad hand. I was just wondering what to do next when you arrived.'

The brothers shared a glance, but Amos's heart was too full for him to find his voice. That she could be so level-headed, so calm at such a time earned his respect, his admiration, his total, unconditional love.

'You're remarkable,' he said, gently taking her arm to lead her away from Reece. She winced at his touch.

'You are hurt?'

'He pulled me along by my arm.'

'Let me see.'

He gently removed the rope binding her wrists, scowling when he saw how chafed and bleeding they were. He rolled up her sleeve and saw ugly red weals all over her lovely skin. Reece had just been pulled to his feet and Amos turned to him, murder in his eyes. The footman, on Zach's orders, was about to bind his hands but Amos stopped him. He then swung his fist and placed it with considerable force in the centre of Reece's cringing face. He had the satisfaction of hearing bone crack beneath the force of the blow as blood gushed from Reece's nose. He screamed and crumpled to the floor again.

'That is for daring to touch Miss Brooke,' he said, indicating to the footman to take him away. 'Come along,' he added to Crista as he shrugged out of his coat and draped it around her to hide her dishevelled clothing. 'Let's get you to safety.'

He swept her from the floor, into his arms, and carried her out into the night.

21

The moment Amos and his brothers arrived, Crista felt the fight drain out of her. She was dimly aware of the duke ordering his footman to secure her uncle's premises and to arrange for him to be taken to the Park. That, apparently, was where she was to go as well, and she was too fatigued and relieved at her narrow escape to argue the point. She was also exhausted. The tension of the past few weeks had taken its toll, and she could scarce keep her eyes open. Besides, being cradled in Amos's strong arms was far too comforting for her to protest about the arrangement.

She didn't remember much about the journey back to the Hall, other than she was in a carriage, and still in Amos's arms. She did recall seeing her uncle. He was pale and tired, and his wound was deep. The duke said it would require stitches, but Uncle Charles appeared oblivious to the pain, frequently saying instead just how relieved he was to see Crista relatively unharmed. Unharmed physically maybe, but she wondered how long it would take for her subconscious to recover from the ordeal. Not that she would ever admit to the degree it had affected her. It would do no good anyway, and besides it was a personal battle to be fought in solitude.

Sunlight filtering across her face woke her from a deep, surprisingly dreamless sleep. She stretched between crisp cotton sheets in a wonderfully comfortable bed and was most reluctant to open her eyes. She did so only because she became conscious of someone sitting beside her. When she turned her head in that direction, she was astonished to find it was the duchess.

'Oh, Your Grace, I — '

'Hush, child, I didn't mean to wake you. I only wanted to reassure myself you were sleeping, nothing worse.'

'I didn't mean to be such an inconvenience.'

'The very last thing you are is an inconvenience, my dear.'

What an extraordinary thing to say. Obviously, the duchess doesn't know the truth. 'How is my uncle?'

'He's sleeping. The doctor has seen you both, but I don't expect you remember much about that. You were totally exhausted. Anyway, your uncle's wound has been stitched.'

Crista glanced down and noticed for the first time that her wrists were neatly bandaged. 'I see,' was all she could think to say. 'Thank you so much, Your Grace.'

'It is I, or rather my family, who should be thanking you.'

Crista wondered if she had suffered a concussion. 'I don't understand, I — '

'My dear, my sons have told me everything.'

'Oh.' Crista bit her lip. 'I wish they had not. Whatever must you think of me?'

'I am very glad they did. I knew something wasn't quite right. We mothers have a happy knack of knowing when our children are up to something, as you yourself will discover one day. Anyway, one of our responsibilities as the leading family in this district is to keep the residents of Compton and Shawford from killing one another. If those rogues had been allowed to get away with what they forced you and your poor uncle to do, there's no telling what that would have done for local relations.'

'I'm not dishonest, Your Grace, and I hated what my father had been forced to do.'

'Because of your mother's ambitions?'

'Yes.' Shame forced Crista to look away from the duchess's sympathetic smile. 'Because of that.'

'Then I have even greater admiration for your courage. You have more than redeemed yourself, as well as helping Lord Romsey to arrest the culprits behind an audacious criminal activity against the state.'

'Have the ringleaders been caught?'

'The duke sent an express to London telling Romsey to arrest them there. It would not be safe to allow them back to Shawford, given the circumstances.'

Crista sighed with relief. 'Then it really is all over.'

'It would seem so.' The duchess stood up. 'But I should let you rest.'

'No, if you please, I would like to get up.'

'In that case, I shall send a maid to help you.'

'Oh, but I have nothing to wear.'

The duchess smiled. 'That, my dear, is a situation easily remedied.'

A short time later, several footmen came into the adjoining sitting room — Crista could hardly believe this sumptuous bedroom had its own sitting room — and set up a bath in front of a roaring fire. When it was filled with steaming water and the footmen had withdrawn, a young maid helped Crista into it.

'Please to keep your wrists clear of the water, miss,' she said, soaping Crista's back, then pouring water over her hair and washing it.

Crista closed her eyes and surrendered herself to the maid's efficient hands. Feeling the tension drain out of her, she slowly came back to life.

'Oh, miss, your poor arm.'

The maid's voice snapped Crista out of her reverie. She glanced at her upper arm and saw colourful bruises forming. Far from disheartening her, they reminded her of her narrow escape, of how she *had* escaped without anyone's help, relying on her wits and determination not to be vilified by Reece. She had survived his attack, and that made her strong enough to survive whatever life threw at her in the future.

'Goodness, to whom does this belong?' Crista asked when the maid held up a beautiful pale lilac muslin gown.

'Lady Annalise thought it might fit you, what with the two of you being a similar height.'

'How thoughtful of her. It's truly lovely.'

'That it is, miss. All of their ladyships' clothes are of the finest quality.'

The maid helped her into the gown and then dressed her hair. When she declared herself satisfied, Crista glanced at her reflection and hardly knew herself. Her complexion was pale, but her eyes were bright, a hint of defiance in them concealing worries about her uncertain future. The cut on her lip where Reece had backhanded her barely showed. Crista would enjoy her afternoon, pretending to be a lady. She had probably earned the right.

And then, tomorrow, she would think about the future.

'You really shouldn't be out of bed, sir.' Amos stood when Chesney was shown into the room, looking pale yet resolute; a large dressing covering the wound on his forehead. 'The doctor recommended bed rest.'

'Nonsense, my lord. It will take more than a tap on the head to disable me.'

'Well said.' Zach nodded to Chesney. 'I'm glad to see you're none the worse for wear.'

'Thank you again for your assistance, Lady St. John,' he said politely.

'It was entirely my pleasure.'

'How is my niece?'

'Sleeping, apparently.' Amos flashed a rueful smile. 'I would like to take credit for rescuing her, but she dealt with Reece without any help from us.'

Chesney roared with laughter when Amos told him the particulars. 'She always was a spirited little chit,' he said, pride glowing from sapient eyes.

'When he was carted off to gaol last night, Reece was still clutching his . . . pardon me, Lady St. John, his private parts where your

326

niece deposited her knee to great effect,' Zach said.

'She should have used more force,' Amos muttered, scowling.

A commotion in the doorway caused all heads to turn in that direction. Amos's breath caught when he saw Crista standing on the threshold. She was beautifully dressed, but looked pale and unsure of her reception. Then she caught sight of her uncle, her face lit up, and she ran to him.

'I am so glad you're all right,' she said as he took both of her hands in his.

'I was about to say the same thing of you.'

'I'm relieved it's all over,' she said. 'I will never forgive myself for what I did to you.'

'You did nothing, child. Besides, you know very well I never do anything unless I wish to.'

'You really would have let Reece kill you rather than admit to how we swapped the stone?' Crista shook her head. 'It is only a diamond, Uncle, and not worth dying for.'

Chesney shrugged. 'If he knew we no longer had it, he would have had no use for us. All the time there was a possibility that we did, I thought we would be safe. I just didn't make allowance for his . . . for his lustful intentions.'

'Come and sit down, Miss Brooke.' Amos

took her arm and steered her to the nearest chair.

'Have the ringleaders been arrested?' she asked the duke.

'Yes, I sent word to Romsey in town, explained the situation, and they moved in. The culprit was a trusted undersecretary in the Foreign Office whom no one had suspected, so the government is greatly indebted to you, Miss Brooke.'

'When I see Romsey again, I shall have a few choice words to say to him,' Amos said, grinding his jaw. 'He was supposed to protect you.'

'He's distraught at the turn events took,' the duke replied. 'And rightly so. It seems he had a crisis in Southampton that required immediate attention from men he could trust. According to the brief message he sent me by express, he doesn't have many completely honest souls under his command. It was something to do with a smuggling ring his police office in Southampton have long been attempting to crack. If he sent in untrustworthy officers, the cargo and half the smugglers would have escaped, and so he called in the ones from Shawford, thinking Reece would be insensible from drugged ale, and Miss Brooke would be safe.'

'He might have warned us,' Amos said, scowling.

'Yes, that was a mistake,' Zach agreed. 'If we had known, we would have taken precautions. It seems Romsey intended to have his people back in place by first light this morning, and didn't count on Reece avoiding the drugged ale. Don't think too badly of him, Miss Brooke. He is a man with a lot of responsibility resting on his shoulders and not enough people to share the burden.'

'I don't blame Lord Romsey,' Crista said.

'I damn well do,' Amos muttered.

'Romsey will be returning to explain himself, and offer you his thanks and apologies, Chesney, and especially you, Miss Brooke.'

Amos growled. 'So he blasted well should.'

'I was obliged to tell your mother you were here at the Park, Miss Brooke,' Lady St. John said apologetically, 'and she is most anxious to come and see you.'

Crista pulled a face. 'Does she wish to see me, or is she using it as an excuse to be admitted here?'

That was what Amos would like to know.

'I came over to ask after your health and ascertain if you would like to receive her.'

'Tell her to come to the shop if she is so concerned about me. Uncle and I will be returning there directly.'

'Not until Romsey has come back and talked to you. We must prevail upon you to remain with us for at least one more night, Miss Brooke,' Zach said with a charming smile. 'And I rather thought to send your family back to London as soon as possible to relieve Lady St. John of the responsibility for them.'

'Oh, very well then.' Crista managed a wan smile. 'I might as well see them, and get it over with. If you know in advance when she is expected, you gentlemen could make yourselves scarce,' she added, smiling more naturally this time. 'That would serve her right.'

'Then I shall return to Farrington House and tell her so. You can expect her this afternoon, Miss Brooke.' Lady St. John stood, as did every gentleman in the room. She leaned over Crista and gave her a brief hug. 'I am so very pleased to see you safe and well.'

'Thank you for looking after my family,' Crista replied. 'They do not deserve your kindness, and I dare say they will forget to thank you for it, and so I shall do so on their behalf.'

'I would not have missed all the excitement for the world.'

'I'll see you out,' Zach said, walking to the door with Lady St. John. A footman leapt forward and opened it for them.

'Excuse me, my dear,' Chesney said. 'I feel a little tired. I believe I shall rest before luncheon after all.'

'Are you sure you're all right, Uncle?' Crista's brow wrinkled. 'I expect the doctor could be sent for again if you — '

'Nonsense, my dear. An hour's rest, and I will be as right as rain.'

The room seemed very quiet, and rife with tension, with just Amos and Crista in occupation of it. She looked everywhere except at him, and he wondered what thoughts occupied her mind. Almost certainly not the lascivious type that gripped his whenever he was in her company, of that he was perfectly sure. He was equally determined she would not be going back to work in her uncle's shop, or anywhere else for that matter.

'I am so very relieved to see you looking well,' he said, sitting beside her and claiming one of her hands. 'I died a thousand deaths when I realised Reece had captured you.'

'It was not a pleasant experience,' she said in a matter-of-fact tone, 'but it taught me a very great deal about my rebellious nature. My mother would say she could have told me as much, of course, but now I have discovered it for myself.'

Amos sent her a melting smile. 'How are your wrists, and your arm?'

'They will soon heal.' She waved his concerns aside. 'My main discomfort is being here where I don't belong, imposing upon you all.'

'Look at me, Crista.' When she didn't turn her head, he placed one finger beneath her chin and compelled her to do so. 'If only you could know the horror I felt when I realised Reece had taken you,' he said for a second time. 'I told Romsey. I warned him . . . damn it. He had no right to behave in such a cavalier fashion and put you at risk!'

'Shush, it's all right.' She reached up a hand and gently stroked his face. 'I was frightened, I will admit that much, but I was equally determined not to let him touch me, no matter what, and it all turned out for the best.'

'But it so easily might not have done. If we hadn't arrived when we did, I . . . well, he would have overpowered you, even with an injured hand.'

'But he did not. It does no good to dwell upon what might have been.'

'I suppose not.' Amos shook his head. 'And at least now you're safe at the Park, where you belong.'

She laughed. 'I hardly belong here.'

'Oh, but you do, my love. Where else would my wife live?'

'Your wife!' Crista opened her eyes very wide, appearing shocked by the suggestion. 'Don't be so ridiculous.'

'Does the idea appal you so very much? I thought we felt something for one another.'

'Just because . . . well, just because we enjoy one another's society, that is no basis for marriage, or reason to enter into one.' She looked directly at him, giving him her full attention for the first time since her uncle left the room. 'If you think you've acted in an ungentlemanly fashion, which you have not, and feel the need to redress the balance, let me assure you such a sacrifice is quite unnecessary. After all, it was I who asked you to educate me.'

Sensing she was serious in her rejection of him, he grasped her hand more tightly, raised it to his lips, and kissed each finger in turn. 'I'm sorry, my love, I'm not doing this properly. You make me nervous, you see.'

'I make *you* nervous?' She laughed. 'I cannot imagine why.'

'Because I so much want you to accept me, but your courage and beauty unbalance me.'

'I'm starting to think you received a blow to the head as well. You're not talking any sense. The last thing I am is beautiful.'

'Ah, love, that's where you're quite wrong. I knew you were unique the moment I set eyes on you. A heady mix of intelligence, wit, and irreverence. You are the lady I've been waiting all these years to find.' He trapped her with an intensely sincere gaze. 'What kept you so long?'

She didn't respond for what seemed like an eternity. The tense, oppressive silence weighed heavily on Amos, but he resisted the urge to break it. He considered trying to convince her with words, or to show her with deeds, just how comprehensively he had fallen in love with her. But that would be unfair. He knew how responsive she was to his touch, and he needed her to be thinking rationally when she made her decision. He ought not to be asking her to make one so soon after her ordeal, he knew, but had a very good reason for doing so.

One that he had yet to share with her.

'You are in earnest, are you not?' she eventually asked, her expression giving nothing away.

'Never more so. I'm coming about this all the wrong way, but what I should have made clear from the outset is that I love you with a deep passion that does not allow room for one iota of doubt. I never want to be parted from you again, never want you to throw yourself headfirst into danger, or behave recklessly in a misguided effort to protect your family. Only by marrying you, can I be absolutely sure you will remain safe.'

Crista laughed. 'There would be nothing

safe about marriage to you, my lord.'

Amos threw his hands in the air. 'Crista, I'm trying to be serious.'

'So am I, and I'm sorry to say that a marriage between us is not possible.' The laughter left her eyes, and she looked desolate yet resolved. 'Your mother would never give her permission, and I would not see your family striven by discord because of me.'

Amos sent her a smouldering smile. 'I address you with my mother's blessing.'

'You what?' Crista's mouth fell open. 'I beg you not to make sport of me. This is already difficult enough.'

'It's true. She came to me immediately after she spoke with you this morning and told me that if I didn't marry you, I would regret it for the rest of my life, which is true. My mother is nothing if not perspicacious. I think she understood my feelings for you before I understood them myself because — '

'Because mothers have a sense for such things,' Crista finished for him, a slow, glorious smile invading her features.

'Precisely.'

'I realise she is anxious to see at least one of you suitably married, but I am hardly suitable. I am no lady. She probably just feels grateful I helped avoid a scandal. She will have come to her senses by tomorrow.'

'But my senses have never left me, and you are more than lady enough to satisfy me. You have been brought up as a lady and instinctively understand how to behave in good company.' Amos grinned. 'You even poured tea for a duke without spilling it on the cloth.'

She laughed. 'If that is what you think, it's fortunate you didn't notice my shaking hands.'

'So, what is it to be, my love?' He fell to his knees in front of her chair and grasped her hands. 'Don't torture me a moment longer by withholding your answer.'

She ran her hands through his hair and offered him a radiant smile. 'If you are absolutely sure, then the answer is *yes*. Of course it's *yes*.' She stood up, still with her hands in his. He came easily to his feet and pulled her into his arms. 'A thousand times *yes*. Pinch me, I must be dreaming. My most secret desire has become reality. Now kiss me, if you please, and seal this bargain.'

22

Crista, still dazed by Amos's offer and her acceptance of it, was even more astonished by the genuine-seeming congratulations she received from all the members of his family when they made their announcement after luncheon.

'Welcome to the family, my dear,' the duchess said, kissing her cheek. 'You are everything I could wish for in a daughter and, I suspect, one of the few women in England capable of keeping Amos in line.'

'You will want Portia and me as bridesmaids, I'm sure,' Lady Annalise said, smiling.

'Thank you,' the duke said, kissing her also. 'You have just removed a heavy burden from my shoulders.'

'Oh no she has not,' the duchess replied, wagging an admonishing finger at the duke. 'I still expect you to find yourself a wife in the very near future.'

A plethora of male Sheridans converged upon her to offer their congratulations, all tall, elegant, and ever so slightly dangerous. None of them moved her in the way Amos so easily could, simply by looking at her in a particular fashion, or sending her one of the devastating smiles he appeared to reserve just for her.

'Congratulations, my dear.' Uncle Charles squeezed her hand. 'Some good has come out of this terrible business after all.'

'There, you see,' Amos said when the rest of the family tactfully withdrew and left them to themselves. 'What did I tell you? They all love you almost as much as I do already.'

'I feel as though I'm living in a dream.' But she also didn't feel quite as euphoric as she knew she ought to. There were aspects of her past she still couldn't put behind her.

'What is it?' Amos asked, frowning.

'Already you understand me so well.' She sent him a wan smile. 'My mother and sister. I still don't know what to do about them.'

'What do you wish to do about them?'

'I must face them, I suppose, and tell them the news before they hear it elsewhere. But . . . oh, I don't know. My mother doesn't even like me very much, but now she will smother me, just to get close to your family. I couldn't inflict that upon you.'

'Why do you continue to make allowances for them when they have treated you so shabbily?'

She shrugged. 'Because I always have, I suppose. Papa made endless allowances for

Mama, and I fell into the habit, too. I feel the distance between Mama and me is partly my fault because I have never been able to please her.'

'Oh, my sweet love.' Amos pulled her into a tight embrace. 'I cannot have you constantly feeling guilty about the woman who happens to be your mother. She will continue to take shameful advantage of you if you do.'

Crista blinked. 'Is that was she does? Do you really think she uses me?'

'Absolutely. And until you speak your mind, allow her to see you are no longer willing to oblige her, she will continue to do so.'

Crista nodded, feeling a great fog lifting from her brain. 'You're probably right about that.'

'Then here is what I suggest.'

★   ★   ★

Crista received her mother and sister alone, aware that Amos was in the adjoining room, just in case he was needed. It was clear they had not yet heard of the betrothal. Her mother bustled into the room and frowned when she saw Crista's fine gown.

'You ought not to be wasting money on gowns for yourself. Think of Amelia first.'

'Yes thank you, Mama. I suffered no lasting

injuries from my ordeal.'

Mama took her time selecting a chair and made no reply.

'This is a very fine house,' Amelia said, glancing around the room, her eyes round with appreciation. 'Far nicer than Farrington House. Where is the duke? Will he be joining us?'

'Yes, you ought to find an excuse to call him in, Crista, since you seem to be on such good terms with the family.'

'Ah yes, about that. I must ask for your congratulations, Mama.' Crista paused to fix her mother and sister with a penetrating look, enjoying her moment of triumph. 'Lord Amos has asked for my hand in marriage, and I have accepted him.'

A stultifying silence greeted this announcement. Crista was unsure what it said about her character when she found it deeply satisfying, especially when Amelia's mouth fell open in a most unladylike fashion.

'He can't have done!' she cried, her face rendered white with jealousy.

'Thank you for your congratulations, Amelia.'

'But, my dear, why did you not mention you and his lordship were attracted to one another?' Mama's entire attitude changed in a heartbeat, and she made to embrace Crista. Since she had not done so when she walked into the room, Crista fended her off. 'If I had known I would have — '

'Would have what, Mama?' Crista asked.

'Well, given him encouragement, or something, but it seems none was necessary. You really are a sly little thing. I didn't realise you had it in you. Anyway, it probably explains why you look almost pretty today. We have so many plans to make. Amelia and I will have to move in here and help with the arrangements. My father will have to receive me now, and you will be thrown constantly into company with the duke and his remaining brothers, Amelia.'

'No help is necessary, thank you, Mama. Arrangements have been made for you to return to London tomorrow. I shall send you an invitation to the wedding, naturally.'

'Don't be so silly, Crista. A girl needs her Mama on the eve of her wedding day.'

'Where have you been on all the other occasions when I have needed you, Mama?' Crista asked softly.

'Oh, you never needed me. You are far too much like your father, self-sufficient, sure of yourself, intolerant of advice.'

'How do you know I never needed you? Did you trouble to ask?'

As always, Crista's mother ignored a question she had no wish to address. 'You see, something good came out of this business with the diamonds after all. I knew you would be all right.'

'You knew?' Crista sent her mother a questioning look, which is when it all suddenly fell into place. The mystery that had eluded her for so long, perhaps because she wasn't ready to face the truth. 'It was you, Mama,' she said slowly. 'You told them I was Papa's apprentice. That is how they knew to come after me, to threaten me and Uncle Charles if I didn't work for them.'

'No, I did not — '

'No one else knew of my skill, not for certain. It had to be you.'

Mama blanched beneath Crista's unwavering glare. 'I didn't mean to, but they would keep on at me. They threatened Amelia. Threatened to go to Mrs. Devonshire with what they knew about your papa's activities.'

'Activities which he only entered into in order to satisfy your greed.'

'Don't speak to me like that, Cristobel Brooke. I am your mother.'

'You're a stranger to me, now.'

'No, don't say that, my dear. Everything worked out well. You are to marry Lord Amos, and naturally your husband will take care of us all.'

'I wouldn't count on that.'

Amos walked through the adjoining doors and stood behind Crista, hands resting protectively on her shoulders.

'But, Lord Amos, things are different now. We are all family.'

'You, madam, will take your younger daughter and return to Chelsea.'

'You can't expect me to live in that hovel. It wouldn't reflect well upon you if I do.'

'I don't much care where you live, but this is what I am prepared to do for you, in spite of the fact that you wilfully put your elder daughter, my future wife, in danger's path. I will give you a generous allowance so you can live in Chelsea without financial concerns. I cannot prevent you from flouting Crista's connection to my family for your own benefit, ensuring Mr. Devonshire marries Amelia. Forget any ambitions you might have with regard to her and any of my brothers. None of them is interested in the scheming little minx.'

Amelia pouted at being thus addressed, but wisely remained silent.

'Oh, this it too much!' Mama swiped imaginary perspiration from her brow and slumped in her chair.

'It won't work this time, Mama,' Crista said, smiling up at Amos and covering one of the hands still resting on her shoulders with her own. 'I suggest you accept his lordship's generous offer before he has a change of heart.'

Crista was deaf to her mother's pleas, wheedles, and entreaties and had the satisfaction of seeing her leave the Park without getting her way. She couldn't recall the last time that had happened.

'Now you look better,' Amos said, pulling her to her feet and into his arms. 'The shadow has left your eyes, and you are as radiant as any bride ought to look.'

'You knew it was Mama who gave me away?'

'I suspected as much as soon as I met her and saw for myself just how single-minded she can be. There's nothing she will not do for her own advancement, and Amelia's. I also knew you needed to solve the mystery of who exposed your talent, which is why I proposed to you before your meeting with your mother. I needed you to face her from a position of strength.'

'It had been worrying me, how the people behind Reece discovered I made jewellery as well as Papa.'

'I realised you would not have settled easily without knowing.'

'Quite. Almost no one knew, you see, and the most obvious candidate was Mama. I just wasn't ready to think that badly of her.' She shook her head against his broad shoulder. 'Now I know better.'

'And feel better, I hope.'

'Yes, my love.' She twined her arms around his neck and smiled up at him. 'Now I am ready to be your wife.'

We do hope that you have enjoyed reading this large print book.

Did you know that all of our titles are available for purchase?

We publish a wide range of high quality large print books including:
Romances, Mysteries, Classics
General Fiction
Non Fiction and Westerns

Special interest titles available in large print are:
The Little Oxford Dictionary
Music Book
Song Book
Hymn Book
Service Book

Also available from us courtesy of Oxford University Press:
Young Readers' Dictionary
(large print edition)
Young Readers' Thesaurus
(large print edition)

For further information or a free brochure, please contact us at:
Ulverscroft Large Print Books Ltd.,
The Green, Bradgate Road, Anstey,
Leicester, LE7 7FU, England.
Tel: (00 44) 0116 236 4325
Fax: (00 44) 0116 234 0205